OLD DOGMA NEW TRICKS

OLD DOGMA NEW TRICKS

THE ELVEN PROPHECY™ BOOK TWO

THEOPHILUS MONROE

MICHAEL ANDERLE

DISRUPTIVE IMAGINATION®

Copyright © 2021 LMBPN Publishing
Cover copyright © LMBPN Publishing
A Michael Anderle Production

LMBPN Publishing
PMB 196, 2540 South Maryland Pkwy
Las Vegas, NV 89109

First US edition, May 2021
Version 1.01, May 2021
ebook ISBN: 978-1-64971-757-3
Print ISBN: 978-1-64971-758-0

THE OLD DOGMA NEW TRICKS TEAM

Thanks to our Beta Team

John Ashmore, Rachel Beckford, Kelly O'Donnell, Billie Leigh Kellar

Thanks to our JIT Readers

Veronica Stephan-Miller
Dorothy Lloyd
Dave Hicks
Diane L. Smith
Peter Manis
Zacc Pelter
Jackey Hankard-Brodie

If We've missed anyone, please let us know!

Editor
The Skyhunter Editing Team

CHAPTER ONE

I was supposed to preach in about five minutes.

And I couldn't get off the toilet.

No, it wasn't anything I ate. I'd finished my business a while ago. I literally couldn't stand up.

I sighed. It was the day after leg day.

Layla had made me do about a thousand lunges and squats, and that's not hyperbole. My lower half was so sore that sitting *down* on the toilet had been challenging enough. Getting up again was going to be damn near impossible.

I just got off suspension as a preacher. Our former bishop, now in jail for drunk and disorderly conduct, had blackballed me for what he thought was heresy. His replacement, Philip Schwartzerdt, was more progressive, and with a unanimous vote of support from my congregation, he'd had me reinstated.

Good news, right?

But there was a problem. I mean, other than my current bathroom predicament.

How in the world was I supposed to preach again when a legion of otherworldly elves was preparing to launch an assault on Earth?

Don't get me wrong; I still had my faith. But the existence of elves, not to mention magic, was a truth that would rattle people to the core. Not that our beliefs were incompatible with such things—at least I didn't believe they were—but accepting it required a bit of an open mind.

What in the world could I preach that would prepare people for something like that? I had something prepared, but I wasn't happy with it. It felt insufficient.

Still, given all the time in the gym, all the time training with Layla to fend off legions of magic-wielding elves, not to mention going to work at my second part-time job as a bartender, I didn't have a lot of time to devote to sermon prep.

It wouldn't matter what I'd prepared, I suppose, if I couldn't get my ass off the toilet.

I looked to my right—handicap rail.

Thank God we were ADA compliant. Usually, older facilities like ours can get away with not following the rules since most of the requirements apply to new construction, but I always thought it was important to provide accessibility. Since most of our congregation was north of sixty, it made sense, too.

I gripped the rail. It didn't help much, mainly because it was back day the day before it was leg day, and the muscles I needed to pull myself up were sore, too.

I grunted, hurled my body off the toilet, and fell on the floor.

The bathroom floor. Gross, right?

I checked my watch. I needed to wrap this up.

I closed my eyes and focused.

Magic. I could use a little magic.

I mean, I was still a novice when it came to this sort of thing, but I'd used magic to fly. All I had to do was clear my mind and visualize it.

I took a deep breath.

Ew. Thankfully, a skunk doesn't know its own scent. Not pleasing, but tolerable. I tried not to think about it.

I envisioned myself standing up. Precision was difficult. When it came to magic, I tended to overdo it. I went from neutral to fifth gear, no problem. It was the level two, three, and four magic I struggled with. I have always had difficulty with moderation.

Rise, I told myself. I mean, I *was* a preacher. All I had to do to make other people stand was open my palms, move my hands up just a few inches, and people always obeyed. It was almost like magic. What I needed now wasn't much more than that. *Keep it small, Caspar*, I told myself. *No more magic than I need to get back to my feet.*

I saw myself, in my mind's eye, standing up. Yeah, my pants were still around my ankles, which looked ridiculous even in my imagination.

Somehow I'd have to bend over and pull them up.

One problem at a time.

I opened my eyes. I was floating in mid-air above the toilet.

"Shit!" I exclaimed, trying to keep my voice down.

My magic failed and I fell, my right foot splashing in the john…which I hadn't flushed.

I'm not one of those name-it-claim-it preachers. I don't believe in that, but I had to wonder if I hadn't just said "shit," maybe my shoe wouldn't be in the middle of a bunch of it.

Somewhere up in the heavens, God was looking down and laughing his divine ass off at my expense.

I didn't have a lot of time to deal with it.

After removing my foot from the toilet, I bent over at the waist, straining my hamstrings.

I caught my waistband with my middle finger—a small but noteworthy success.

I pulled up my pants, flushed, removed my shoe, and washed it off the best I could in the sink.

I put it back on my foot, which was a challenge all its own. I had to lean against the wall, cross one foot over the other leg, and try to slip it on.

Thankfully, these were loafers and didn't have laces.

I lowered my foot and squished, feeling the delightful sensation of toilet water between my toes.

I sighed.

This was what I got for letting Layla work my ass off at the gym.

Don't get me wrong; I love her. She's the first woman I've loved since my divorce. And she's an elf princess, which, in a way, adds a little allure to the relationship. I don't know—it's exotic and a little taboo. There's an extra thrill in that.

Despite everything I loved about her, there was something about the door of that gym that turned her into something else. It was like a magic portal that changed her from a sweet, empathetic, attractive female into a total monster.

She was an exercise freak and pushed herself to the absolute limits. It was impressive. I'd be okay with it if she hadn't taken it upon herself to train me, too.

I was sure she'd get a kick out of it when I told her this story.

Yeah, that wasn't going to happen.

No one could ever know about this other than God Almighty, and that was only because He was all-knowing. Sometimes God's omniscience was embarrassing. I mean, you'd think He'd respect someone's privacy. Just because He could see all and know all didn't mean He had to creep on me in the bathroom.

I washed my hands; I'm not a barbarian. I'd end up shaking a lot of hands in short order. I added a pump of hand sanitizer for good measure. After the handshaking, I'd have to use it again since I was reasonably sure that at least a few of the folks in the congregation were non-hand-washing Neanderthals.

I quickly vested up since Holy Cross was an old-school church. Wasn't my style, but it wasn't my place to mess with people's traditions, not without a good reason. Not as long as they gave people comfort.

I had a long white robe and a purple stole. Purple because it was the first week of Lent, and that was the prescribed color of the season.

I did a double-check in the full-length mirror before stepping out into the chancel.

People started applauding. Were they cheering me?

I don't think I'd ever heard anyone clap in our church. The denominational powers that be discouraged it. We shouldn't praise people, we should praise God; that was what they said. Clapping was *irreverent*.

But they were applauding my return.

The last time I was there, just as I was starting my sermon, Doris had a stroke. She was one of my favorite members. She was an older lady, not theologically trained or well-educated, but she had the kind of faith that could move mountains. Compared to me, she was a spiritual giant.

At the time, I didn't know what had happened. I'd been stabbed by a magic blade and the mysterious elf who had since become my girlfriend had healed me somehow, not leaving so much as a scar. But that blade had connected me to Earth's magic. When Doris collapsed, I'd healed her before the paramedics arrived.

That particular event was, oddly enough, what my former bishop had used as cause to suspend me. He didn't believe it was a miracle. In truth, I didn't think it was either, but in his mind, I'd healed Doris by the power of Satan. Yes, because that's the sort of thing the devil likes to do. Human sacrifice. Ritual orgies. Healing old ladies from strokes. Makes sense.

I had resigned myself that my career was likely over, and if my former bishop, Matthias Flacius, hadn't gotten himself into alcohol-induced legal trouble that triggered a review of his decisions, I wouldn't be a minister anymore. I wouldn't be standing there in front of my congregation, awkwardly receiving their applause.

Ironic, I thought. I mean, why cheer me on for something they believed God did?

I raised my hand and lowered it slowly, a universal gesture meant to signal it was time to sit down and shut up.

"Thank you," I said, smiling. "It's great to be back here with you all, and I thank you for your support and prayers."

No sooner did I start speaking than there was a loud knock on the church's front doors.

I cocked my head. "Did someone lock the doors?"

"Yes, Pastor," Doris said. "The minister who filled your place in your absence insisted we lock them to prevent interruptions."

I sighed and rolled my eyes. No wonder this church didn't look at all like our community. Holy Cross was located in a part of the neighborhood that was seventy-five percent African American, but there wasn't a single person in attendance who wasn't white.

"Someone open the door," I said. "We welcome everyone."

"But Pastor," said Jim, one of the elders, "it's probably just a beggar looking for a handout."

"Then let them come," I said, meeting Jim's concerned stare with a determined one. "Blessed are the poor."

No one was applauding now. There was nervousness in the air. In my experience, a lot of Christians talked a good game, gave a lot of money to good causes, and supported ministries that were supposed to care for the poor. But like a lot of people, they'd rather throw money at a problem than get their hands dirty. They'd rather not get involved in the lives of real people who have genuine problems.

Another knock on the door, louder this time.

"Is someone going to open the door?" I asked again.

No one moved.

I walked down the aisle. The whole place was silent. I

unlocked the door, and the click of the latch echoed throughout the sanctuary.

I swung open the door.

A nice-looking man stood there. A black man. He had a look of desperation in his eyes. He grabbed my hand and knelt in front of me. "Please, man of God!"

"Stand up," I said. "I'm just a man."

"But you are a healer, man of God!"

I bit my lip. I turned and saw Doris, who was beaming with pride. I surveyed the rest of the room and saw looks of concern mixed with curiosity. I turned my attention back to the visitor and smiled. I gripped his hand and helped him to his feet. "Like I said, sir, I'm just a man."

"But you wield the power of God!" the man declared.

I looked at the congregation again. Their expressions hadn't changed. Funny how news of my supposed "miracle" had spread. No wonder the visiting minister who'd handled services during my absence kept the doors locked. It wasn't just to keep the poor out; it was to keep the miracle-seekers at bay.

"In the future," I told the man, "don't kneel before anyone but God."

The man smiled at me and nodded. "Only trying to show respect to a man of God."

I returned the smile as best I could. "Sir, would you like to join us for worship?"

"No, Pastor," the man said. "But I was hoping you could help my daughter."

I cocked my head. "What's wrong with your daughter?"

The man reached out the door and waved his hand. A few moments later, a woman appeared, pushing a young girl in a well-used and outdated wheelchair. The child couldn't have been more than twelve. She smiled at me sweetly.

I smiled back at her. "What's your name?"

"Grace," the girl told me.

I smiled. "I love that name. It is by grace that we are saved."

The girl turned to her mom. "I like him!"

"Can you help her, preacher?" the man asked.

"What's your name, sir?" I asked.

"I'm Cecil, and this is my wife Shanda. You've already met Grace."

"What's wrong with her?" I asked. "Why can't she walk?"

"The doctors say spina bifida in the top part of her back," Cecil said. "But God can heal her."

"I'm sorry to hear that," I said, nodding. "Do you need assistance with her medical bills? Maybe a better chair?"

"You're the one they call Caspar. You're the healer, right?" the man asked.

"That's my name. I'm just a regular preacher."

"Not true," Doris piped up. "He healed me!"

I glanced at Doris. "I don't know what I did, Doris. And this young lady. Sir, I'm sorry, but…"

"Please, Preacher. Just try! We've been coming every week, hoping to find you here. We've got Medicaid, but there's only so much the doctors can do."

I bit my lip. I really didn't know what I could do, but if there was a chance, if I could use my magic to help this girl, could I turn her down? To have the ability to help but not use it would make me worse than my former bishop. I had to try.

I prayed I wouldn't make things worse. My propensity was to overshoot magic-wise.

I nodded at Cecil and Shanda and placed my hand on Grace's back.

I took a deep breath.

I released it.

I didn't know a ton about Grace's condition. I knew what it was, more or less, but it wasn't as important to understand her problem as to visualize her healthy and whole. That was how I'd inadvertently healed Doris. I'd remembered her as I knew her, full of life and vigorous for her age. I focused on this girl, her spine normal, running and playing with other children. I imagined her jumping rope, playing hopscotch.

I felt a familiar tingle. I was drawing on magic.

Then I heard a giggle.

Grace had leaped from her chair and hugged her parents, whose eyes were full of tears.

Gasps broke the silence in the congregation, then they cheered again.

"Thank you, Preacher!" Cecil said. "Praise God!"

I smiled, nodded at Shanda and Cecil, and walked back down the aisle toward the front of the church.

I bit my lip.

People were laughing in jubilation.

Grace grabbed the side of one of the pews. She'd jumped up pretty quickly, but she hadn't used her legs much until now. Even if she *was* healed, she'd need to develop lower-body strength, and that would take time.

If I could use magic to build muscle, I wouldn't have fish for legs at the moment.

Grace was still giggling as she made her way down the aisle towards me and hugged me. "Thank you, sir! Thank you so much!"

I smiled and briefly rested my hand on the top of her head. I was happy for her, don't get me wrong, but this was just the start. If people had heard about Doris, an old white lady who didn't even live in the neighborhood anymore, word of this was going to spread like wildfire. And with a previously paralyzed girl walking again, the evidence to prove the veracity of the story was there.

So much for coming back to the church quietly, trying not to make waves.

I'd probably be suspended again by the end of the week.

CHAPTER TWO

I grabbed my duffel bag from the back seat of my Mitsubishi Eclipse and slung it over my shoulder. Didn't have much in there: a couple of changes of clothes, a set to work out in, and another set for afterward, along with a relatively new pair of cross-trainers I was still breaking in. Other than that, a stick of deodorant, a padlock, and a massive bottle of ibuprofen. The essentials.

For the first time, I looked forward to the gym. Layla didn't go to church with me. Our relationship wasn't public, and her being an elf made it complicated.

She covered her ears with a hoodie most of the time, but the old-timers would insist she remove it. If only they were a little more old-school. Then she could get away with a bonnet, maybe.

Layla's hair was long, straight, and blonde. If she wore it down, though, it only partially covered her ears. They tended to poke through, giving her elvish identity away.

At some point, if the world didn't fall to her father's elven legions, we'd have to figure it out. It wasn't that I was afraid people would know she was an elf, but there was a cult that had arisen, the Order of the Elven Gate. People called it the Elf Gate Cult or the Cult of the Elven Gate, and it was privy to the otherworldly elf king's plans, thanks to Layla's ex, the late Hector, for creating it. They mostly hoped to get on the elves' good side so as to remain in the favor of the king after the elves conquered the world.

Most people thought they were just another run-of-the-mill crazy cult. And since many of the members wore fake ears or even had their ears surgically altered to resemble the elves' ears, showing up as a recently reinstated minister with what people would think was a cultist as a girlfriend probably wouldn't go well for me.

So, we'd planned to meet at the gym immediately after Sunday service.

I wobbled through the doors, my legs still weak from the day before. Layla was standing there in tight fitness pants and a tank top. Her body was flawless, and her workout clothes accentuated every curve perfectly. Most people would think she was my trainer, or maybe my daughter—certainly not my girlfriend. By human standards, she was in a whole other league. Thankfully, she wasn't human. Apparently, hot elf chicks have a thing for the Pillsbury Doughboy look.

Layla didn't require her hoodie in the gym to hide her pointy ears. Sure, the gym rats could be plenty judgmental, but they were more likely to damn you for excessive carbohydrate consumption than for membership in a fringe organization.

Perhaps that was one reason she loved the gym so much. She didn't have to worry about being singled out.

"How was church?" Layla asked. "Everyone happy to see you back?"

I smiled. This was the obligatory friendly small talk she'd make before the workout began, a strategy meant to remind me that I did love her, no matter what she was about to do to me.

"Someone came looking for a miracle," I said. "I wasn't going to do it, but I couldn't *not* help her. It was a young girl."

Layla nodded and smiled. "You had compassion. Just be careful. You realize now that your services aren't going to be the same ever again."

I nodded. "That's what I'm afraid of. Those people don't like change. They're committed to their ways, their traditions, and for the most part, the denomination supports that. Once other people show up, people not like them, looking for healings…"

"Things will change," Layla said. "Sometimes change can be a good thing."

I nodded. "And a painful thing."

Layla's smile turned from kind to devious. "Which is exactly why we're here. No pain, no gain, right?"

"Yeah, about that. Could we take it a little easier until my body adjusts? I can barely walk, and standing up and sitting down is a real challenge."

Layla shook her head. "You just have to get through it. We don't know how much time we have, so we can't afford to start slow."

I sighed. "All right, what is it today? Arms?"

Layla shook her head. "Yes and no. Chest and triceps."

I made my way to the men's locker room and changed clothes.

Layla put me through a warm-up set of push-ups. No, not standard push-ups. Most of them I did from my knees, but I got through them. The hardest part was standing again. Thankfully, Layla was willing to help me to my feet.

After that, it was the bench press.

You know, the barometer of gym-rat manliness? "How much you bench, bro?"

The question was meant to size you up to other dudes. Thankfully, no one had asked me yet. I wasn't competition, and even if someone asked, I didn't know how I'd answer. But I'd overheard other guys talking their bench press max in the locker room.

I tried not to think about it. Layla only had ten pounds on

each side of the bar. I bench a twenty-spot, bro. Yeah, I wasn't going to say that…ever.

Less weight, I wagered, added to the bar than the bar itself weighed. I could handle it. Seemed like for once, Layla had listened to me and was going easy on me.

So I thought.

First set, not too bad.

Then the second, and the third. Started to get a little more challenging.

The fourth set? It took everything I had just to raise the bar from my chest. Layla was spotting me. She'd prevent me from dropping the thing across my windpipe, which wasn't entirely unlikely.

I finished my tenth rep and racked the bar. "Holy crap, that sucked!"

Layla smirked and took the weights off. "Go again."

I raised one eyebrow as I laid on my back, staring up at her. "That was all the weight I could lift. Now you're going to make me press the bar by itself?"

"It's called a drop set. You have to shock your muscles. Keep going until failure."

"You're going to make me fail with just the bar?" I asked. "I'll look like a wimp."

Layla snorted. "If the shoe fits."

"Hey!" I protested. "I might *be* a wimp, but that doesn't mean I want to *look* like one."

I glanced to my right. Some hulk of a man in a tank top, sporting a mohawk and a smorgasbord of tattoos, was bench-pressing the bar with three forty-fives on each side. I didn't bother to do the math.

"You want me to sit here and struggle with the bar right next to that?"

Layla shook her head. "Who do you have to impress, anyway? I'm your girlfriend, and I'm not judging you."

"Sure you aren't," I said, gripping the bar again. My arms were still trembling from the last set. Even the bar by itself felt heavy. I had no idea how much the bar weighed, but it wasn't zero pounds. I'm sure Layla knew…and if she told me, I'd probably be embarrassed by how little I was barely managing to press. After four sets, my arms were ready to give out.

"Up," Layla commanded.

I gripped the bar as it rested in the rack.

"Slow and with control," Layla said. "You don't want to give your muscles a break on the way down. It's all about time under tension."

I rolled my eyes. Time under tension. Drop sets. Supersets. Reps. All that gym speak. It was like I was in a foreign country.

The few times I had gone overseas, I didn't know much more than how to ask where the bathroom was.

Wo ist die Toilette? That was Germany.

Ou sont les toilettes? That was what I asked when I had to go pee in France.

Onde e o banheiro? I once took a dump in Portugal.

But now I was in a gym in America's heartland, and most of what the denizens said didn't make a lick of sense.

"Where's the shitter?" I asked.

"Nice try," Layla said. "You know where it is. You were just in the locker room. Besides, you have to finish your set first."

"But I'm going to poop my pants!" I protested.

"No, you aren't," Layla said. "You just know I can't follow you into the men's locker room."

"*Fick dich,*" I replied under my breath. Not that I was fluent in German, but I knew how to f-bomb someone. "Where's the toilet?" "Fuck you." You know, the essentials. Enough to survive in most civilized nations, anyway.

Layla raised her left eyebrow. "What does that mean?"

"It's German. It means 'I love you.'" I smiled.

"For some reason, I don't believe you."

My eyes darted back and forth nervously. "What? Why would you think that? I mean, don't you trust me?"

"I do trust you," Layla said. "I also know you."

I snorted. "How am I supposed to go to work if I can't even walk tomorrow?"

"Legs were yesterday. Today we're working your chest and tris," Layla said. "By tomorrow, you'll be able to walk just fine. Besides, you work as a bartender and as a preacher. You don't need a lot of leg strength for that."

I chuckled. I almost told her about my stuck-on-the-toilet incident at the church, but I was still too embarrassed to mention it. Besides, citing that event as told-you-so-moment would only turn up her workout intensity. Instead, I rambled on about the ridiculousness that was my existence. "A sober alcoholic preacher walks into a bar... Not a joke, it's my life. Now that I think about it, I guess it is a bit of a joke."

Layla shook her head. "Your life isn't a joke. I don't think that girl's parents would call you a joke. Every day she walks, every step she takes, is a gift you've given them. And that's just the start. The world depends on you, Caspar. Once my father sends his legionnaires here, you'll need to be able to do more than heal people. You need to be ready to fight."

I looked at Layla wide-eyed and parted my lips slightly. "I'm a lover, not a fighter."

"You're a cliché machine is what you are. Especially when you're trying to put off your next set."

I grinned. "You caught me. I'm ready to do that drop set now."

Layla cocked her head. "No, a drop set means you reduce the weight and hit another set immediately without rest in between. Now that you've bullshitted for a couple of minutes, you need to do another full set, then the drop set."

I grunted.

"*Fick dich* too, sweetheart," Layla murmured, smiling sadistically. "And pardon my French."

I almost choked on my tongue. It was German, not French, but I wasn't about to correct her. Since she was asking for pardons, she must've figured out what it meant. Or she thought I was trying to tell her to flick a dick, which was how it sounded. Either way, she got the gist of it. "All right. But after this, we're calling it a day."

"After you do a set of dumbbell flies and stretch," Layla said. "If you're going to be a fighter, you need to be more than strong. You need to be flexible and agile."

I shook my head. "Isn't that why you have me doing yoga?"

"Ioga," Layla said, correcting me. Technically, what she'd brought from New Albion was a tradition that was similar to yoga. When she said "ioga," it sounded almost the same as "yoga," and other than the terminology, I couldn't tell the difference between the two practices. Not to mention, she usually had me doing yoga videos on demand. Apparently, the one time she'd tried to do it with me, I had been too much of a smart ass about it to maintain the state of mind that yoga, or ioga, requires.

Since Tony Horton wouldn't talk back at me through the television, I suppose she figured leaving me in the hands of the ageless fitness wonder was better than trying to teach me yoga herself.

"You need to do that, too," Layla said. "But immediately after a workout; that's when your muscles are warm and the most pliable. It's the best time to make flexibility gains through your stretching."

I sighed. "All right. Load me up."

Layla slid ten pounds onto either side of my bar. I glanced at He-Man, who was still pressing something in the range of three hundred pounds. And he made it look easy.

"Light weight, baby!" the man next to me shouted as he re-racked his weights.

"Why'd he say 'light weight, baby?'" I asked. "He's lifting more than my entire body weight."

Layla shrugged. "I don't know. Why don't you ask him?"

I started to open my mouth and say something to the man.

"After you finish your sets," Layla interjected before I could speak.

"Set," I said. "Singular. You just said sets, plural."

Layla added the safety clamps to the outside of each of the ten-pound weights. "Ten reps, then no talking. Straight to the drop set."

CHAPTER THREE

Why is it the older someone is, the wrinklier their ass is, the more likely it is that they stroll nakedly and carelessly across the locker room? They're also the ones most likely to engage you in a conversation at the same time.

I turned my eyes the other way as I headed to my locker.

All I wanted was to quickly change and go home.

But on the bench right in front of my locker was the mohawk sporting bodybuilder from before.

I stood to the side and waited my turn.

He turned and looked at me.

"You need in here, man?"

I nodded. "Yeah, sure. But I can wait."

The guy shook his head. "No, come on. I wasn't trying to hog the space."

I nodded. "All right. Thanks."

"No problem," the man said. "Name's Jag, by the way."

"Jag?" I asked.

He shrugged. "Short for Jagger. That's my last name. It's what I go by."

I nodded. "Caspar. Nice to meet you."

"So, your trainer is hot," Jag said.

I nodded. "She certainly is."

"Think I could get her number?"

I snorted. "She's also my girlfriend."

Jag raised an eyebrow and looked at me curiously. "Seriously? Congrats, man. How'd you pull that off?"

I shrugged and jiggled my gut. "It's my magnificent physique."

Jag looked at me blankly. "No, really."

"What can I say? I have a fantastic personality." I smiled.

Jag smirked. "Well, good for you, bro."

"Yeah, good for me," I said. I slithered around Jag and opened my locker, which was just below his. At the moment, even the location of our lockers seemed a display of the man's dominance.

And we were invading each other's personal space. And at the moment, Jag wasn't getting anything out of his locker. He could have moved down, but I wasn't about to ask him. I didn't know this dude. I was hoping he'd get the hint.

Instead, he just sat there, his legs spread, smelling like man. I quickly retrieved my bag and found a spot on the bench about five feet away. Jag reached into his locker, pulled out a giant tub of who knows what, and a shaker cup. I glanced at him.

"Mind if I ask you a question, Jag?" I asked.

Jag shrugged. "Sure."

"When you were lifting in there, why'd you say 'light weight, baby?'"

Jag smiled wide. "Channeling the king, bro."

"Elvis?" I asked, cocking my head.

"No. King Coleman," Jag said, rubbing some kind of oil on his body. "Ronnie Coleman. Eight-time Mister Olympia."

I tilted my head to the side. "The only Mister Olympia I've ever heard of was Arnold."

"King Coleman was bigger than Arnold. Much bigger. And Arnold only won the Olympia title seven times. Anyway, Ronnie Coleman didn't work out at a great gym. Not a fancy place like this one. Worked out at some shit hole-in-the-wall. But whenever he lifted heavy weights, he'd say, 'Light weight, baby!' Maybe he was being ironic. I think it was sort of a mind trick. Tell yourself you're lifting light, it kind of feels lighter."

"So, it's a mind-over-matter thing?" I asked.

"Exactly," Jag said with a definitive nod.

"And he's who you're trying to become?" I asked.

Jag shook his head. "Don't get me wrong. I admire what he did. But when I do competitions, I'm not competing against other men."

I bit my lip. "So, you compete in the women's bodybuilding competition?"

Jag snorted and chuckled. "No, that's not what I meant. I mean, I don't compare myself to other people. That's the secret to success in the gym."

"Hard to do," I said. "I can't help but feel like I'm the weakest guy here."

Jag nodded. "Yeah, you probably are."

I smiled. "Thanks for the confidence boost."

Jag smiled back. "I'm not your therapist. I'm not trying to make you feel better. Not trying to make you feel worse, either. Just the truth. You are where you are, and that's your journey."

I nodded. "Seems like you've been on this path a while."

Jag bit his cheek. "I saw you watching me over there while you were pushing your weight. You know, I didn't always lift this much. I used to lift what you do."

"What," I asked. "When you were fifteen?"

"Four years ago," Jag said. "Sure, I'm only twenty-nine. But I used to be no bigger and no stronger than you. And back then, if I'd looked at the other lifters and tried to be them, I'd have quit before I started."

I nodded. "I can see why someone might do that. I'm having a hard time staying motivated myself."

"The trick is to become your own competition," Jag said.

"Every time you come here, the only one you're trying to beat is your previous self. As long as you're winning that battle, you'll hit your goals eventually."

I smiled. "You know, that's pretty good advice."

Jag grinned. "Yup. Learned that from the King, too. You realize after he won the first time and there was no one bigger than he was, he still came back the next year larger than the year before?"

I shook my head. "That's impressive."

Jag nodded. "It's because he was still competing with himself. Ronnie just wanted to be a better version of Ronnie. The other men on the stage with him, the way he saw it? They weren't even there. He didn't worry about them. That's why he dominated the Olympia for almost a decade."

"So, you don't think I'm a pussy for only lifting twenty pounds and the bar?" I asked.

Jag bellowed a laugh as he scooped some kind of powder into a shaker cup. "I didn't say that. You're still a pussy."

I smiled. "Thanks, man. Encouraging."

"Just keeping it real, bro. That's the thing. If you don't want to be a pussy, come back tomorrow stronger than you were today."

"What are you drinking there? Protein?" I asked.

Jag nodded as he started shaking his cup, the blender ball inside clicking as it banged back and forth inside. "It's partly protein, several kinds. Whey isolate, whey concentrate, casein, and collagen. But this baby is also packed with glutamine, creatine, BCAAs, and a lot of other shit."

"So, that's your magic sauce?" I asked.

Jag shrugged as he gulped it down. "It helps. But the real magic sauce is what happens out there on the floor. None of this stuff would do squat if I wasn't pushing myself in the gym."

I bit my lip. "Well, thanks for sharing, Jag."

He snorted as he gulped down the rest of his drink, then ran his hand across his now-sweat-filled mohawk. Then he stood, walked up to a mirror, and roared.

I pressed my lips together hard. I was trying to suppress a giggle.

Jag pointed at himself in the mirror. "You're going down, asshole!"

He took the whole "competing against your former self" thing seriously. It was a very different approach to utilizing a mirror than I was used to. I had grown up with Daily Affirmations with Stuart Smalley. Sure, it was just a Saturday Night Live act, a character by Al Franken. But I'd be lying if I said I'd never tried it.

You're good enough, Caspar. You're smart enough, and gosh darn it, people like you.

It never occurred to me to call myself an asshole.

I glanced at Jag.

He was still fixated on his reflection.

"What you looking at, you little bitch? You want some of this?"

That time, I had to press my whole hand against my mouth to prevent myself from laughing. I mean, part of the comedy of what was happening was that this hulk of a man wasn't just dissing himself in a mirror. He was doing it in his tighty-whities.

Don't laugh, Caspar. Hold it in.

Sure, Jag seemed nice enough, but he didn't strike me as the sort of dude you'd want to make angry. And I doubted he'd appreciate being laughed at. I mean, I've heard of 'roid rage, and there was a reasonably good chance that his witch's brew of proteins and whatnot wasn't the only thing he was taking. I know a dedicated regiment of diet, exercise, and basic nutritional supplementation can lead to decent gains, but this guy's thighs were the size of my waist. His biceps were as big as my skull.

I'd never seen a human that big before. He was almost as big as B'iff, the elven giant, which Layla's people refer to disparagingly as "orcs." B'iff, oddly enough, was the one responsible for vesting me with my relatively newfound powers. He'd inadvertently stabbed me with a mystic blade imbued with Earth's magic. Little did I realize at the time that he was trying to bring magic back to his people on New Albion.

While he looked like a prototypical villain with greenish-brown skin, massive incisors overhanging his lip, and a serious case of resting I-want-to-eat-you-for-dinner face, he was committed to protecting humanity from the elves.

The elves, Layla's father and his kingdom, intended to leave their planet and return to Earth. A couple thousand years ago, give or take a few centuries, the Earth had been their home. They were druids in what I suppose would be modern-day Britain and Wales. They had fled under persecution from the Romans and then the Christians. The elven giants had gone with them, and ever since, they'd been fighting some kind of otherworldly war.

The elves believed they were destined to return to exact vengeance on humanity for what had happened to their ancestors. They wanted to take over and use Earth's magic to dominate the globe. The elven giants, aka the orcs, were committed to staying on their new world, New Albion.

The only reason they fought was to prevent the elves from coming here.

But the wars had taken a toll on their new world. The magic they'd brought with them from Earth to make their planet habitable was waning. Too much magic had been used for fighting wars. As their supply failed, the condition of their world worsened.

B'iff had come to Earth with the Blade of Echoes, the enchanted dirk that had been used by the ancient druids to bring magic to New Albion, intending to recharge the blade and return to their world to reinvigorate their planet. The elves had other designs: to take the blade from the giants before they could do it and instead use it to forge a permanent gateway to our world.

Long story short, we'd managed to prevent the elves from

getting the blade. B'iff had given his life to see the blade destroyed.

The problem? When we did that, a surge of energy coursed through the ley lines and blasted the gateway between our worlds open.

The elves ultimately got what they wanted, and the giants didn't have any magic left on New Albion that they could use to stop them from coming.

It seemed there was only one reason the elf king, King Brightborn, hadn't marched on our world yet.

To his chagrin, I had convincingly fulfilled the five known facets of an elven prophecy. He wasn't happy about it because in his mind, the chosen one should have been an elf, not a pipsqueak human.

Also, Layla was his daughter, and she'd sided with the giants and me against her people. If he came here before trying to smooth things over politically, he'd have a real mess on his hands. He might have little choice but to try his daughter for treason. Also, since I'd fulfilled most of the prophecy, he needed some time to sort things out with the elven priests.

Layla was reasonably confident, and the king had confirmed as much when we'd confronted him, that he was looking for some loophole in the elven dogma, something he could use for waging his war without setting himself up as the enemy of the chosen one.

While I didn't know much about the elven prophecy I was fulfilling, I did know enough about Biblical prophecy because of my theological education to know that most prophecies were cryptic and could be interpreted in a variety of ways. There probably isn't a book in the Bible, for instance, with more varied interpretations than Revelation.

In short, the elven king would have to do some complicated political gymnastics to justify his war while also setting himself up as the true defender of the prophecy rather than its enemy. He needed the elven priests to help him with that, and, according to Layla, they'd be inclined to do so. And the elves would likely buy it. The common elves were utterly dependent on the priests when it came to such matters. They didn't have their own copies of the prophecies. What the priests said, the elves would believe.

While all that was going on, though, we were preparing. It wasn't likely I could defeat an entire elven legion on my own. It was more than likely the king would try to take me out or at least capture me before bringing his legions through the gate. He'd send assassins and maybe a few death squads my way.

I needed to acquire a lifetime's worth of skills as soon as possible. I needed to master my magic, yes, but I needed to be in good physical shape, too. I needed to learn to fight.

Thus, the whole gym routine Layla was subjecting me to.

It gave me the opportunity to meet interesting people like Jag, who was now flexing in the mirror and demeaning himself.

"Look at you," Jag said to his reflection. "You're soft! A wimp! I'm going to crush you!"

I finished changing my clothes now that I had the bench to myself. It still wasn't easy. The soreness in my legs hadn't disappeared. I would have tried to use magic to soothe the pain, but that would be counterproductive since Layla said the pain was a part of the process. It was how my muscles were being torn down and rebuilt. If I healed the pain, I'd hijack my gains. No pain, no gain.

CHAPTER FOUR

The worst part about my apartment was that I had to climb a bunch of stairs to get there. I'd never counted them until now. The bar below my apartment had high ceilings, so that meant twenty-four steps of agony. I know, it's not *that* many. Under normal circumstances, it would have been nothing. But with legs like hams dangling from my hips, every stair sent pangs through my thighs, hamstrings, and glutes.

I chuckled to myself even as I winced from the pain.

Moons over my hammies.

Shorthand for my butt and hamstrings. Also, a breakfast plate at Denny's.

"Excuse me," Layla said as she whizzed past me, skipping every other stair on her way to the top.

"Showoff." I grunted.

Layla shrugged and grinned widely. "I promise, Caspar. The next leg day, you'll just be a little sore. After that, you'll hardly be sore at all. It gets better!"

I shook my head. "Next leg day? Why does there have to be a next leg day?"

"Come on," Layla said. "You're through the worst of it. I promise."

I finally made it to the top. I tried to put my key into the deadbolt, but it was the wrong key. I had new locks, but I hadn't removed the old key from my keychain. No reason, just lazy. After my apartment door was busted in recently, my landlords had installed a heavier door and an extra lock. I swapped keys for the correct one and tried again.

The lock was stiff, but it clicked.

I turned the knob and went inside.

"Agnus, what the hell?"

My cat was sitting on the couch, watching Animal Planet and licking his junk. His body flailed for a second before he fell on the floor, then he got back to his feet. "Casp!" Agnus said. "You should knock before barging in on me like that!"

I rolled my eyes. One side-effect of the magic I had recently acquired was I could hear my cat speak. We could have conversations. Since Layla was an elf and could access magic, she could hear him, too.

And from the looks of things, despite lacking opposable thumbs, he'd figured out how to use the remote to navigate to his favorite channels.

He'd found a program on the mating habits of Bengal tigers. Apparently, he found it alluring. It was narrated by some British guy because you have to be British to narrate animal documentaries.

I guess it made sense. I mean, I couldn't imagine someone with a Southern or, closer to home, an Ozark hillbilly accent detailing animal mating habits in any dignified way.

"Agnus," I said, "why would I knock? It's my apartment. Besides, you have great hearing. Didn't you hear me try the wrong key first?"

Agnus shook his head and sat back down. "I guess my mind was someplace else."

I raised my eyebrow. "In Bangladesh?"

Agnus looked at me. "Bang-la-who?"

"It's where Bengal tigers come from," I said. "They're native to Bangladesh."

Agnus cocked his head. "Not interested in banging la desh, whoever that is. But I'd sure bang la tiger. Look at those stripes on her!"

I bit my lip and looked at Layla. She shrugged. At least now, he was appropriately interested in felines and wasn't flirting with my girlfriend.

I smiled and, bracing myself to bend over the best I could, given my soreness, scratched Agnus behind the ears. "Yeah, she's a real beauty. A bit large for you, though, don't you think?"

Agnus looked at me. "I like big Bengals and I cannot lie."

I smiled. "You other kitties can't deny?"

Agnus wiped his paw across his head. "Don't try to piggyback off my joke, Caspar. It's lame."

"Sorry," I said.

Agnus sprang to his feet and took off across the floor.

Layla was opening a can of tuna. No sooner did the opener pierce the top of the can than he was at her feet, meowing loudly and pawing her leg.

I used to just open the can for him and let him go to town. Layla insisted that wasn't a good practice since he could cut himself on the can. I tried to explain I had one of those extra safe can openers that left a dull edge, but she wouldn't hear it. She always put it in a bowl for him.

I sat down on the couch. Layla came over and sat next to me as Agnus went to town on his food.

"Anything else on television?" Layla asked as the screen showed two Bengal tigers licking each other. "After what just happened, it feels oddly dirty watching this."

I chuckled. "Well, you're sitting right where he was doing his thing."

Layla shrugged. "Trying not to think about it."

I grabbed the remote. It was Sunday, but we were now out of football season. My Chiefs, despite being favored, had been trounced in the Super Bowl. Not a bad season, all things considered, but you can only get away with so many injuries on an offensive line. Sadly, they didn't have a chance from the start, but there was always next year.

I loved football. I don't know why, always had. I looked forward to it every week, and now, only a few weeks into the off-season, it felt like I had to wait an eternity before my team would get another shot at redemption. It also meant we had to find something else to watch on Sundays.

It was the one day of the week I didn't pull an afternoon shift at O'Donnell's, the Irish pub underneath my apartment. The pub's owners doubled as my bosses and also my landlords. They'd given me a job as a bartender when I'd lost my position at the church. Now, even though I was back in the ministry, I just felt bad leaving the job after they'd been so generous. Besides, they'd said as long as I worked for them, they'd waive my rent.

I needed the money. If push came to shove, I supposed I could always pawn my old wedding ring. I wasn't holding onto it for sentimental purposes. My sentiments regarding my marriage were mostly in the form of regrets. But the price of platinum was down at the moment, so I left it in the bottom of my underwear drawer. With free rent and a modest second income from bartending, I wasn't destitute. I had enough to eat, and I had credit cards.

Not to mention, Holy Cross was such a small church that it wasn't a full-time gig anyway.

A lot of folks might think it wouldn't be wise for a recovering alcoholic to work behind a bar. They'd be right, in some instances, but the AA Big Book says that if you're in a fit spiritual condition, you don't need to avoid being in places where alcohol is served. Hell, we even had a guy in our meeting who owned a local vineyard and winery, and he had a few more years of sobriety than I did.

I had a lot of issues with my religion. I didn't agree with everything they told me I was supposed to preach. It was one reason my former bishop had tried to oust me. Healing Doris had been the straw that broke the camel's back. He'd been trying to get rid of me since I'd gone through my divorce. Every time he'd tried, he couldn't get past the fact that my congregation supported me completely, and while they were a small group, our membership consisted of a few wealthy benefactors who were primarily responsible for supporting the district over which the bishop presided.

The healing, though, had given him the excuse he thought he needed. It had been a risk, I suppose, but my healing someone—which, according to our denomination's teaching was the sort of thing that was no longer normative in the Christian experience, being a gift that belonged to the age of the Apostles—was the first time he'd seen me do something he felt was intolerable.

Philip was more understanding. He was what you'd call a more progressive bishop. More like me. While he didn't always vote in my favor, when he had just been an ordinary minister in our district, he'd secretly harbored views more aligned with my own. He'd just felt at the time that since we were a minority, it was to his benefit to vote with the bishop—a wise career move that left him without a target on his back. That had allowed him to move into his current position, which, in the end, saved my career.

I mention all that to say that I didn't begrudge him his past voting habits. It had all worked out. I was the hard-headed one who consistently voted my conscience.

We had a council meeting later that evening, the first since my reinstatement. Philip had promised me we'd revisit the question of partnering with the Methodists to run a local soup kitchen. Under the previous bishop's regime, the question had been dismissed out of hand. Since we didn't fully agree with the Methodists about doctrine, it was argued that partnering with them would give the false impression that we agreed with their abominable teachings. Thus, we'd be complicit in possibly leading people to hell.

It was as stupid as it sounded, but that was the argument.

We had a few hours to burn before that.

Layla interlaced her fingers with mine. "How about a round of ioga?"

"Yoga?" I asked. "I mean, I know that's not what you do, but the videos you've been making me do are actually yoga."

Layla bit her lip. "I'm not talking about that. No videos. I thought maybe I could show you a few moves."

"Like what?" I asked. "I spent all evening perfecting one of the poses. Shavasana. It's my favorite."

"Corpse pose?" Layla asked. "The only thing you do for that is lie on your back and breathe."

"Like I said, I've got that one mastered." I grinned.

"You can do that one if you like. But I could show you a few others while you're doing it. A few poses from on top."

I dropped my jaw and widened my eyes. "I think I follow where you're going with this now."

Layla nodded, stood, and helped pull me off the couch. She winked.

I followed her to the bedroom.

CHAPTER FIVE

Originally I had hoped to catch an AA meeting before the council meeting, but Layla and I found other ways to fill the time. I couldn't believe it. Usually, I was only good for a few minutes, but in my current state of soreness, unable to move much, she was in complete control—and she made it last. Oh, how wonderfully long it lasted!

Before I realized it, too much time had passed. I wasn't going to make a meeting. I'd get over it.

I usually tried to make two or three meetings a week, and they weren't all at the same time of day. Our AA group had an old mansion where they held multiple meetings daily. Technically it wasn't owned by AA since that would violate the twelve traditions, but several members had formed a not-for-profit and used the proceeds to purchase the old house for meetings. Suffice it to say, I'd find another meeting. If not tonight, probably in the morning.

Oddly enough, my legs were feeling better. Hell, after all the things Layla did, everything about me felt better.

I mean, I hadn't expected she'd massage me for that long.

Yes, it was a massage.

Why would anyone think anything else had happened? I'm a minister, so I can't do that sort of thing outside of marriage. As far as anyone knows, at least. That's my story, and I'm sticking to it.

Funny thing about sore legs. Going *down* the stairs is more challenging than climbing them. Despite feeling better, I was still a bit sluggish as I made my way down the stairs. When I got outside, I pulled my keys out of my pocket, then noticed the front driver's side tire on my Mitsubishi was flat.

I sighed and popped the trunk. Not the first time I had to change a tire. Not even the first time in recent memory.

But then I noticed the rear driver's side tire was flat, too.

"Well, shit," I said to myself.

I walked around the car. *All* of the tires were flat. It couldn't be an accident.

Someone had probably taken a knife to them. I didn't see any damage to the sidewalls, but a blade stab to the treads wouldn't be easy to see.

The only question was, who would do that? I mean, random vandalism wasn't entirely out of the question, but something in my gut told me it wasn't random.

Unfortunately, the pub was closed, one of few places that still stayed closed on Sundays. I mean, the place was owned by Irish Catholics. Otherwise, I'd have asked Donna if I could borrow her car. She ran the pub. Her parents, who owned it, only showed up on occasion.

I couldn't miss the council meeting, not after everything I'd been through. Not after Philip had agreed to revisit the soup kitchen issue.

I quickly texted Layla about the tires. Best to keep her on guard. She'd gradually gotten better with her phone. Elves typically dislike technology, but she'd been coming to Earth to learn about our culture for years. She'd gotten a phone by necessity. When she'd been learning about our world, she hadn't realized the whole point of her mission was to discover the best way for her father's legions to attack. She'd thought they were keeping tabs in case they couldn't save their planet. She had believed that coming to Earth was Plan B. She thought she was learning about how to fit in and join us peaceably if it ever came to that.

Her father had deceived her, and the discovery had been harrowing for her.

And anytime anything bad happened, even something as innocuous as someone cutting us off on the highway, she was afraid some assassin from New Albion was responsible.

My phone dinged. It was Layla.

You should come back. But I'm guessing you won't.

Nope, I typed back. **This meeting is too important. I'll be fine.**

B careful, Layla responded. I grinned. She was getting the hang of this texting thing if she was abbreviating two-letter words with one letter.

Two seconds later, she did it again, this time reducing three letters to one. Even more impressive. **Love u**.

Love u 2, I texted back. Yes, abbreviating "too" with 2 was a whole other level of texting expertise. Still, I doubted she was impressed. We'd work on the art of the emoji at a later date.

I had one choice; I had to take the Metro.

It wasn't a far ride to St. Matthews, where the council meeting was supposed to be held. Philip had temporarily taken over my ex-bishop's post there in addition to continuing to serve his congregation. Not sure why he'd decided to cover the vacancy himself, but since he was reviewing Matthias' decisions, I imagined assuming his previous post was part of that. And since the council generally met there, he'd decided he wouldn't rock the boat.

Not rocking the boat was not the strategy I hoped he'd

embrace as the new bishop, though perhaps his decision to rein-state me was bound to be controversial enough. Without good reason, avoiding unnecessary changes was wise, I supposed.

I boarded the Metro bus, and after taking my seat, I checked my phone.

Everything ok?

Yup. Agnus is onto a Cheetah documentary now.

I chuckled. **Yeah. He has a thing for fast felines**.

Layla replied with a laughing-crying emoji. She'd figured out how those worked.

I generally avoided making eye contact with anyone when I had to use the Metro. Not trying to be antisocial, but I also didn't want any trouble.

It usually took two to three times longer to get anywhere by Metro than by car. Thankfully, I'd left early, and we only had a few miles to go. I'd make it in time.

The bus moved from my stop to the next. A massive man got on, massive like Jag. Even larger than B'iff.

And he had a mask on. I mean, it wasn't unheard of. People sometimes wore masks to prevent the spread of sickness. No one used to, but after that Covid situation, mask-wearing in public was less a matter of looking like you were about to rob a convenience store and more about public safety. He was also wearing a hood.

The whole bus shifted as he boarded. He wasn't only large, he was heavy. He barely made it through the door.

He looked straight at me.

I diverted my eyes before it became apparent that I was watching him.

Then he took the seats just beside me. Yes, I said "seats." He filled two of them, almost three.

From my peripheral vision, I could tell he was staring at me.

"We need to talk," the man said. His voice was gravely and unusually deep, but I'd heard a similar cadence and accent like his before.

I bit my lip and looked at him. His eyes had an oddly golden hue. I'd only seen eyes like that once before, and the leathery skin around his brow confirmed it. He wasn't human. He was an elven giant, and he apparently knew who I was.

CHAPTER SIX

"You must be Caspar. The human my brother told me about."

"Your brother was B'iff?"

The giant nodded. "I am Brag'mok. I've been sent to collect my brother's body. He must be granted the proper rites."

I cocked my head. "Wait, you know he's dead?"

"Connected," Brag'mok said. "All of our kind. What happens to one of us, all of us feel. The closer kin we are, the more agonizing the pain. For some giants, the death of one is but an itch, a discomfort. They feel it, they sense it, but the pangs wane quickly. For those closest to the deceased, the pain lingers indefinitely. We will have no peace until he is granted the proper rites."

I took a deep breath and exhaled. "That must be awful. I mean, with all the wars on your world. Every death."

Brag'mok nodded. "Whatever it is that connects us, that which creates the death pangs reaches across worlds."

I shook my head. "I can't imagine what that must be like. Well, you should know, your brother died a hero. He died destroying the Blade of Echoes."

"And fulfilling a prophecy while also saving you from what we assumed would be the death of the chosen one. When the seal broke, the prophecy was revealed."

I nodded and bit my lip. "There might be a problem. When he died, your brother's body went into the source. The heart of Earth's magic. I don't know if there's any way to recover it."

"Please," Brag'mok said. "It is to everyone's benefit that we do this."

I folded my arms. "I want to help. Trust me. And truthfully, I'm thrilled to see you because we could use your help."

"To stop the elves from coming through."

I nodded. "You should know, when he died, his body disappeared along with the blade in the light of Earth's magic. I can't say for certain that it is even whole anymore."

Brag'mok shook his head. "Trust me, his body remains intact."

"If that's true, I'd love to help you," I said. "I just don't know for certain how much help I can be."

"It is worth an attempt," Brag'mok said. "You should know that it might benefit your world if my brother is returned to us. It is B'iff's body, now filled with Earth magic, that has disrupted the ley lines. It is because of that the gates will not close."

"Then I suppose it is to *everyone's* benefit we do this," I said, shrugging. "Somehow."

"Our intelligence said you were a minister. One who does many funerals."

I nodded. "That's true. I do more funerals than I'd like, I suppose. Comes with the territory when you're pastoring an older congregation."

"Apologies, human," Brag'mok said, shaking his head. "I do not know all this language. This is my first time in your world. You say you are a pastor?"

I nodded. "Comes from a word that means 'shepherd.' It means I'm supposed to guide and protect the people in my care, and doing funerals is a part of that."

Brag'mok tilted his head. "And these people are not offended that you think of them as sheep?"

"It's a metaphor," I said. "Do you have sheep on New Albion?"

Brag'mok nodded. "I believe they were brought by our ancestors. Dumb creatures. Helpless. By this metaphor you use, you are saying that your people are stupid?"

I chuckled. "No, not the point. Only that they need a guide."

"Because you think they are dumb," Brag'mok repeated.

I sighed. "It's not a perfect metaphor, I guess. But I don't think they're dumb."

Brag'mok snorted. "No matter. You understand the importance of a death rite, do you not?"

I nodded. "While we don't feel the kind of pain you're describing, we do ache when we lose loved ones. Our funerals, our death rites, are a part of giving people a little closure. Not that the pain completely goes away, especially when family or people are close, but it's part of the healing process."

"I agree," Brag'mok said. "Our rituals are also important. We must sever our connection with the deceased. Only when he has ascended the stalk of bean and assumed his place in the sky fortress will the agony of his death be released."

"The beanstalk?" I asked, raising an eyebrow. "I thought that was just a fairy tale."

Brag'mok grunted. "Fairies. Annoying buggers, they are. It is no surprise that their lore makes a mockery of our own. Why would such stories persist when none of our kind has dwelled on the Earth for centuries?"

I scratched my head. "So, giants and fairies don't get along?"

Brag'mok rolled his eyes. "No one gets along with fairies."

I nodded understandingly, which, I suppose, was mildly deceptive. I'd never met a fairy. Hell, it had never occurred to me that fairytales came from real fairies. Of course, I hadn't realized that fairies were real until now, either. I'd only recently learned that elves and giants were more than folk legends. Of course, *Jack and the Beanstalk* wasn't a flattering tale when it came to the giants. I could see why, if it was a literal fairy tale, Brag'mok might find it offensive.

"About your brother," I said. "You said if his body was consumed by the magic, the gate would close."

"It is the magic that preserves his body," Brag'mok said. "That and the cold water of the spring. There's no telling how long it will take to degrade, if ever. The best way to prevent the elves from coming to Earth is to remove my brother from the core. We must burn his body in accordance with our rites for the sake of your world and so my family can rest."

"You deserve peace," I said. "I get that."

Brag'mok nodded. "The death pangs are part of it, but this kind of pain you describe, the pain humans have when one dies. We feel that too."

I took a deep breath. "There's a time to mourn. I'm very sorry for your loss."

"Thank you," Brag'mok said.

"I want to help, but I was down there with your brother before he died. I don't know if I could go any deeper. The power is all-consuming."

"We must try, human."

I grinned and put my hand on Brag'mok's shoulder. I was both mildly impressed and taken aback by how solid he was. B'iff had been big and strong, but this giant? He was on another level.

"I *want* to help," I said. "I'm just not sure if I can. I have a meeting right now, but when I get back, I'll talk to Layla about it. I'm sure you know of her. Layla Brightborn, the elven princess?"

Brag'mok grunted, "I know of her, and my brother was in communication with us. Before, I mean. We understand she is with you. But you mustn't tell her what we plan."

"Mustn't tell her?" I folded my arms in front of my chest. "Why wouldn't I tell her?"

Brag'mok sighed. "Given what we intend to do, I cannot say for sure if the gates will ever open again. I hope to take B'iff and quickly pass through the gate before it closes. If we get to the gate, passing through it will likely force it shut, and this time, there is a chance it will never open again. Not even on a full moon."

"Which means Layla would be stuck here." I took a deep breath.

Brag'mok nodded. "And if you tell her, she will undoubtedly find cause to return for one last time that she might settle whatever affairs she must. But if she does, the other elves will arrest her. And if they arrest her…"

"They'll execute her as a traitor," I said, finishing the giant's thought.

Brag'mok nodded. "Most certainly."

"But I don't understand," I said. "If I'm the chosen one, if I'm supposed to unite all people…"

Brag'mok clasped his hands in his humongous lap. "Much is assumed about the role of the chosen one. All we know for certain is what the first five prophecies have said and that you've fulfilled each of those. The other two prophecies are yet sealed. We must do what is prudent without making assumptions about what the prophecies might reveal. Until the seals break, we have to work only with what we know."

I nodded. "I'll do what I can, but getting away and trying to help you without her knowing will be a challenge."

Brag'mok nodded. "You need to find a cover."

I bit my lip. "Find a cover" was another way of saying I needed to come up with a clever lie. I didn't like that, but what choice did I have? Something with the church, maybe. That was the one thing I did other than AA meetings that didn't involve her. And AA meetings were only an hour. They wouldn't provide sufficient cover for the time Brag'mok and I would need to go to Meramec Springs, recover B'iff's body, and get back again.

"One question," I said. "Did you slash my tires?"

"I needed a way to get you alone. To a place where you could talk and you wouldn't be able to run away."

"Why would you think I'd run away?" I asked.

Brag'mok shrugged. "You did not know we knew what we know. I thought you'd assume we'd come to avenge B'iff."

"I wouldn't assume anything," I told him.

"Still," Brag'mok said. "I wanted to be sure."

"So you slashed my tires? Do you realize how much a new set of tires costs?"

Brag'mok shook his head. "Sorry about that."

"How'd you even know I'd be leaving? That I'd be going to a meeting tonight and need to take the Metro?"

Brag'mok pulled a small device from his ear. It looked almost like an earbud, but it was crystalline. "With this."

"What is that?" I asked.

"Call it a bug. There is another small device hidden in your car. I've been listening to your conversations, so I knew what your plans for tonight were."

I raised an eyebrow. "Impressive. Do you have any more of those things hidden around that I should know about?"

"If I had hidden them," Brag'mok said, grinning from ear to ear, "I certainly wouldn't tell you about it."

"So you are still spying on me?" I asked.

Brag'mok snorted. "No. But I could be."

The brakes on the bus squealed as it came to a stop.

"This is where I get off," I said.

"I know," Brag'mok said. "Just get in your car and tell me when you can go, and I will meet you at the source."

I sighed. "All right, but it might be a few days."

"Days?" Brag'mok said. "Why days?"

"Because now I have to buy new tires," I said.

"Take this Metro bus to where the rivers meet. From there, you can travel the ley lines. Did my brother not teach you how?"

I sighed. "He did."

Brag'mok nodded. "Then no need to wait for tires."

CHAPTER SEVEN

I imagine I looked stunned as I walked into St. Matthews. I was not sure what had been most off-putting about my Metro encounter with B'iff's older brother. Whether it had been that he wanted me to lie to Layla, or maybe it was a reminder that everything else I was doing, the things I cared about, had to take a back seat to these potentially world-saving endeavors. I mean, how could I even begin to focus on convincing the council to participate in a cross-denominational soup kitchen when elven legions could come bursting through an otherworldly portal at any moment with designs on world domination?

Brag'mok had been patient despite how pressing his need was and had not insisted I leave with him straight away. He hadn't balked about the meeting I was attending getting in the way of things. Surely he knew what this meeting was about. I'd discussed it with Layla more than once recently while driving, so the elven giant had known I was going there, which was how he had been able to arrange our encounter.

On top of all that, I was more than a little annoyed about my tires. I mean, surely Brag'mok could have figured a less destructive way to corner me and force the discussion he meant to have.

It was the least important issue on my mind at the moment, but it still irked me. Sometimes, it's the little things that kill.

I grinned. "The little things that kill." There was a Bush song that said that, one of my favorite bands of all time. I still remembered when I showed up for the first day of school, and half the kids were wearing shirts with the band name modeled on the logo from the old TV show, *M*A*S*H:* B*U*S*H.

I didn't have a clue who they were at the time. Apparently, they'd become a sensation over the summer. It was news to me. But when I picked up their album, you know, back when people bought compact discs, I was hooked. I was a machinehead. Alas, I missed the days of nineties alternative.

"Caspar?" Philip said as I approached the table. "You all right?"

I nodded. "Yeah, sorry. It's been a long day. Someone slashed my tires for some reason."

"I'm sorry to hear that." Philip gestured to an open seat, not the one I was used to claiming. At council meetings, sort of like when people went to church or any other sort of gathering, I tended to take the same seat. I was a creature of habit, I suppose. This time, I was sitting right next to my bishop, a less confrontational position than across the table, like it used to be with his predecessor. Perhaps it was a subtle but symbolic gesture to emphasize that in Philip's mind, we were on the same side.

I sat down and reached to the middle of the table, where there was a carafe of coffee alongside a stack of Styrofoam cups and the usual non-dairy creamer, sugar, and pink fake-sugar packets.

I scooped a little cream into my cup but bypassed the sugar before nearly burning my tongue with the first sip.

I glanced around the table.

Everyone was looking at me.

These guys weren't my friends. They were my colleagues, but I'd always been something of an outsider.

"Shall we begin with a prayer?" Philip asked. It wasn't really a question, more a signal that we should assume the proper posture.

I smiled a little as Philip started speaking. His prayer hadn't been prepared in advance. It wasn't from one of our denominational manuals. That was what the ex-bishop used to do. He was praying what in seminary-speak was known as *ex corde* prayer. That is, extemporaneous prayer. Praying from the heart.

I found it refreshing. It was also controversial, as dumb as that might seem. I still remembered being told by one of our old-school professors at seminary that out of the heart came all things ungodly: evil thoughts, murder, adultery, sexual immorality, theft, false testimony, slander. For that reason, he said, praying from the heart was ill-advised.

What brilliance.

I raised my hand and asked why, then, we were always told that Jesus was moved by his heart, motivated by compassion, when he healed. Also why the prophet Ezekiel had declared that we'd be given new hearts and why, elsewhere, the Bible said we should love God and our neighbor with all our hearts.

I don't remember the professor's reply, but I recall it was dismissive.

"Grant us a spirit of peace and harmony," Philip continued after beginning his prayer with a litany of gratitudes. "Ensure that our deliberations are modeled after your heart, your love of all people, rather than fueled by fear and blind ideals. Amen."

"Amen," I replied, nodding enthusiastically. The other men around the table echoed their obligatory amens. Yes, they were all men because, well, our denomination only permitted men to preach.

Not an issue for local districts to dispute.

It was the sort of matter that would require deliberation at our denomination's national convention, and since each district only had one representative who was chosen from the clergy in that district, my status as an envelope-pusher had never earned me so much as a single vote to become the delegate. And being recently off suspension, I was sure they wouldn't select me this time. Sure enough, selecting a delegate was one of the items on our agenda for the evening.

Philip distributed sheets of paper outlining our meeting's agenda. I habitually licked my thumb, took mine from the top, and passed the rest of the stack around.

Probably not the most sanitary practice, now that I thought about it.

I mean, since the last time I washed my hands, I'd ridden the Metro, opened a couple of doors, and shaken a few hands.

Nasty. What was I even thinking?

I glanced at the agenda.

I wasn't sure why "opening prayer" was listed since he hadn't handed these out until after the prayer had taken place. But after that, there were two items, mostly to do with me, and the third, electing our convention delegate. That one most certainly wouldn't have a damn thing to do with me.

It listed "Rev. Cruciger's reinstatement" as the first item to address, followed by "Reconsidering participation in the Methodist soup kitchen."

"First," Philip said, "I'd like to welcome Reverend Cruciger back. Everyone here knows Caspar and the reason my predecessor initially suspended him. As we discussed in our emergency session, it seems our former bishop's decisions might have been made in haste and with compromised judgment. I believe today was Caspar's first service back at Holy Cross."

I nodded. "It was."

"I presume that today was less eventful than your last?" Philip asked.

I winced. "Not exactly."

Philip smiled. "Well, I'm sure the people were glad to see you nonetheless."

"It's not that," I piped up. "After what happened, word spread. People are coming looking for healings."

"We're aware of that," Philip said, nodding at one of my colleagues. "Reverend Otten managed the situation in your absence. Care to share your experience, Daniel? It might be helpful for Caspar as he navigates this challenge."

Daniel Otten had historically been a loud-mouth advocate of the hardline approach the former bishop Matthias Flacius had taken. A kindly enough man, older than the rest of us, but also the one most likely to turn over a fellow minister if he felt he'd crossed the line when it came to denominational rules. For instance, he ran a blog dedicated to what I've often called "heresy hunting." He was looking for folks like me, those willing to push the envelope and test the boundaries of our dogma and denominational rules.

Otten had once published a scathing blog on the evils of using guitars in worship. Only a pipe organ, he believed, and a piano in a pinch, could be used, and then only to lead a congregation in doctrinally reviewed and approved hymns.

His article included a list of several hundred ministers whom he believed had aligned themselves with Satan on account of offering "contemporary" worship alternatives in their churches.

He also wore a white-tabbed collar almost all the time. In fact, I don't know if I'd ever seen him without one. He once posted a picture of himself canoeing with his wife, and he had been wearing his collar under his life preserver.

"We had to start locking the doors," Otten said. "The first week, we had three or four miracle-seekers show up."

I nodded. "They're still coming. We had one today. A girl with spina bifida."

Otten shook his head. "I know the couple. They've come every week in your absence. I suspect, though, they're faking their daughter's condition to elicit our sympathies and a handout."

I snorted. I wasn't about to argue with him. It was a fairly bold accusation, not to mention a gross assumption hidden under a veneer of racially charged assumptions about the family.

But this was one of those opportunities when winning the battle would come at the expense of losing the war.

I wasn't going to convince Otten that the girl was genuinely in need, and I'd make even less progress asserting that I'd healed her.

"Would it be so wrong," I suggested, "if we established a fund for folks who are in need? I don't know about the girl's condition, but it strikes me that a family must be in dire need if they're willing to go to such measures to secure assistance."

"Not that I'm opposed to helping the poor," Otten said, "but once you start doing that, trust me, their kind multiplies like rabbits. You'll have five more, or even twenty, the next week, expecting additional handouts."

I sighed. "I understand that can be a challenge, but surely there's something we can do to help. I feel like we're wasting an opportunity. We're an all-white congregation in the middle of the city where minorities are the majority. Most of our members drive thirty minutes or more to come to worship."

"And they drive so far," Otten said, "because Holy Cross was their parents' church, the place where they learned the faith, and their grandparents did the same. They come because the traditions of their youth continue to serve them well."

I shook my head. "I have no problem with traditions if they are genuinely helping people. And I agree, most people do value them. But surely there's a reason why our church remains viable, even if only barely so, in a community of need."

"Where would you propose such funds come from?" Philip asked.

I shrugged. "We have wealthier members who might be persuaded to contribute. Perhaps if I led the charge and donated half my salary to the cause."

Daniel was laughing while shaking his head. "If that's what you want to do, there's no one here who will stand in your way. But don't say I didn't warn you. Even Jesus was overwhelmed by crowds of miracle chasers. After he fed the five thousand, he had to flee across a lake because more people came looking for a free meal."

I nodded. "He left so he could have time to pray, not to get away from the people. He did feed the five thousand, after all, and he empowered his disciples to do it."

"I'm not questioning your heart or your motives," Otten said. "But you should act wisely."

I shook my head. "We're not just going to hand out cash, but what if we use our funds and pay utility bills for people in need? We could pay people's rent directly. And if we add our resources to what the Methodist soup kitchen is already doing in our community…"

"Would you like to move on to that item on the agenda?" Philip asked.

I shrugged. "Might as well."

"The situation hasn't changed," Otten said. "They still espouse dangerous doctrines that might deceive the faithful."

I shook my head. "Have you been to the soup kitchen, Daniel?"

"I have not."

"They aren't preaching there, and most of the people who come don't know the difference between Methodists and Baptists and Lutherans, or any of the other thousand denominations that hide behind the notion that they're the only ones doing it right."

"That doesn't mean," Daniel said, clenching his fists, "that the differences don't still exist, nor that such matters are unimportant."

I sighed. "I agree, such issues are important. But we don't sort out those issues by retreating into conclaves of like-minded persons while assuming that everyone else has somehow been infected by the devil's influence."

"So you're suggesting we go so we can convince the Methodists of their errors?" Daniel asked, a hint of intrigue in his voice.

I rolled my eyes. "No. I'm suggesting we go so we can contribute to the infrastructure they've already established and help more people in the community."

Otten was about to speak, but Philip raised his hand, cutting him off. "For the sake of argument, let's say that you're right, Daniel. The Methodists espouse doctrines we believe might conflict with our interpretation of scripture. But if you believe that their teachings are dangerous, wouldn't you want to be there so that those who are reached at the kitchen don't all end up in their churches rather than ours?"

I bit my tongue. That point had occurred to me too, but the idea that this was some bait-and-switch scheme to grow our membership rolls was aggravating.

That wasn't the point.

There were hungry people in the community. Some might not eat if the soup kitchen wasn't there, and from what I knew, the Methodists were stretched thin. They didn't have enough volunteers to oversee the place seven days a week. They didn't have the financial resources to do it, either. The fact of the matter was whether or not the folks who benefited from the kitchen ended up in our churches the following Sunday, if we participated, they'd be able to eat on evenings when they might otherwise go hungry.

"A fair point," Daniel said. "But I'd suggest we propose to the Methodists taking over the kitchen on the nights when it isn't open. We run our nights how we see fit. They do the same on the evenings when they are in charge."

"It's a possibility," Philip said. "Is that an agreeable proposal, Caspar?"

I shrugged. "Better than not participating at all. Still, I don't see any harm if our volunteers and theirs are allowed to contribute on any night of the week, regardless of who is in charge that evening."

"We can't prevent our members from volunteering whenever they like," Philip added. "And trying to enforce rules like that would be untenable."

"Still," Otten continued, "on our nights, we will offer prayers before meals. We will be the ones answering questions of a religious nature. We will be the ones handing out invitations to our churches."

I bit my lip. I thought that was silly, but as a compromise, it was preferable in my estimation to refusing to participate. "I think we could work with that, provided the Methodists agree."

"Very well," Philip said. "Then it's agreed. Caspar, please initiate a conversation with the Methodists in charge and communicate our terms. Pending a final vote to approve this course of action, of course."

I nodded. "I can do that."

Philip took a voice vote. On this occasion, the ayes were universal. There were no nays, a small victory. It was progress, anyway.

"With that matter settled," Philip said. "I'd like to open the floor for nominations for the denomination's convention."

"I nominate Daniel Otten," one of the ministers piped up.

"Any objection?" Philip asked.

No objections were voiced.

"In that case, Daniel, are you willing to serve as our delegate should you be chosen?"

"Of course," Otten said. "It was an honor to serve at the last convention, and I'd be glad to do so again."

Philip nodded. "I'd like to also nominate Reverend Caspar Cruciger. Do you object to your nomination, Caspar?"

"No, I don't." I scratched my head. "But, I mean, I was barely reinstated."

Otten grunted. "And he'll be distracted by his duties at the soup kitchen. Provided the Methodists agree to our terms."

"Are you objecting to his nomination, Daniel?" Philip asked.

"No," Daniel said. "No objection."

I didn't win, but I did secure five out of eleven votes, which was darn close. One more and we'd have ended up in a tie. Technically, I abstained, and Otten voted for himself, so one could argue that effectively we did tie. If I'd voted for myself, we'd be six-to-six. But in this case, unlike other formal matters, we'd voted by secret ballot. No one knew for certain that I was the one who abstained.

Though, from the look on Philip's face when he announced the tally, he suspected it.

I was assuming Otten had cast his vote for himself, but there wasn't any way he'd vote for me. Cows would fly before he did that.

Truthfully, it was the best-case scenario. I didn't want to go to a convention, not when elven legions might burst through the gates at any time. Not when, according to Layla, I'd be the best shot my fellow humans would have to stop them. I probably should have declined the nomination, all things considered, but I didn't think I'd get more than a single vote. And even then, I suspected, Philip had only nominated me as a good-faith measure.

But for some reason, half the council believed I was preferable to Otten. I, the one who was always challenging church dogma, as opposed to my colleague, who believed himself to be a defender of it.

An odd position, given that the God of the Bible had created the universe, decided the outcomes of wars, flooded the world, and raised himself from the dead. Why would anyone think that a God who could do things like that needed us to defend him?

I exhaled a sigh of relief. Now, in addition to making my mind up about whether to help Brag'mok behind Layla's back, I had to contact the Methodists, make our council's proposal, and if they agreed, start organizing things at the soup kitchen.

Then again, if I still needed a cover to help Brag'mok, working the soup kitchen would be ideal. It would give me a whole evening, not to mention since it was a church function and Layla and I still hadn't gone public with our relationship, she wouldn't be able to attend.

CHAPTER EIGHT

"I'm not doing anything called downward dog," Agnus said. "That would be humiliating."

I smirked as I got on all fours and stuck my ass in the air. "It's just what it's called, Agnus."

"So, if I told you to get in a pose and called it pansy bitch, you'd do it?" Agnus asked.

"Well, probably not."

"Why not? It's just a name. Doesn't mean you'd become a pansy bitch if you did it."

"Fair point," I agreed.

"Because you can't become something you already are!" Agnus shot back.

I cleared my throat, did my best to jump my feet back to my hands, and stood up slowly.

Layla had gone for a jog, and I'd decided to take advantage of her absence to knock out my yoga routine before bed. Since I only had one television, and Agnus had nothing better to do, he'd decided he'd try to show me up. I mean, he's a cat, and cats are more flexible by nature. Until now, I'd assumed he had better balance.

"You're seriously going to try tree pose?" I asked as I stood up and lifted one leg, pressing my foot into the thigh of the other and extended my arms toward the ceiling.

"If you can do it, I can do it," Agnus retorted before perching on his hind legs and trying to push himself up with just one. He collapsed in a pile of fur and hissed. I chuckled, which caused me to lose my balance. Thankfully, all I had to do to come out of the pose was lower one foot. "This is human yoga, Agnus. It's fine if you can't do every pose."

Agnus stared at me and burst into song. *"Anything you can do, I can do better. I can do anything better than you."*

"No, you can't," I replied

"Yes, I can," Agnus insisted.

"No, you can't. Besides, isn't that from some musical?" I asked.

"Sung by Ethel Merman," Agnus informed me. "My love."

I cocked my head. "You think you're in love with Ethel Merman?"

"The way she moved across the stage, she was like a cat."

I shook my head. "You realize she died a long time before you were born?"

"What!" Agnus exclaimed, placing one paw to his chest. "Say it ain't so!"

I paused the video and grabbed my phone. "Here it is. It says on her Wikipedia page that the musical you're talking about was done in the forties. She died in the early eighties."

Agnus huffed and hopped onto the couch. "Probably for the best. I'm still holding out for my beloved Bengal. It's a more appropriate match anyway."

I bit my lip. "You realize you're neutered, right?"

"All that means is I can't knock her up. That doesn't mean I can't have my fun!"

"First, I'm not sure a small tabby house cat can knock up a Bengal Tiger. And second, I somehow doubt it would be as much fun as you're imagining unless getting eaten is your idea of a good time."

Agnus shook his head. "Once you go cat, you never go back."

I scrunched my brow. "That doesn't even rhyme properly, and I can't imagine that's true."

I grabbed the remote and unpaused the video in time to see Tony Horton release his tree pose and go through another vinyasa sequence.

I did my best to follow suit.

"I'm just staying right here," Agnus said.

"Embarrassed about the last stumble?" I asked.

"No," Agnus said. "This exercise is beneath me."

"Because of downward dog?" I asked.

"Amongst other things," Agnus said, licking his paw, then dragging it across his head.

I rolled my eyes and proceeded through my vinyasa before Tony introduced the next balance posture: crane.

There was no way in hell I was pulling this one off. It was a miniature handstand with your knees tucked in and resting on your elbows.

I just sat there and stared at the screen.

"Pussy!" Agnus blurted. "You won't even try?"

"Look who's talking!" I snapped.

"When you call *me* that, it's no insult. I'm immune to pussification."

I cocked my head. "Is that even a word?"

"Maybe not according to the King's English. But whoever decided the king gets to define what is or isn't a word anyway?"

I shrugged. "They do call our language 'English.'"

"And I've been known to call you an asshole, asshole. Does that make you the master of all things butthole?"

I squinted. "Your analogy is flawed. Besides, I think it's the Queen's English as long as the reigning monarch is a queen, not a king."

"Doesn't matter," Agnus said. "You aren't in England, and even if you were, what kind of jerk thinks he's so high and mighty that he can dictate proper grammar?"

"I don't know," I said. "I don't think the King or Queen of England has much governing power beyond that."

"And that's no power at all," Agnus said. "Besides, I don't technically speak English. You just hear me in English because that's how your mind processes what I'm telling you."

I shrugged. "I don't care. How'd we even get on this topic to begin with?"

"You were distracting yourself from doing yoga by challenging my use of the word pussification. Mostly because you're a pussy."

I sighed. "Whatever. I can't clear my mind enough to do this tonight anyway."

Agnus cocked his head. "Want to talk about it?"

I sighed. I wasn't sure I could trust Agnus not to blab about it. "No, not really."

"Good. Because only pussies talk about their feelings."

"That's not true!" I objected. "It's healthy to talk about your feelings. If you don't talk about them, you just bottle them up until you blow up. It's one of the benefits of my AA meetings. It's a place to air my feelings without worrying about being judged."

"And you think I'd judge you?" Agnus asked.

"All you ever do is judge me," I replied.

"True," Agnus said. "But all I'm doing when I judge you is state the obvious."

"That I'm a pussy?" I asked.

Agnus nodded. "I somehow doubt I'm the only one who has ever called you that."

I snorted. "Some dude at the gym said as much earlier today. But the way he said it, it didn't come across as judge-y."

"Judge-y?" Agnus asked. "And you're challenging the legitimacy of *my* word choices?"

"How do you even know that's not a word if I only hear you in English?" I asked.

Agnus stared at me blankly, then slowly shook his head.

"So, according to this prophecy, you're supposed to be my familiar, right? A source of wisdom and guidance?" I asked.

Agnus continued staring at me. "Obviously."

I snorted. "Can I trust you to keep a secret?"

"A secret? There are only two people who can hear me speak, you and Layla."

"Right." I pulled myself up on the couch. "Unless anyone else who wields magic shows up."

"Oh. My. God. You're planning to propose!" Agnus exclaimed.

I laughed. "Good guess, but no. Too soon for that."

Agnus cocked his head. "Then what could it possibly be?"

I sighed. "B'iff's brother is here on Earth. He thinks B'iff's body is charged with magic and still in the source, and that what's keeping the gate open."

"So we help him get it out. What's the big deal? Why would that be a secret?"

I bit my lip. "Because Brag'mok, B'iff's brother, said that once we remove his corpse from the source and the gate closes, we cannot guarantee that it will ever open again."

"And Layla would be stuck here indefinitely," Agnus said.

I nodded. "Brag'mok cautioned that she might try to go back to say goodbye to people she loves and tie up loose ends. But if she does that, he said they'll arrest her and probably execute her immediately."

"How can this orc be certain?" Agnus asked.

"They don't like the world 'orc.' They prefer 'giant,'" I said, correcting my politically incorrect cat. "And I'm guessing he has keen intelligence on elven politics. Since she helped me by defying her father, even if the elf king wants to save her life on account of being her father, his hands might be tied if sentiment against her is too strong."

"If you do this but don't tell her, she might not ever forgive you."

"But she'll be alive. As much as I hate to think about her being angry with me, that's something we can get past. Her being executed, though…"

"Layla is smart," Agnus said. "But she's also overly confident about her skills. This Brag'mok is right. She will likely return to New Albion no matter what you say. She'll think she has the skill to avoid capture."

"So I can't tell her."

"I didn't say that," Agnus replied. "She could be right. You don't know for sure that she will be captured."

"But if there's a chance, even the slightest chance that she'd get caught and killed…" I took a deep breath and leaned over, my elbows on my knees and my face in my palms.

"Despite what the orc said—"

"Giant," I coughed into my hand.

"Whatever," Agnus said, licking his chops. "Despite what he said, if you start making choices for her, even if you're afraid she'll make the wrong ones, she might never forgive you. You aren't her owner any more than you are mine."

I wasn't about to correct Agnus about being his owner. I suspected he figured he was *my* owner. I mean, don't all cats think that way? I scratched my scalp and took a deep breath. "I don't like this. Not at all. I have the perfect out. I need to spend time at the soup kitchen. What harm is there in at least checking first to see if it's even viable? I mean, if we can't even get B'iff's body from the source like Brag'mok suggests, the point would be moot."

Agnus nodded. "Very well. But I'd suggest before you do anything that can't be undone, you tell Layla the truth. She's given up everything for you. Her family. Her world. Everything she's ever known. You owe her the truth."

I pressed my lips together. "I'll tell her once I know for certain what the plan is, then. Part of me hopes it's a moot point and we won't be able to get B'iff out of there, but another part says if we can, we might be able to prevent any chance of an elven invasion."

"Isn't that life?" Agnus asked. "It's not often that we are confronted with cut and dried decisions. I mean, consider the conundrum of bathing myself before versus after using the litter box."

"I'd think after would make more sense," I said. "You know, sort of like washing your hands after going to the bathroom."

"Ew!" Agnus protested. "After digging through litter with my paws?"

"Fair point," I agreed. "Hadn't thought of that."

"But at the same time, I feel dirty after using my box. I have an urge to clean myself."

"I don't blame you."

"The point is, there isn't an easy answer," Agnus said. "But if you do decide to go through with it, you should tell her."

"But won't she be pissed that I didn't tell her from the start?" I asked.

"Probably," Agnus said. "But she'll get over that. If you are going to potentially close the gate to her home without telling her, though, that would be unforgivable."

The door clicked and Layla walked in, still breathing heavily from her jog. I don't know why, but I do the slightest amount of work, and I sweat like a pig. Layla goes for a long run, probably several miles, and has just a touch of sweat on her temples.

"What are you two up to?" Layla asked.

"Just talking about things," I said.

"Things like what?" Layla asked.

I shrugged. "Discussing the meaning of life."

"When you have nine lives," Agnus piped up, "you can try out a few different meanings."

I cocked my head. "Cats don't literally have nine lives. That's just something people say because of how cats seem always to live on the edge, narrowly escaping major disasters."

"How do you know that?" Agnus asked.

"Have you ever died?" Layla asked. "Even once?"

"Well, no. I don't want to waste any of my lives."

"Because you only have one," I said. "You won't test it because deep down, you know I'm right."

Agnus meowed before he turned, jumped off the couch, and walked away, displaying his hindquarters. "Silly mortals."

CHAPTER NINE

"How'd the meeting with the council go?" Layla asked.

"Better than I expected," I said. "They agreed to allow me to explore an arrangement for working the soup kitchen on alternate evenings with the Methodists."

Layla nodded. "Well, I suppose that's progress."

I looked at the wall. When there's something I know but can't share, I get uneasy. I'm a horrible liar, and I don't keep secrets well. "Yeah. Going to take a lot of work, though."

"Are you going to be able to handle it all?" Layla asked. "You really can't afford to cut back on your training."

I sighed. "I know. I guess something will have to give."

"The bartending gig?" Layla asked.

I nodded. "Probably, but I need it this month. I won't get my first paycheck from the church in time to pay rent, which I'll have to do if I quit that job."

"How are you going to get everything in?" Layla asked.

I shrugged. "Just the same for now, only two or three evenings each week I won't be here. I'll have to work in the kitchen. Presuming, of course, the Methodists agree to our proposal."

"Do you expect they will?" Layla asked.

I nodded. "Most likely. They'll probably think it's a little silly to divide the evenings by denomination, but their goal when asking us to participate was to offer dinners seven days a week. This arrangement would accomplish that."

"I suppose we'll just have to make the most of our time at the gym, then," Layla said. "It isn't like this is going to be forever."

I chuckled. "Yeah, because the way things are going, I'll end up slaughtered by your father."

"Don't say shit like that," Layla snapped, rolling her eyes. "You are coming along well. You might not notice, but you're getting leaner, you're getting stronger, and the flexibility will come eventually. You just have to stick to that yoga, which should also help you focus and get a better handle on your magic."

"Layla," I said. "We're talking about me taking on a whole legion of magic-wielding elves. A legion that is strong enough to defeat every human army on Earth."

"Only because they can use their magic to control nature," Layla said. "But once you're in full control of your power, you should be able to neutralize anything they do."

I shook my head. "Which means that killing me will be their number one priority."

Layla sighed. "Most likely. Which, as you know, is why we're trying to get you into fighting shape. Even if you don't fight, at least to give you a chance if you have to run."

I bit my lip. "What if there was a way to close the gate?"

Layla shook her head. "I don't know how we could do that."

"But say there was a way. What would that mean?" I asked.

Layla scratched her head. "I'd be afraid we couldn't open it again. I love you, Caspar, but I am still holding out hope that you *will* find a way to unite the people. All people—elves, giants, and humans. Maybe even fairies."

I bit my lip. This was the first time Layla had mentioned fairies. I'd only just learned of them from Brag'mok, but Layla didn't know that. "Fairies? Are you serious?"

Layla nodded. "They mostly stay to themselves. They don't like elves much. Or giants or humans, for that matter. But now that you're wielding Earth magic, there's a good chance they'll make an appearance eventually. They believe themselves to be the protectors of magic."

"How do they protect magic?" I asked.

"They used to wage massive assaults. Swarms of them would overwhelm a practitioner and strip him of his power. But for the most part, they're tricksters. They don't have the numbers they used to, so they'll do what they can without you noticing it to make it seem like every spell you cast has consequences."

"Like the idea that magic comes with a price in the *Once Upon A Time* series?" I asked.

Layla chuckled. "Binged a few episodes of that on Netflix while you were working. Funny you'd say that, but yes, that's sort of what the fairies do. Not that there is a natural price that comes with magic, but if you think there is, they believe you'll be more careful about how you use it."

"And these fairies are on New Albion, too?" I asked.

Layla nodded. "Not many, but yes. Their numbers on both planets have dwindled over the centuries. That's probably why we haven't encountered them yet. They surely know you've tapped into Earth's magic, but they're likely observing from afar, making sure you aren't doing anything too foolish, not risking their lives by getting involved until they feel like they have no other choice."

"Well," I said, "I guess I'll look forward to it."

"I wouldn't," Layla said. "I've only had a handful of encounters with them, but in my experience, such confrontations are never pleasant. They don't trust that anyone who isn't a fairy will use magic properly."

"Wonder why they'd think that? Given that on your planet, it's been wasted for the sake of war for centuries."

Layla nodded. "They aren't wrong. But if the fairies had their way, they'd prevent all of us from using it. If there were more of them, they'd probably succeed. Instead, though, they'll just watch you. You might not even realize it—unless they catch you doing something naughty, magic-wise, that is. Then they'll become something of a nuisance."

"A nuisance how, exactly?" I asked.

Layla shrugged. "No one knows all they're capable of, but they'll find ways to fuck with you. They usually start small, little pranks to get your attention. Like warning shots, I suppose. But then, provided you don't get the clue and keep using magic, they'll escalate their attacks."

I scratched my head. "I don't get it. You say you have fairies on New Albion. How is it that you've been able to wage wars for so long? Wouldn't the fairies stop you?"

"They've tried," Layla said, "but fairies can be killed. The elves have been hunting them down for years. There are hardly any left on New Albion, and those that remain are too scared to get involved."

"I see," I said.

"Here on Earth, no one has hunted them for centuries. Their numbers still aren't huge, but they're more numerous here than on New Albion. And since there are only a handful of people on Earth who can wield magic, it won't take many of them to quickly become a nuisance."

I shook my head. "Why haven't we talked about this until now?"

Layla shrugged. "No need. As long as you keep using magic the way it's intended, it shouldn't be an issue. The only reason it came up now was that you asked when I mentioned that the chosen one is supposed to unite all the peoples."

I nodded. "Yeah, I suppose that makes sense. Still, it would be nice to know what other magical creatures might be out there that could cause problems."

"On Earth, that's pretty much it. As far as I'm aware, anyway."

"As far as you're aware?" I asked. "Aren't you supposed to know about this stuff?"

Layla shook her head. "Remember, our people haven't been on Earth for centuries. I'm one of just a handful of visitors who've come here to study human society. Beyond that, all we know about the Earth's magical history is whatever knowledge our ancestors passed on through the elven priesthood."

"The priesthood." I huffed. "The ones who only share however much of the prophecies they want the people to know?"

"The same," Layla agreed.

"So there might be more about this stuff that your ancestors meant for you to know that the priesthood has kept from the rest of the elves?" I asked.

Layla bit her lip. "I suppose that might be true, now that I think about it. Keep in mind, until just recently, I believed the elves were the good guys."

I snorted. "Yeah, seems kind of funny that the giants, the so-called orcs, are the noble ones."

"The elves used to be, too. Originally, before we became elves, before we left Earth, our druid ancestors were sages, brilliant and honorable. But that was when they were connected to the Earth. Centuries apart from the Earth with only a bit of stolen magic used to invigorate our planet changed us, it seems."

"I can see why your people would want to come back," I said. "I mean, if Earth is a part of what your people used to revere."

"'Used to' is the key," Layla said. "Now I think they only worship power. They use the whole idea of reverencing the Earth as justification for their plans to come here and punish humanity. You know, for pollution and whatnot."

I chuckled. "Yeah, all that whatnot is destroying the planet."

Layla snorted. "The ecological hazards that shall not be named. Too many to count. 'Whatnot' is an all-inclusive term."

"I'm all for inclusivity," I said. "We need a more welcoming world."

"You see, that's why you're the chosen one. Why you're the one who is supposed to unify all the people. However, that pans out once the last two seals are revealed."

I nodded. "We'll see, I suppose."

"Want to watch a show or something?" Layla asked.

I sighed. "I was thinking of trying to catch an eight o'clock meeting. With the car vandalized on top of everything else, I could use one."

In truth, I needed a meeting because I still was incredibly uneasy. I wasn't going to drink over it or anything. Given all that was happening, the one thing I knew I couldn't do was take a drink. If I wanted everything to get even more stressful, that would be the way to do it.

Layla grabbed my hand. "Do what you need to do. I'll be here when you get back. Maybe we'll have a little time before bed? Need to make sure you're getting your eight hours of sleep, though, so your muscles can adapt to the workouts."

I nodded. "I think I can make it back by nine-thirty, ten at the latest."

Layla leaned over and kissed me on the cheek. "All right, I'll see you soon."

I pulled her close and kissed her forehead.

CHAPTER TEN

Every AA meeting begins with the Serenity Prayer. After that, there's a reading from the "How it Works" chapter of the Big Book. Part of that reading says the program demands rigorous honesty.

I'd reflected on those words before. I had to be honest with myself that I just couldn't drink like a normal person. No matter how much I wanted to, no matter what methods I tried, one drink would always turn into twenty.

But tonight, those words struck me to the core. How could I embrace a life of rigorous honesty while lying to the one person who'd risked everything and effectively given up her family and her entire world because she believed in me?

But Agnus hadn't said anything to change my mind. Why not figure out if what Brag'mok said was even possible first? Make sure that we *could* retrieve B'iff's body before the prospect of the gate closing was an issue. Then I could tell Layla.

It made sense.

It minimized the chance that she might freak out and go back to New Albion and get herself arrested, but it also meant, even if for a short time, that I wasn't rigorous about my honesty. It meant having to use the soup kitchen as a cover to go to Meramec Springs with Brag'mok. It meant not telling her about why the tires were slashed.

"Caspar," Rusty said when it was my turn to share, "do you have something to say tonight?"

Rusty was my sponsor. He was an older man, an electrician with more years of sobriety than I had fingers and toes. He was the guy I had done my fourth step with, the one where you make a list of all your character defects.

Mine had been a tome.

Rusty knew it all, and he could see right through me. No one other than my mother could read me that well.

If I passed my turn to share, he'd know something was up.

I never passed. Preachers never pass up a chance to hear themselves talk, and I was no exception to that.

"Yeah," I said. "I have something I'd like to say. I'm sorry if it's off-topic. In truth, I wasn't paying much attention to the topic because my mind is stewing on something. As some of you know, I'm in a new relationship. It's going well, but something came up that I was told I should hide from her. Something that if she knew about it, it might cause her harm. But here's the thing. If I don't tell her the truth, I'm going to have to create a whole web of lies, and I don't know if I can handle that. Part of me thinks I should just tell her. I should trust that she's not going to take the information and do anything rash. But then again, I'm worried that I'd only tell her for selfish reasons. Because I'm afraid if I keep this information from her, she'll hate me for it once she finds out. But I don't want to see her get hurt, either. I don't know what to do."

Rusty cleared his throat. "Thanks, Caspar."

I nodded. We weren't supposed to cross-talk in meetings. If someone talked, it wasn't the place for other members to directly address the person. It was a rule meant to prevent people from giving unsolicited advice. Not all advice, even in an AA group, was helpful. The rule also prevented one person's issue from taking over the group. But I knew Rusty would have a few words for me after the meeting. As my sponsor, I'd given him permission to verbally slap me sideways when I needed it. He wasn't a shrink, and he didn't have any training as a therapist, but he did know what it took to stay sober.

There were another half-dozen or so folks who shared. Usually, I try to listen. It's not a good thing to be in your head during a meeting. Hard to get something out of it without listening. But I was overwhelmed by my dilemma.

The meeting finished, as was our custom, with the Lord's Prayer. Then, as I knew he was bound to do, Rusty pulled me aside.

"What's going on, Caspar?" Rusty asked.

I shook my head. "I'd tell you the details, but it's kind of unbelievable, and it involves secrets that aren't mine to share."

Rusty nodded. "I can respect that. But I'm concerned about you."

I sighed. "I am, too. I don't like this. Hiding things. Not being truthful. Having to use other things as a cover to get away with the lie. Reminds me of when I was drinking."

Rusty nodded. "That's why sobriety demands rigorous honesty, Caspar."

I bit my lip. "I'm scared. If I tell her the truth…"

"Why do you think it's your job to protect her from information she probably wants to know?" Rusty asked.

"I don't know," I said. "Maybe because the person who asked me to help him with the thing that would impact her asked me not to tell her."

Rusty shook his head. "If someone is telling you to lie to someone you love, if they're putting that burden on you, then what they're asking of you isn't right. It isn't fair."

"I get that," I said. "But I also feel like I owe this person something. He's sacrificed a lot for my sake. It feels like I have to respect his request for a secret."

"Well, there are a couple of ways to think about this," Rusty said. "But you said in the meeting that this woman you're with, you're afraid she'll leave you if you don't tell her. Why did you say that?"

I shrugged. "I don't know. Because if I were in her position, I'd want to know."

"And you don't think she'd understand why you felt obligated to keep it a secret for the sake of this other person who you said sacrificed something significant for you in the past?" Rusty asked.

I took a deep breath. "I think she'd understand, but she'd also be angry about it."

Rusty scratched his head. "Why don't you give her the choice?"

"What do you mean?" I raised one eyebrow. "How can I do that without telling her the truth?"

"Just the way you told us tonight," Rusty said. "Tell her that you've been presented with something, and someone asked you to keep it a secret from her. Tell her what you're afraid of happening either way. Then let her decide if she wants to know."

I grinned. "You know, that's not half-bad advice."

Rusty patted me on the shoulder. "That's what I'm here for. Remember, rigorous honesty. It's not always easy, but there's always a way."

CHAPTER ELEVEN

I hated to admit it, but I felt like Rusty's advice was probably better than the idea I'd sorted out in consultation with my cat. Not that Agnus wasn't a good familiar and didn't provide decent council.

But at the end of the day, he was a cat.

And since they didn't have Al-Anon groups for the pets of alcoholics, groups where people could go to gain some understanding of what their loved one is going through, he didn't understand why hiding the truth for even a moment was so terrifying to me.

I can't live with half-truths and lies lurking over my life.

Brag'mok might be pissed, but even he'd only urged me to lie for Layla's sake. At least, that was the reason he gave me. If there was more to it than that, if there was another reason he didn't want Layla to know what we were doing, all the more reason to tell her. I mean, could I trust the giant who'd slashed my tires to lure me into a conversation more than the elf I loved? The one who'd saved my life and had given up so much for my sake?

I reached into my pocket and grabbed my phone as I walked out of my meeting so I could switch it off silent.

Fifteen missed calls, all from Layla.

One text message.

Caspar. Emergency at home. Couldn't wait. Had to go back to New Albion. Don't worry, I'll be fine. Keep training. Agnus has details. Love u. Xoxo Layla.

"Fuck!" I shouted out loud, garnering a few stares from a few AA members who were still lingering in the hall.

Don't go, I quickly typed back. **Something I have to tell you first**.

As I took off running, I double-checked the bus schedule on my phone. What were the chances that if I took the Metro I'd catch her in time?

No reply to my text, either. Not yet.

I found a dark corner behind the dumpster in the back of the AA club. I didn't care if people saw me, given the urgency of the situation. Still, all things being equal, it would be better if they didn't.

I took a deep breath and did my best to clear my mind. The hardest thing about magic was that it took a focused mind, but the times I needed magic the most were usually urgent situations like this one, when focusing was practically impossible.

Still, I'd done it before. I could do it again.

Breathe, Caspar.

I visualized myself taking off into the sky and flying home. I had to do it all in my mind's eye, but it was possible.

This was one reason Layla had me doing yoga—all the chaos of the body trying to hold impossible poses while, at the same time, clearing my mind. That was what I needed. It wasn't just about flexibility.

I felt a breeze against my face and opened my eyes.

"Shit," I said, still seeing the back of the dumpster in front of me. It was just a gust of wind, and it smelled delightful, given that I was crouching behind a dumpster.

I tried again. I inhaled slowly. I exhaled.

My body soared through the skies just like Superman.

Again nothing.

My phone rang in my pocket, *A Cloak of Elvenkind* by Marcy Playground. It was Layla's ringtone.

A video call.

I quickly answered.

"Layla!" I said just before Agnus' face appeared on my screen.

"Seriously?" I asked out loud. "Where's Layla?"

"She's gone, Caspar. She left her phone here. Some other elf came and grabbed her. Said something had happened to her father. Assassinated by Hector."

I raised my eyebrow. "Hector is dead, Agnus."

Agnus shook his head. "Apparently not. And since he says he survived a stab by the Blade of Echoes, he's claiming he's the chosen one."

I bit my lip. "How long ago did Layla leave?"

"You're not going to catch up with her," Agnus said. "The guy that showed up, I think it was one of the elven priests. They went through some kind of gateway, probably back to the portal."

"Maybe if I can fly there?"

"Caspar," Agnus said, "you can't stop her. This is her father, her family. Even if you got to her, what would you tell her?"

I sighed. "The truth, Agnus. I'd tell her the truth."

I had to take the Metro. Even if I could fly, I was too late, based on what Agnus had told me.

But things didn't add up.

I'd seen Hector's body dissolve into a cloud of golden dust. He'd stabbed himself with the false blade, thinking it was the genuine Blade of Echoes and thereby proving he was the real chosen one, but by so doing, he'd attuned his soul to the fake. When I'd overwhelmed the fake blade with magic and destroyed it, he'd died, too.

It wasn't like his body lingered somewhere and could have been revived.

He was in more pieces than Humpty Dumpty. Not even all the king's horses and men could put that elf back together again.

A strange fairytale, now that I thought about it. I mean, how much help did anyone expect the king's horses to be in the Humpty Dumpty reassembly project, anyway? And the king's men? Come on. Humpty Dumpty needed serious medical attention.

I half-wondered if it was a genuine fairytale, a story told by real fairies, now that I knew fairies were real. Who was Mother Goose, anyway?

I clenched my fists.

If only I'd told Layla from the start. I don't know what she would have done, but it might have prevented this from happening.

Now, if I helped Brag'mok retrieve B'iff's body, if we closed the gate, there was a chance I'd never see Layla again.

I wanted to go after her. I knew where the portal was, but I hadn't dared go through it.

Who was I kidding?

The only advantage I had here was that I had a unique connection to the Earth's magic. I could access it in insane quantities. I'd barely scratched the surface in terms of what was possible.

But if I went to New Albion where magic was in short supply, I'd be helpless.

That was not why Layla had said I needed to get into fighting shape. She'd never once mentioned having to go to New Albion for any reason, much less to rescue her.

She'd said she'd be fine. She'd said I should keep training. Why was I even thinking she needed rescuing?

I shook my head. Maybe I just wanted to play knight in shining armor. I suppose I've always had a hero complex in my relationships.

My ex-wife had had issues I knew about before we were together. I thought I'd save her from it all. Part of me went into ministry because I thought by doing that, I was saving people. And now, I was the chosen one who was supposed to save the world.

Going after Layla would be a suicide mission. Frankly, she could handle herself better alone than if I was there and she had to worry about keeping *me* safe. She was the badass warrior princess, not me. I wasn't badass, I wasn't a warrior, and I wasn't a princess, though Agnus might dispute that last part.

Once the bus arrived at the stop nearest my apartment, I ran as fast as I could. First things first.

If Brag'mok had some kind of bug in my car, maybe I could let him know what was going on. He might be able to help.

I pulled my keys out of my pocket and clicked the fob to unlock my Mitsubishi, which still sat in my usual parking spot in the back of the pub parking lot with four flat tires.

"Brag'mok," I said. I took a deep breath. It felt a little strange talking to some kind of bug that supposedly existed. "I need to talk to you. Something has happened, and I don't think I'll be able to help you until it's resolved. But I need your help. And this time, just come to my apartment or something. I'd rather not meet you on the bus. I'm sick of the bus. Someone slashed my tires, you know."

I cleared my throat. I didn't know how much sense I was making. I was rambling. I tended to do that when I was anxious.

No sense waiting in the car.

When I walked into the apartment, Agnus was sitting at the door, waiting for me.

"About time you got home," my cat said.

I sighed. "I had to take the bus. Do you know anything else? Did Layla tell you more about what I should do while she's doing whatever it is she's doing?"

"Nothing," Agnus said, head-butting my shin. "There was a knock on the door. Some elf dude was there. He told her that her father had been assassinated and there was a struggle for control. And Hector was suspected to be responsible. He was trying to claim the throne in her absence."

I sighed. "They want to make her the queen?"

"Hell if I know," Agnus said. "But the elf priest didn't want to see Hector or whoever they think is Hector in charge."

"It can't be Hector," I said. "You were there when he died. You saw his body turn to dust, right?"

"That was what we thought we saw," Agnus equivocated.

A loud thud on the door startled me. "I wonder if that's Brag'mok?"

I checked the peephole. All I could see was a massive chest, so it probably was. I opened the door, and, sure enough, Brag'mok stood in my hallway, ducking to avoid hitting his head on the ceiling.

"Thank God you came," I said.

"I know a little about the affairs on New Albion. Do you have some time to chat?" Brag'mok asked.

I nodded. "Of course. I'd offer you a place to sit, but—"

"Never mind it," Brag'mok said as he ducked even lower and walked in. He barely fit through the doorframe.

"I'm sorry, Brag'mok. I can't do anything to close the gate. Not until Layla gets back."

Brag'mok nodded. "I understand. Nonetheless, my need remains what it was until my brother is given the proper rites."

"It hurts," I said. "I get that."

"But you are right," Brag'mok said. "The situation on New

Albion is volatile. I've been in communication with our prime minister."

"Prime minister?" I asked. "You have a parliamentary government?"

"We borrowed the system from what you would call Old Albion or Great Britain. Our people, like the elves, have studied your world. Not so we could take it over, but so we could defend it from the elves if need be."

I nodded. "Makes sense."

"Upon King Brightborn's return, his request that the elven priests revisit their interpretations of the prophecies in the light of all that had happened was met with resistance."

"And you know this how?"

"Our intelligence network is extensive. There are friends of the giants even amongst the elves. Many do not agree with the former regime's plans to conquer this world."

"So King Brightborn was assassinated. I mean, aside from the fact that Layla just lost her father, from a political standpoint, that's a good thing, right?"

Brag'mok shook his head. "The revolution against the king was of his own making. They believed he'd gone soft in the wake of his daughter's entanglement with a human. When he suggested the priests consider what it might mean if the chosen one was a human, it caused outrage."

"And Layla is going back into that climate?" I asked.

Brag'mok nodded. "Presumably, she's going to support the faction that would see her inherit her father's throne. Since the revolutionaries want to see her family's dynasty replaced by Hector, you can be sure she'll fight for whatever's left of the establishment."

I sighed. "So if she becomes queen, she might not come back?"

Brag'mok shook his head. "I do not know. But if the prophecy binds you two together, I should think she would come for you one way or another, either to bring you back to New Albion with her should she succeed in ascending to her father's throne, or she would come back to you if the revolutionaries have their way."

"And the matter with B'iff at the source?" I asked.

"It might be wise that we table that matter for the time being. I would like to see my brother put to rest, and it is no small pain to see this issue delayed, but we must do what must be done."

"So what do I do in the meantime?" I asked. "Layla said I should train, but I don't know where to start, other than to keep going to the gym."

"I cannot go to your gym. It is best if I remain in the shadows. But you should continue to do what she told you. And if you like, I can teach you orcish combat."

"Orcish?" I asked. "I thought you found that term offensive."

"We do not like to be called orcs," Brag'mok said. "We are giants. The word 'orc' to us is what 'barbarian' might be to you. In terms of combat, it describes an old, primal style of fighting that we giants still use today."

I snorted. "So, you're going to teach me to fight like a primal giant?"

Brag'mok nodded. "That is what I know."

"One question," I asked. "How much of the style depends on brute strength and size? Will I be able to master it without those assets?"

Brag'mok smiled wide. "Even the weakest of creatures who master this art are fierce in battle."

"Good," I said. "Because you're about to teach the weakest person you've ever met how to fight."

CHAPTER TWELVE

"Hit me as hard as you can," Brag'mok directed, bracing his core and clenching his fists. The breeze fluttered through the single tuft of black hair he'd tied like Poppy's pinker version in *Trolls*. We didn't have access to a boxing ring, not even a dojo, so a clearing in the woods in the middle of St. Louis' Forest Park had to do. It was early enough on a Monday that the only people we were likely to encounter were morning joggers.

I rolled my eyes. "I'm not going to hit you."

"How can I teach you to fight if you won't even throw a punch?" the giant asked.

I sighed. "Just don't hit me back."

"How can I teach you to fight if you do not learn to block a strike?"

"Your fist is the size of my head," I said. "If you hit me—"

Thump!

Right upside my head.

Another thump.

This time, it was my body hitting the ground.

"Dude!" I shouted. "Concussions are real."

"You will heal," Brag'mok assured me.

"I can't use magic to heal myself!" I protested. "It doesn't work that way."

"Then *I* will heal you," the giant nodded confidently.

I sighed. "Not if you kill me."

"I've killed before. I know what I'm doing."

I wobbled as I got back to my feet, still dazed. "Why don't I find that comforting?"

"If you don't want to be hit again, learn not to be." Brag'mok nodded self-assuredly.

I took a deep breath. Brag'mok's way of training someone to block a punch was akin to how my father had taught me not to drown. No, I didn't learn how to swim when he tossed me into the lake without warning. All I figured out was how to kick my legs furiously and barely keep my head above water…and to avoid being near both my father and a body of water at the same time.

After this, I'd be heading to the gym. Thankfully, unlike Layla, Brag'mok couldn't hide there. He wasn't just massive. The greenish-brown skin and oversized lower incisors overlapping his upper lip made it much more challenging for him to blend into human society than it was for Layla. All she had to worry about was hiding her ears, and even then, at places like the gym, most people didn't give them a second thought. It was becoming a regional trend because of the Elven Gate cult.

"Now hit me back," Brag'mok said.

"What the hell is this teaching me?" I asked.

"Just do it."

I clenched my fist, reared back, and struck him in his rock-solid abdomen. The giant didn't flinch.

"Again," Brag'mok said.

I shook my head. "Do you even feel that?"

Brag'mok nodded. "I *feel* it."

"Sort of like when a fly lands on your skin?" I asked. "Probably feels like I just threw a cotton ball at you."

"More or less," Brag'mok confirmed. "Try to make it hurt."

"I don't know if I can hit harder than that."

"Focus your mind. You have magic, do you not?"

I sighed. "But using magic for war... Isn't that the reason your planet is running out?"

"This is not for war," Brag'mok said. "It is to end the war."

I shook my head. "Said every person ever who led an army into battle. Always the battle to end all battles."

"But you will not throw your fists, using magic or not, in order to win a war. You will only do it to protect your world. To save your elf. Such reasons are not beyond the purview of what the Earth's magic is meant to accomplish."

I rolled my eyes. "Are you saying that the Earth will examine my motives?"

Brag'mok huffed. "The Earth is a mostly peaceable place, is it not? It provides you air to breathe and its soil nurtures crops, so it feeds you, too. But the Earth can strike back. Hurricanes. Tornadoes. Extreme temperatures. Such things are not acts of vengeance, nor do they occur because the Earth wishes to kill you. But they are a part of the Earth's mechanism to defend and protect itself."

"So, you're saying I should strike like a hurricane?" I asked, raising my eyebrow. "That sounds like something a boxer would say."

"Float like a butterfly, sting like a bee," Brag'mok agreed.

"How do you know that phrase?" I asked. "I think I learned it from playing *Mike Tyson's Punch-Out* on my Nintendo."

Brag'mok cocked his head. "We have butterflies on New Albion. And we have bees."

I cocked my head. "And you just happened to put those things together in a metaphor that corresponds precisely to the one I learned from a video game?"

"It was Muhammad Ali," Brag'mok said. "He was the one who said it first, and we've studied your world's most influential persons. But now, you can harness the power of the butterfly *and* the bee. You can draw from the well of nature, Earth's magic, and hit me."

"What good is that going to do if we have to go to New Albion to rescue Layla?" I asked. "If there isn't much magic and the elves there are more proficient with it than I am?"

"First, who said we were going to have to go to New Albion? Did she tell you to prepare yourself to rescue her?" Brag'mok asked.

I shook my head. "Well, no. She wanted me to keep training."

"She said she'd be fine," Brag'mok reminded me.

"But you're the one who told me if she went back there, if I told her the truth about what you wanted me to do at the wellspring, she'd be in peril."

"That was before the situation with the elves changed. Before the revolutionaries assassinated the king," Brag'mok said.

"And you think they're going to be any kinder to the king's daughter, who is the heir-apparent to the throne that they're trying to usurp?"

"The upheaval in the elven kingdom will work to her advantage. Unless she attempts to assert a claim on her father's throne, chances are that no one will even notice she's returned."

I cocked my head. "Then why did she go back?"

"I cannot say," Brag'mok said. "I have no intelligence on the matter, which is probably a good thing. It means that so far, her return has gone unnoticed."

"I just hope she's okay," I said, staring into the distance, watching the trees' limbs wave in the wind.

"Hit me," Brag'mok said. "Focus all your worry, all your anxiety, into the punch."

I bit my lip. "I thought I was supposed to clear my mind?"

"Clear your mind of distractions, but focus on how you want your magic to manifest. A punch is an act of aggression. Focus on the emotions you'd channel into that."

I took a deep breath. I thought about Layla. I felt helpless. I hated feeling like I needed to do something but not knowing what I could do. I hated that I was training for what might amount to nothing, but I had to in case the fate of the world depended on my physical fitness. Most people worked out to lose weight. To be more attractive to potential love interests. To reverse diabetes or improve their overall heart health. But I was working out to save the world.

Usually, when I'm pressured to do something, it motivates me, but that only works to a point. Once the pressure becomes crushing, I freeze. I had that pressure, combined with the temptation to gamble on the possibility that one way or another, we'd close the gate. If we did that, I wouldn't need to fight. I could go back to eating Twinkies and frozen pizzas without any sense of guilt. I had mixed feelings about that, too.

If Layla came back, it probably meant she'd failed to stop the coup for her father's throne. I couldn't imagine she'd make it back, at least not for any reason other than to say goodbye if she succeeded. Then I could do what Brag'mok wanted: retrieve B'iff from the source and close the gate.

My relationship with Layla had progressed quickly. Maybe too quickly. Faster than you'd think it would, considering that I hadn't been in a relationship since my divorce. Now, it felt like I was about to lose her. Not because we'd fallen out of love, not because we decided to end it, but because of some elven bullshit. Because the ghost of an elf I was sure had died had shockingly killed the elf king. It was all too much. Hector, besides being dead, had been one of the former king's most loyal subjects. But was his loyalty to the king's person or to the elven dogma he felt had been violated by my fulfillment of the elven prophecy?

I was pissed that there wasn't anything I could do. I was ticked off that I didn't understand what was going on. I was furious that Layla had left without telling me face to face what was happening before she went.

I channeled all those feelings into my fist and threw it at Brag'mok.

The giant went flying, struck a large oak, and crashed to the ground.

"Shit!" I shouted, running to Brag'mok. "I told you I didn't want to hit you!"

The giant stood up, wobbling as he tilted his head. "Good punch, human."

"Thanks," I said. "Are you okay?"

"My bones are strong and my skull is thick. I'll be fine. Remember how that felt. I will meet you back here tomorrow."

"All right." I couldn't help but notice that the giant still hadn't recovered his balance. "You sure you're fine?"

"I'll survive," Brag'mok assured me.

"Do you have a place to go until tomorrow?" I asked.

"I've found a few places to hide. Again, human. I'll be fine. If you need me once again, you can speak to me from the confines of your car."

CHAPTER THIRTEEN

It was strange walking into the gym without Layla at my side. I felt like a fish out of water. With Layla here, I just did whatever she told me to do. Now, I stood staring at the gym floor, unsure of where to start. She had me on a schedule, working certain body parts each day. We'd had a leg day. I still wasn't over the last one. We did chest the day before. I was pretty sure that today was supposed to be back day. What the hell do you do to work your back?

Chin-ups, maybe? I mean, that's a lot of arms, but I think it works the back, too. Forget free weights. Maybe I'd just focus on the machines. They had little pictures showing what muscles they were supposed to work. Maybe I could just do all the back machines and call it a day.

Then there was a hard thud on my back.

I turned. Jag was staring down at me, smiling.

"Ready to crush it?" Jag asked.

I nodded. "Yeah, if only I knew what to do."

Jag smiled wide. "That's why I'm here. I didn't think you'd show."

I furrowed my brow. "Why you're here? I figured you were just here because don't you live here?"

"Almost," Jag said. "But your girlfriend called me last night."

I bit my lip. "Let me guess. After eight o'clock?"

Jag nodded. "I thought she was looking for something on the side. No offense, but a man with some girth if you know what I mean."

I stared at Jag blankly. "Why would you think that?"

"Never mind," Jag said. "I'm just fucking with you, little man. She asked if I could train you."

"Fuck," I said, laughing to myself. Not just because she'd signed me up for personal training without consent, but because he'd just called me "little man" with a straight face. "Of course she did. And how much did she offer to pay you?"

Jag shrugged. "She said she'd pay me with favors."

"No, she didn't," I said. "Really, how did she say she'd pay you?"

"She said you had a credit card."

I snorted. I wasn't sure if I was more upset that she volunteered my credit card for personal training sessions I didn't want or that she'd managed to talk to Jag before she left but hadn't gotten hold of me. Not that she hadn't tried, but couldn't she have waited an hour until I was out of my meeting? Was the issue on New Albion so pressing that she couldn't spare that much time?

"How'd she even get your number?" I asked.

Jag nodded at the front counter. "I assume she took one of my cards. I'm certified, and the gym lets me train any clients I recruit here provided they maintain membership and I give them a percentage."

I sighed. "So, what sort of ass-kicking do you have in store for me today?"

"First, we have to get your mind right," Jag said. "Let's do some self-deprecations."

"Self-deprecations?"

"You need to tell your old self that he isn't worthy of your future," Jag said, gesturing at one of the wall mirrors. "Call yourself a pussy."

"I thought positive affirmations were supposed to be good for you?"

"Affirmations are for pussies. Deprecations are for men!"

I looked at Jag blankly. "I'm not calling myself that."

"Do it!" Jag shouted. "Or are you too much of a pussy to call yourself a pussy?"

"No, I'm not," I said. Then I realized that contradicting him and rejecting the notion that I was a pussy set me up for contradicting myself if I did what Jag wanted. Whatever. Consistency probably wasn't the point of this exercise. Might as well play along. I took a deep breath and stared myself down in the mirror. I curled my lip. "You pussy."

"There you go!" Jag said, slapping my back hard enough that I almost slammed into the reflection of my pussy self. "How did that feel?"

"Honestly?" I scratched my head. "It felt strangely empowering. Like I was forbidding myself from ever being the same again."

"That's the point," Jag said. "Affirmations tell you that you're fine the way you are. That's the crap we tell kids. It's why kids these days are so soft. If you want to change, you can't affirm your present. You need to embrace the future you. A better you."

"So, you're saying fat-shaming is a good thing?" I asked, raising my eyebrow.

"Heavens, no," Jag said. "You should never fat-shame anyone else, but if you want to change, there's nothing wrong with fat-shaming yourself."

I snorted. "I'm not sure that makes sense."

"Why would anyone change if they were comfortable with what they are?" Jag asked.

I shrugged. "I don't know. I mean, can't you be comfortable with how you look but decide to get fit for health reasons?"

"Health is important," Jag said. "But you want to get huge. You want to be ripped. You want to turn heads!"

"Why?" I asked.

"What else is there?" Jag replied.

I wanted to go through a litany of things more important in life than attaining a beach-worthy body. I was reasonably confident, though, that Jag would dismiss anything I suggested. I mean, who needs to work on living more virtuously, learning new skills, or acquiring knowledge about important things when you could get ripped instead?

"I see your point," I lied.

Jag nodded. "Go get changed and meet me at the free weights."

"Free weights?" I asked. "Can't we just do machines?"

"That's what your old self the pussy would have said. Now you're a man. We're doing free weights."

I didn't waste time in the locker room. I half-expected that Jag would crush me like a bug if I waited too long. Besides, I suspected I was paying him by the hour.

And I had an advantage working with Jag that I didn't have with Layla.

He didn't know I could use magic.

I know, by cheating in my workouts, I was only cheating myself. I wouldn't do it every time, but just once, I wanted to see Jag flip out when he saw me lift more weight than he could. And with magic, it was possible.

"Let me see you do a pull-up," Jag said, pointing at the bar.

I nodded. Focused my mind, I leaped and grabbed it. I felt the tingle of my magic course across my back as I raised and lowered myself, maintaining steady control.

"Good," Jag said. "Let's see if you can do two?"

"Two?" I asked. "I'm not a pussy."

I did twenty.

"Good enough?" I asked.

"Impressive," Jag said. "Must be because you're a lightweight."

I smirked. "Yeah, maybe. How many can you do?"

"I'm two hundred and eighty pounds worth of solid muscle," Jag said. "It's apples and oranges. There's a reason you don't see big men like me on *American Ninja Warrior*. Layla made it clear that performance, not size, was your primary goal."

"Then why'd you tell me a few minutes ago that getting huge was the point?" I asked.

"Are you going to let your woman set your goals for you? She wants you to perform, but trust me, size matters."

I cocked my head. I was about to challenge his assertion, but I wasn't sure that what I assumed he meant was what he was saying, so I shifted the subject back to him.

I nodded. "So, you won't tell me how many you can do?"

"I told you the last time you were here that it's not good to compare yourself to others."

"Yeah, I'm my own competition," I said. "I remember."

I chuckled. I had to admit, it was a clever way of getting out of admitting he couldn't do as many pull-ups as I'd just performed. Jag took an adjustable bench and lowered the back until it was flat.

He grabbed a twenty-pound dumbbell from the rack.

"We're going to do a dumbbell row," Jag said, putting one knee up on the bench, the corresponding hand with his arm locked straight, and his other leg extended to the ground. With his free arm, he raised and lowered the dumbbell slowly.

"I think I get it," I said.

"Just don't let your elbows fly out. You want to keep your arm close to the body. That will help recruit the lats."

I nodded as Jag set the twenty-pounder he'd used to demonstrate the move on the floor next to the bench.

I got into the position he had demonstrated.

"Brace your core," Jag said. "You don't want the weight to tweak your body."

I nodded, then grabbed the dumbbell and imitated his motion. Twenty pounds was challenging. I only used a little magic to assist. "Can we go heavier next set?" I asked.

Jag nodded and grabbed a twenty-five-pound dumbbell from the rack.

I shook my head. "Heavier."

Jag nodded and grabbed a thirty-pounder.

Again I shook my head. I walked over and grabbed a hundred-pound dumbbell. It was the heaviest one on the rack. It took all the magic I could muster to drag it back to the bench.

Jag raised his eyebrow. "Are you sure about that?"

I nodded, got into position, and hammered my way through twelve reps, then set the dumbbell gently back on the floor. It took a lot of focus and more than a little magic, but the look on Jag's face was priceless.

Jag stood there, his jaw hanging. "You must be a lot stronger in the back than in the chest. We're going to have to get you into balance. Don't get me wrong, if there's an imbalance, it's better to have a stronger back and weaker chest than the opposite. That's the problem most men have. They work their chest too much and have weak backs."

I smiled. Sure, I was paying for the session. I should have let the process work. But I've paid for entertainment before, and this was pure comedy.

We went to the lat pull-down machine. I pulled the whole stack.

Jag's ego, meanwhile, was melting in front of my eyes. I could see from the look on his face that he was bothered. Maybe it was cruel, but doing it to a guy who'd insisted I call myself a pussy was worth it. Not to mention, it was good for us to have our egos checked from time to time. The way I saw it, I was doing Jag a service.

We wrapped up the workout, and I hardly broke a sweat.

"What muscle group are we doing tomorrow?" I asked as I handed Jag my credit card. He swiped it through his Square reader.

"Back again," Jag said.

"But you just said my back was strong. Don't I need to catch up on my chest?"

"You lifted a lot of weight today. Tomorrow, how about you try the same workout without magic?"

I almost choked on my tongue. "What did you say?"

Jag reached into his gym bag, pulled out a set of silicone elf ears, and put them on. "I'm a member of the Order of the Elven Gate. You think I don't know who you and Layla are?"

I snorted. "Well, damn."

"Tomorrow," Jag said. "Don't be such a pussy."

CHAPTER FOURTEEN

I scratched Agnus behind the ears when I got home. His eyes were plastered on the television.

"*Cats,* the musical?" I asked.

"It's the movie version from a couple years ago. That Victoria!" Agnus purred loudly.

"You realize she's played by a human, right?"

"Shush!" Agnus piped back. "Don't ruin it for me!"

"Well, enjoy," I said. "I have to get to work. Donna's expecting me at the bar in ten minutes."

"Well, hurry up," Agnus said. "I need my privacy."

"Whatever," I said, shaking my head. I hadn't sweated much at the gym because I hadn't done any work, but I needed to change my attire for my shift at the pub. Usually, a good pair of jeans and a button-up shirt were sufficient. I quickly changed and slipped past Agnus, who ignored me as I headed out the door.

"Look who the cat dragged in," Donna said as I stepped through the door. The pub was pretty empty in the early afternoon, now that the lunch crowd had gone. It was ideal because, while I'd been in training for a while, with my limited hours, I still had several drinks to learn. Not to mention, they still needed someone to man the bar even when it wasn't busy. Since I wasn't living off the tips but mostly working the job for the sake of the free rent perk, I wasn't particularly eager to change shifts.

"Yeah, I'm here," I said.

"How's Layla?" Donna asked.

I bit my lip. "Had to leave town. Family emergency."

"How are you handling that?" Donna asked. Donna was also an AA member. We'd known each other for years. While she wasn't my sponsor and never had been—AA generally advises against selecting sponsors of the opposite sex—we had a pretty open relationship when it came to sharing our feelings. And, since we happened to work a bar together, it wasn't bad to have that kind of accountability and support at work.

"I'd be lying if I said I wasn't anxious about it," I said. "I mean, the relationship is new. I think we're still in that infatuation phase."

"When all you ever think about is each other? When you still whisper sweet nothings in each other's ears?" Donna was smiling.

"Yeah, that's about where we're at," I said. "But she's the first woman I really felt like I could have a future with since my marriage fell apart."

"Young love is fragile," Donna said. "It's also when you're most vulnerable. Just make sure you can handle it."

I nodded. "I'm not going to drink over it if that's what you mean."

"I know you won't," Donna said matter-of-factly. "But make sure you don't lose yourself in the relationship."

"I won't," I said. Though, if I was honest, it was a little late for that. Not that I was losing myself in the relationship, but with everything that had happened since I met Layla, truth be told, I wasn't entirely sure who I was anymore.

Yes, I was a minister again. But when I'd first gotten involved in the ministry, it was part of who I was. Now, it was just something I did.

I still believed in it. My faith hadn't changed all that much.

But I suppose nearly losing my career and not falling apart over it meant I knew I was a lot more than that now.

Not to mention the elven prophecy and my role in it. There were bigger issues afoot. However, even Layla had learned that a lot of what she'd assumed about the prophecy wasn't complete. The elven priests had hidden some of the truth from the elven people. And everything about the prophecy had been in limbo since we fulfilled the last seal. And the last two seals of the prophecy hadn't yet been revealed.

Something about being the chosen one gave me a little hope.

I had to assume that since I'd fulfilled five of the seven seals and the princess' love for the chosen one was part of the prophecies, our story wouldn't end. Not as long as there were more seals and more prophecies to be revealed.

At the very least, I imagined, we wouldn't be cut off from New Albion. At the same time, though, the seals broke at random intervals. The last one had been revealed just days before I fulfilled it. There was a chance that the other two could break at any moment and be fulfilled, somehow, without me even realizing it.

Two businessmen came in and sat at the bar, probably to negotiate some kind of deal.

"Two O'Donnell's stouts," the older of the two men said.

I grabbed a glass and started to fill it.

The glass slipped out of my hand and shattered on the floor.

The two men didn't notice. They still wanted their beers, and my clumsiness wasn't a matter of significant concern to them.

I grabbed another glass and filled it, twisting the glass as it filled to pinch off the head. The perfect amount of foam, just grazing the top.

I set the glass in front of one of the men.

Then I proceeded to fill the next one.

And the first one inexplicably fell over. It slopped over the younger man's lap.

"What the hell!" the man shouted.

"I'm so sorry," I said. "I don't know how that happened. Must've been some water on the bar."

The man looked at me dumbly. "A towel, please?"

I quickly grabbed a rag from beneath the bar and handed it to him. "I'll replace those beers for you."

"Never mind," the young man said. "We'll go someplace else."

I sighed as the two men stood up and left, stomping their way through the door.

"Sorry," I said as Donna looked at me from across the room.

"Not your fault," Donna said. "That was a freak thing. I don't think I've ever seen a glass just spill itself all over a man like that before."

I shrugged. "Like I told him, I wonder if there was just a little water on the bar. Maybe the glass slid across a puddle or something. Or maybe he bumped it with his elbow, and I didn't see."

"No worries," Donna said. "I think that's your first spill. It happens to all of us eventually."

It was going to be one of those shifts. Ever have a morning or a moment in time when it seems like Murphy's Law has set its sights exclusively on your life? If anything could go wrong during this shift, it did. We were even five dollars and some change short in the drawer at the end of my shift, and since I was the only one who'd accessed it, the difference was on me.

Part of me wondered if fairies were to blame.

Layla had said that they were tricksters. They'd make sure that if you used magic irresponsibly, you'd experience negative consequences. Magic had a price, that whole idea. I shook my head. I was overthinking it.

I hadn't done anything awful with magic. I couldn't imagine I'd done anything to force the fairies to start interfering. If anything, my distraction with the uncertainty of what was happening with Layla and the elves was likely to blame.

I'd probably caused the drink to spill because I hadn't paid attention to the condition of the surface where I'd set it down. And the glass I dropped? That happened often enough that it could have been a coincidence.

And the five and change missing from the drawer was easily explained by my mind being elsewhere.

CHAPTER FIFTEEN

I still needed to reach out to my contact from the soup kitchen. Evelyn Smithe was a kind woman, and she'd been at it for a while. Now in her late fifties, she'd been a pastor in the Methodist denomination the better part of two decades. I didn't know what she'd done before that. Her being the one in charge of the soup kitchen was one of the major hurdles my council had had to overcome.

After all, in our denomination, they took St. Paul's injunction that women should be silent in the churches and another statement that he did not permit women to teach, not as a reflection of Paul's own time and situation, but as a universal dictum meant to limit the ministry to males indefinitely.

Many of our ministers were so chauvinistic about it that they disparagingly referred to female pastors as priestitutes.

Yes, it was offensive as hell. But in their minds, these women were violating some kind of holy ordinance.

Of course, they usually only used that word in conversation with like-minded male ministers. They'd never dare call Evelyn or any other female pastor that to her face.

That was because although those men viewed the male organ

as a divine scepter conveying special privileges upon its bearer, at their core, they were pussies.

At least, that was what Jag would say.

I say all that to indicate the sort of challenge I was facing, trying to convince our district to participate. What was even more surprising was the Methodists' willingness, especially Evelyn's, to tolerate our participation.

It was a Monday evening, so when Evelyn didn't return my text message, I knew I'd be able to find her at the soup kitchen. Might as well meet up with her there.

Not to mention, after the comedy of errors that had been my afternoon shift at the pub, I figured donning an apron and helping a few folks would be mildly therapeutic.

Pretty much any spirituality worth its salt, whether it's found in AA's spiritual program, the Bible, or some other tradition, encourages acts of service. Not that that's the point. I think if you only do things that appear loving because you're hoping to reap benefits, then you don't really love your neighbor.

Still, I couldn't deny that serving other people was good for me. It kept me sober, and, strangely enough, it gave me a sense of peace. Not a good reason to get involved in charity, but it was undoubtedly a fringe benefit.

And as much as anything, I needed to feel like I was doing something good. Something more than carving my physique at a gym, learning to fight, or filling pint glasses for patrons.

"Reverend!" a man said as I walked through the door.

There were Cecil and Shanda, along with their daughter, Grace, standing between them. She was using a cane.

"Well, hello!" I said. "How nice to see you."

I looked at Grace. "How are you doing?"

"I'm great!" Grace piped up.

Cecil smiled. "Her legs are weak. The cane helps her balance, but she's managing. And I'm sure her strength will come in time."

"Most definitely," I said, grinning. "So, have you come for dinner?"

Cecil nodded. "Sloppy Joe night."

"Grace's favorite," Shanda added. "We'd never miss it."

"Well, enjoy your meal. And if those Sloppy Joes are as good as you say, I might just have to get one myself."

"They're the best!" Grace said, still smiling.

"Reverend," Cecil said, pulling me aside while Shanda helped her daughter to her seat. "Thank you, again. She's been smiling for two days straight, ever since you healed her. I know you were reluctant, but thank you."

I extended my hand. Cecil grabbed it and gripped it tightly. "It was my pleasure, Cecil. Enjoy your meal."

"What was that about?" a voice asked from behind me. I turned, and it was Evelyn, peering at me curiously. "Nice to see you, Caspar."

"You too, Evelyn. That family, they came to our church on Sunday."

Evelyn raised one eyebrow. "So you're the minister they say healed her? I figured it must've been a Pentecostal church."

I chuckled. "Not this time. I'm just grateful she's doing well."

"So, how'd you do it?" Evelyn asked.

"I can't say for sure how it works. I visualized her getting better."

"Not that," Evelyn said. "The bigger miracle is, how did you convince your council to let you assist? I got your text. I was as surprised as anyone."

I smiled. "Well, they are still reluctant, but they agreed we could handle the evenings you aren't already serving."

Evelyn nodded. "Well, I suppose that's a start. I don't see why they wouldn't be willing to serve together on the same evenings."

I rolled my eyes. "Stodgy bastards."

Evelyn laughed out loud. "I like you, Cruciger."

"But they can't prevent me from helping out. Tell me what I

can do," I said. "Show me the ropes. If we're going to start doing this on other evenings, I need to learn whatever I can."

Evelyn extended one finger in the air. "One second. I'll be right back."

A minute later, Evelyn returned with a mauve apron.

"Don't you have any other colors?" I asked. "Mauve isn't my favorite."

"When it's covered in sloppy joe, you won't even notice." Evelyn handed it to me.

"Mauve it is," I said. "That's a pretty word. 'Mauve.'"

Evelyn smirked. "I suppose it is. If you'd like, you can work the line. Just grab a ladle and scoop. Not much more to it than that."

I nodded. "Will do. Thanks, Evelyn."

I slipped my apron over my head and reached around my back to tie it, then stepped toward the buffet bar where the servers were dishing out the food.

And my foot caught on something.

I lost my balance and fell directly into the path of one of the volunteers carrying a tray of warm sloppy joe sauce.

It was it all in slow motion: my body hitting the floor, the look on the volunteer's face turning to shock, the tray tumbling end over end and the sloppy joe sauce flying.

Thud!

I hit the ground.

Splat!

The tray flipped over and fell right on top of my head.

I sat up and wiped sloppy joe from my eyes.

Three kids were giggling in the distance.

I looked down.

My shoelaces were tied together.

Those kids?

I would have noticed.

Fairies! It had to be fairies!

I heard a snicker. I turned and looked up at Evelyn.

"You aren't in mauve anymore. That's something, at least."

I licked my lips. "Well, it is delicious. I can see why the kids like this stuff."

"Caspar, bathroom's in the back. Let me see if I can find you another shirt from the donation pile. And another mauve apron."

I nodded. "Thanks."

It felt like a walk of shame. My face, hair, and torso were covered in sloppy joe.

"Bad day?" a random passerby asked.

I nodded. "You could say that."

The bathroom wasn't large. The soup kitchen was in an old, closed-down cafeteria, and the bathrooms hadn't been updated since the seventies. They contained a small mirror and a sink big enough to splash water on my face and make myself nearly presentable.

The sink was too shallow to douse my head. I grabbed a paper towel and wiped away as much mess as I could.

I heard a high-pitched giggle.

No, it wasn't a child. It was too squeaky to be a kid.

Then a bright green orb-shaped glow whizzed across the bathroom, flushing all the toilets before disappearing in thin air.

Must've been a fairy. Neither Layla nor Brag'mok had told me what they looked like, but what else could it be?

"Where are you?" I asked. "Come out, wherever you are!"

I heard tapping in one of the bathroom stalls.

"Someone in there?"

No response. More tapping.

I pressed on the door.

A fountain of water sprayed out of the toilet directly into my face.

I gagged.

Just the thought! It was toilet water.

I quickly went back to the sink and splashed my face with clean water.

I heard a squeak, and the warm water was turned off.

"Stop it!" I shouted, not seeing how the fairy or whatever it was had pulled it off.

I reached into the water again, then yanked my hand out of it. This time, it was scalding hot.

I sighed, grabbed a paper towel, and quickly ran it under the water before the heat could get to me. A warm paper towel; I'd have to settle for that.

I looked in the mirror and sighed again.

Presentable enough.

I walked out of the bathroom.

Someone tugged on my arm.

It was a boy, and not one I recognized.

"Sir," he said. "Your fly is down."

I shook my head.

Fucking fairies.

CHAPTER SIXTEEN

So much for making progress with the soup kitchen.

Why was a fairy messing with me?

Was it because of the whole ordeal at the gym? Maybe it was an accumulation of things. Healing folks. Flying around like a superhero. Wielding more magic than any other human had in centuries, as far as I knew. If the fairies deemed themselves the Earth's magic police, I suppose my emergence had given them something to do, if nothing else.

I was waiting for the next prank.

I guarded every step as if I was walking across eggshells. I looked all around as I made my way back to the Metro for a ride home, expecting a ball to fly toward my head, a car to swerve over the sidewalk, or a manhole cover missing in the middle of the sidewalk. Anything unexpected. That was the problem. It was hard to keep an eye out for pranks or fairy tricksters when there was no telling what they'd do.

It seemed like none of this stuff had happened until *after* Layla left. Was that a coincidence? Maybe, maybe not.

And what did the fairies want? Layla had said they acted up as a warning. To show the person that there were consequences to using magic. That magic had a price, one that was exacted by their antics.

I made it home safely, but I was still uneasy.

My stomach was churning from anxiety.

I unlocked the door to my apartment. Agnus was snoozing on the couch. Everything appeared to be in order.

I took a deep breath and exhaled. It seemed like the fairies hadn't messed with the apartment.

But my stomach was still unsettled.

I made my way to the bathroom, undid my trousers, and sat on the toilet seat.

And something cold squirted me in the ass.

"What the…"

I stood up. It looked like…was that ketchup on my ass?

I lifted the lid, and two ketchup packets fell from the rim into the toilet bowl.

"Dammit!" I shouted. Ketchup is good on a lot of things. A butt cheek isn't one of them.

I grabbed some toilet paper and cleaned myself up.

At least this one had been moderately humorous and painless.

But it had also spoiled the illusion of sanctuary I thought my apartment represented.

I finished my business without incident.

It could have been worse. They could have cellophaned the toilet bowl—an old college dorm prank. I wasn't about to mention that one out loud.

Didn't want to give them any ideas.

There was a knock on my front door.

I quickly tidied myself the rest of the way.

Who in the world was stopping by at this time in the evening?

I opened the door.

As the door swung inward, a giant trash barrel fell toward me, and water flooded the entryway of my apartment.

"How the hell!?!?" I shouted. "They're so small. How the hell did they lift a trash barrel full of water?"

Agnus was awake now, and he was staring at me, his head cocked to one side. "You going to clean that up?"

I narrowed my eyes and glared back at my cat. "What choice do I have?"

It took every towel I had in my closet. Thankfully, I didn't have carpet in the entryway. The only part of my apartment with carpet was the bedroom. This prank had been a much bigger pain than the ketchup under the toilet seat, but it was still relatively harmless—nothing I couldn't handle.

But what would be next?

That was the point, I imagined. To keep me worried about the next shoe to drop. To convince me to stop using magic.

Or at least to be more careful about *how* I was using it.

I tossed my towels into the washer, added detergent, and turned it on. They weren't all that filthy, but I didn't know where the water had come from. For all I knew, it was fairy piss. Or sewer water.

It didn't smell bad, but that didn't mean anything.

I needed a shower, then I was going to bed. How much more could go wrong?

I checked the shower. Butter hadn't been spread on the floor. I turned on the water and checked the temperature. It was normal.

So far, so good.

I stripped down and got in the shower. I washed my body. I shampooed my hair.

I rinsed off and sighed in relief as I turned off the water and grabbed my towel.

I examined it carefully—no scorpions in the towel. No snakes. I was good.

I dried my hair first. Why the hell were there chunks of hair in my towel? I pulled at my hair. More chunks, falling out.

I looked in the garbage can and shook my head. A bottle of Nair hair removal cream.

The damn fairies had put it in my shampoo.

I stepped back into the shower. More hair came out, circling the drain.

I didn't have any extra towels because I'd used them to clean up the water.

I shook out my towel as best I could, then dried off.

I looked at myself in the mirror. My hair was now patchy.

There was only one solution to this problem.

I had a beard trimmer under the sink. I hadn't had a beard for a while, but I used to have a goatee and had used the trimmer to maintain it.

I plugged it in and switched it on, half-expecting that it wouldn't work.

But it did, so I shaved off the rest of my hair.

CHAPTER SEVENTEEN

Brag'mok tilted his head as I approached him in the park for our day's training. "What did you do?"

I sighed. "I think I pissed off a fairy."

My giant friend grunted. "I was talking about your hair. But since you mentioned a fairy, I'm sure that had something to do with it."

I snorted. "You could say that."

"What did you do, magic-wise, to anger a fairy?" Brag'mok asked.

I bit my lip. "Nothing. Just used a little magic to push through my gym routine."

"Why would you do that?" Brag'mok snorted. "You need to get the most out of your training."

I sighed. "Because Layla hired a trainer for me, and he's a douche bag. I was just fucking with him."

Brag'mok shook his head. "Then that's why. You didn't use magic for good, although also not for evil. You used it to pull a joke, a prank, on someone. Now, you're getting your just desserts."

"Sweet justice? How is *that* justice? I pulled one prank. Since yesterday, this fairy has been going after me non-stop. How do I convince him to quit?"

Brag'mok shrugged. "Karma's a bitch."

I rolled my eyes. "If this is karma, you'd think one prank would suffice. That's all I did, just one."

Brag'mok shook his head. "And he'll keep going at it until he's convinced you've changed. Until you've balanced things out."

I sighed. "I healed a girl on Sunday. You'd think I'd earned enough good karma with that to counter-balance one prank. Enough that one joke wouldn't elicit fairy wrath."

Brag'mok shook his head. "It doesn't work that way. That's like saying because you did a lot of good in your life, you have a free pass to commit crimes."

"Not a free pass," I said. "But even in cases like that, the judge will usually consider character witnesses and such. Give you a lesser sentence if the crime was an isolated out-of-character act."

"Fairies don't see it that way," Brag'mok assured me.

"Obviously." I huffed. "So what sort of good do I have to do?"

Brag'mok shrugged. "It's not just about doing good as much as it is about demonstrating you're sorry. Achieving balance through contrition, not charity. After all, fairies don't care about your love for your fellow man. They just want to know you won't use magic recklessly again."

"How would I do that?" I asked.

"Humiliate yourself, so the fairy doesn't have to." Brag'mok stared at me intently.

"Like, go streaking through the park?" I asked.

"If you don't mind getting arrested," Brag'mok said. "That might do it."

"Fair point," I said. "Not to mention a streaking minister would almost definitely make the front page of the Post-Dispatch. Well, maybe not the main article. They'd need a picture for that."

"What is the one thing that would embarrass you more than anything else?" Brag'mok asked.

I sighed. "I don't know. I mean, after years of drinking, I've pretty much had my share of embarrassment."

"You can't think of anything you could do to embarrass yourself?" Brag'mok asked.

"Well, there's that show where those friends go around and have an earpiece in and have to do or say whatever their other friends say. That's pretty embarrassing."

Brag'mok grinned. "We can work with that."

"We don't have an earpiece," I said.

Brag'mok shook his head. "Not exactly true. I have one. It's how I could hear you when you were in the car. Also, how I communicate with my contacts back on New Albion. I have another one."

"Convenient," I said, rolling my eyes. Brag'mok reached into his bag and pulled out a small crystal. I took it. "What do I do with this?"

"Just stick it in your ear," Brag'mok said. "You should be able to hear whatever I say."

I sighed and stuck the little device in my ear. Not as comfortable as earbuds and not contoured to the human ear, but it stuck.

"Now," Brag'mok said. "See that jogger?"

I nodded. "The lady in the yoga pants?"

"Go up to her," Brag'mok said. "I'll tell you what to say when you get there."

I narrowed my eyes. "Just go easy on me, all right."

"That would defeat the purpose, human. Hurry up before she gets too far away."

I sighed. "All right, here goes nothing."

I darted across the grass, angling my trajectory so I'd catch up with the woman. I waved my hands to get her attention. "Excuse me, miss?"

The woman stopped, cocked her head, and removed her

headphones as I approached her, nearly out of breath. "Can I help you?"

Brag'mok gave me instructions in my ear. I bit my lip. I didn't want to say what he wanted me to say. Everything in me said not to do it. But that was the point, right?

"Ma'am, I don't mean to be rude or anything. But I noticed your pants are a bit too tight. I wondered if you'd like to get into mine?"

The woman busted out laughing. "I have to say, that's maybe the best pick-up line I've heard in a while. But I'm married. Happily. So, no, thank you."

"It wasn't a pick-up line," I said.

The woman rolled her eyes, and put her headphones back on. "Try someone else."

"Did she turn you down?" Brag'mok asked, cackling through the earpiece.

"Of course she did," I said as the woman jogged away. "I can't believe I just asked a random woman that."

"Let's try another one," Brag'mok said. "For good measure?"

I sighed. "Might as well."

"There, at two o'clock," Brag'mok said. "She's pretty, don't you think?"

I looked at the woman I assumed he was referring to. I wasn't sure where two o'clock was because I didn't know what the fixed point was I was supposed to use to orient myself. "Yeah, I mean. Of course, she is. But I'm with Layla. Don't make me…"

"You're not going out with her, and it isn't like she'd say yes. Remember, embarrassment is the point."

I sighed. "Fine. What do you want me to say?"

"I'll tell you when you get there," Brag'mok said.

I shook my head and took off toward the pretty girl. She was probably in college; I'd say she was in her early twenties. Since I was nearly twice her age, I was reasonably certain she'd find whatever Brag'mok was about to make me say creepy. But that was the point, right?

"Excuse me, miss?" I asked as I jogged up beside her.

The girl smiled at me. I mean, she was the sort of girl who would have intimidated me with her beauty when I was her age.

Brag'mok told me what to say.

"Are you a peanut M&M?" I asked.

The girl laughed. "No. Why would you ask that?"

Brag'mok told me the second part. I gulped.

"Never mind. Have a nice day."

The girl scrunched her brow. "Yeah, you, too."

I shook my head and ran back to Brag'mok. "There's no way I was going to tell her that. Totally inappropriate!"

Brag'mok laughed out loud. "What's the worst that could happen?"

"Are you a peanut M&M because I'd like to nut inside of you?" I asked, raising my eyebrows. "It's called harassment, Brag'mok."

"But was it embarrassing?" the giant asked.

"Even though I didn't say it, randomly asking a beautiful girl if she's a peanut M&M is humiliating. Maybe even more so since it was obvious, I chickened out on what was clearly a lame attempt at a pick-up line."

Brag'mok nodded. "Then perhaps we've succeeded. Only time will tell."

Brag'mok extended his open palm.

"One thing's for certain," I said, removing my earpiece and laying it in his hand. "The fairy's methods work. I'm not going to use my magic for anything trivial again. Hopefully, he realizes I've learned my lesson."

Brag'mok nodded. "Now, are you ready to fight?"

I sighed. "I'm not going to use magic to hit you. Not like yesterday. For all I know, that was a part of what elicited the fairy's wrath."

"No need for that," Brag'mok said. "We have a different lesson to learn today."

"Which is?" I asked.

"When you're going against someone much larger and stronger than you," Brag'mok explained, "your best bet is to use your opponent's size and strength against him."

I scratched my head. "How do I do that?"

"Momentum," Brag'mok said, nodding definitively. "The larger your opponent, the bigger and stronger, the more momentum they have when they charge you or try to attack you."

"Which is precisely why it's so frightening. When I first met B'iff..."

Brag'mok cocked his head.

"I'm sorry. I didn't mean that. It was insensitive."

Brag'mok brushed his hand through the air. "Your first meeting with my brother was confrontational, was it not?" he asked. "I assume he overpowered you with his size."

"More or less," I said.

"Do you know what else has a lot of momentum?" Brag'mok asked.

"Other than a giant's body flying toward you?" I chuckled.

"A ship," Brag'mok said. "A giant ship is directed and steered by a small rudder. Be the rudder."

"Be the rudder?" I asked. "I mean, I get the concept. Something small can redirect the momentum, right?"

"Exactly," Brag'mok said. "And with a few moves, a step to the side, and a short push, you can use your opponent's size and strength against him."

"Again," I said, "the idea makes sense, but how do I implement that? How can I put that into practice in a way that works?"

"If I'm charging after you," Brag'mok said, "you don't want to leap out of the way. I'll still have control of my momentum, so you'll waste the opportunity. But if you're in a wide stance, if you pivot around your back foot, then when you evade my charge and give me a small shove, you can redirect me. Perhaps into a tree or a rock."

"And if you're trying to punch me?" I asked.

"Again, you pivot on your back foot, you use the force of my body that I've focused into the punch, and push me using the momentum I've channeled into the strike."

"The concept makes sense," I said. "Pivot, don't jump away. Be in a position to push you one way or another."

"In the direction of my momentum," Brag'mok said, repeating his point.

"Right," I said. "But in a real fight, it happens fast."

"Which is why we need to practice," Brag'mok agreed.

The giant clenched his fist and drew it back.

My eyes went wide. I tried to dodge, but he clocked me right upside the head. I crashed to the ground.

"Dude!" I exclaimed.

"Next time," Brag'mok said, "pivot."

"That's what I did!" I insisted.

"No, you didn't," Brag'mok said. "Not properly. Here, try to hit me."

"My punch isn't going to hurt," I said. "Not without magic."

"That's not the point. I'm going to show you the move."

I nodded. I cocked my fist back and swung it. For a giant, Brag'mok moved gracefully. With a single motion, he swung his back foot around, pivoting on his front. He blocked my punch with one arm, even as he swung himself around it, then pushed me on the backside of my arm and shoulder, leaving me once again with a face full of grass.

I rolled over and brushed myself off. "All right. It'll be a lot harder for me to do. My fist is smaller than yours. Your fist is harder to dodge."

"Bigger targets are easier to strike. Don't focus on avoiding my punch. Focus on using it, moving around it, so you can use my strike against me."

I nodded. "All right. Just try to avoid hitting my head this time. I'm sure you gave me a concussion last time."

"No, I didn't. You're fine."

I sighed. "Okay, I'm ready."

Brag'mok clenched his fist, but this time, he didn't draw it back as far. It came hurtling toward me faster than before, but I knew what to do. I swung my back foot around. Used his punch against him. That was the strategy.

I probably wasn't as graceful as he'd been, but I raised my hand, guarding my face with my forearm, as his punch grazed my block. Then, I used my blocking arm and my other hand to push with all my force in the direction of his momentum.

Brag'mok stumbled, then hit the ground.

He turned over, grinning. "And if this were a real battle, if you had a blade in your opposite hand, you could end me here and now."

I nodded. "Or I could just get a gun."

Brag'mok shook his head. "Elves use magic, remember? A gunshot wound, while more devastating to your medical doctors, is nonetheless a small wound. With magic, it heals more easily than a wound from a sword or a knife. Particularly if the blade strikes an artery."

"Good to know," I said. "So, what's next?"

"Practice," Brag'mok said. "Last time, I still clenched my fist. I gave you a chance to anticipate. We need to do this over and over until it becomes a reflex."

I nodded. "Brag'mok. Any word on Layla or what's going on with the elves?"

Brag'mok shook his head. "Not really, but I suppose no news is good news. If your girlfriend has gotten herself caught, or worse, killed…"

"Brag'mok, please!"

"Sorry. I'm just saying. She's the most important elf on New Albion. If anything happened to her, if she was even spotted, I'd have heard something."

"All right. Let's keep practicing. I want to get this move down."

CHAPTER EIGHTEEN

We probably did the move a hundred times in less than an hour. I took a few punches at first, enough to leave me with a black right eye.

It was only Tuesday. Hopefully, it would be gone before church on Sunday. Holy Cross had put up with a lot from me. I wasn't sure how they'd respond to the idea that their pastor was training to become a world-saving MMA warrior. Then again, I could always blame it on a baseball.

It wouldn't be the first time. I was notoriously bad at playing catch. Ever since I was a kid and I made the mistake of turning my glove palm-up to catch the ball my dad had tossed, causing it to roll up my glove and into my face, I'd had an irrational fear of flying balls.

You'd think after the day I had, I'd feel the same way about fists, but all things considered, it wasn't as bad as you'd think, taking a giant's right hook. Of course, I was sure he was holding back. It still hurt enough to inspire me to pick up the pivot move quickly, but it didn't hurt so badly that I was left cowering in the fetal position in the middle of Forest Park, either.

I was getting there. One move down, a hundred more to learn. But progress was progress, right?

Maybe I wasn't going to be the next Bruce Lee, but I could certainly kick the ass of yesterday's version of myself.

Jag would be proud.

Hopefully, he'd be satisfied, at least, when I met him at the gym to re-do my back workout, sans magic assistance this time.

I'd had enough nonsense from the fairy that I wasn't about to cheat a second time. Not to mention, when I spotted a fifty-burger on my credit card activity statement for my wasted session, I was determined to get my money's worth this time.

A shit-eating grin split Jag's face as I walked into the gym. Of course, he was waiting for me.

"What happened to you?" Jag asked.

"Shaved my head," I said. "I just got sick of dealing with split ends."

Jag tilted his head. "I don't care why you changed your hair. I was talking about the black eye."

"You should see the other guy," I quipped.

"Does he have a thing for clichés too?" Jag smirked.

I snorted. "I took a right hook from a giant."

"I'm pretty sure it was something much less cool than that," Jag said. "But since you're dating an elf, and you're all wrapped up with prophecies and whatnot, I'm inclined to believe that you got into a tiff with a giant."

I smiled. "There's a reason Layla wants me in fighting shape."

"Ready to do this right today?" he asked.

I nodded. "Yeah, sorry about that. I was kind of an ass about it."

Jag shrugged. "No skin off my back. I got paid."

"Right," I said. "No sense in wasting another half a Ben Franklin on trying to show you up."

"This isn't about me," Jag said. "Don't make it about me. You're never going to look this good."

I snorted. "Thanks for the vote of confidence."

"Seriously," Jag said. "You're pushing forty, right?"

I nodded. "Your point?"

"I'm not saying you couldn't build some serious mass, but I've been working for years to craft the masterpiece that is my body. Even if you work that hard and that long, at your age, your testosterone levels will be significantly diminished."

"I'm sure they already are," I said.

Jag nodded. "T-levels start declining in the thirties for most men. More rapidly for sedentary men."

"Good to know," I said. "Thankfully, my goal isn't to look like you."

Jag nodded. "I encourage SMART goals: specific, measurable, achievable, realistic, and I don't remember what the hell the t means."

"Time-based?" I offered.

"Whatever," Jag said. "Looking like me might be a specific goal, but it's not measurable since sexy is subjective. And it wouldn't be realistic or achievable."

"You're so encouraging." I rolled my eyes.

"And if I'm honest, it's not the best goal, given your purpose. Don't worry, we'll build you some size. We'll get *huge.* That's the most important thing. But we also need to focus on strength and agility. Layla said to train you like a fighter."

I nodded. "Well, I'm ready. Let me just get changed."

I was already in workout-appropriate clothes due to my sparring session in the park, but I preferred shorts and a tank top in the gym. Not to show off my guns, which were more like peashooters, but because it kept me cool.

I met Jag back at the chin-up bar. When I was in high school, I used to crank those things out like nobody's business. I didn't think I'd done a chin-up or pull-up since. Not minus the assistance of magic, anyway. The workout the day before didn't count.

I jumped up and grabbed the bar. I was surprised how much just gripping it hurt my hands.

"No kipping. Keep your body still. The focus is on pulling all the weight, making you stronger."

I nodded. I braced my core and tried to hold my body still. My legs flailed a little, but it wasn't as bad as it could have been. I grunted as I pulled my chin up to the bar. Then I lost my grip and fell to the floor.

"Good," Jag said. "That counts as half a chin-up."

"Half?" I asked. "I got all the way up."

"Half the effort is on the negative. That's the way down. Some lifters believe you achieve *more* gains, in fact, on the eccentric contraction than the concentric one."

I bit my lip and nodded. I'd been called eccentric before; that wasn't new. Not language I was used to using when it came to exercise, though.

Of course, as a minister, I'd probably used the word "exorcise" more often than "exercise." Not that I'd had any confirmed cases of demon possession, but there were a few exorcisms in the New Testament that popped up a couple of times a year on the lectionary, which was our schedule of Bible readings for each Sunday. A couple of times a year was more often than I'd done any exercise in years.

Until Layla.

I sighed. Damn, I missed her. And I was worried about her.

"Try again," Jag said. "This time, relax your body. You tensed up last time. That takes extra energy. And don't let go when you get to the top. Let yourself down slowly."

I nodded. I managed to get one full chin-up in, and it burned like a bitch when I let myself down. "Woo, you're right," I said. "I can feel it when I go down slow."

"For every exercise we do," Jag said, "I want you to focus on that. Explode into the work, slow and controlled on release."

This time I didn't challenge his best guess of a twenty-pound dumbbell for my rows, and he was right. The more I focused on controlling the release, the more it hurt.

I wouldn't admit it, of course, but it felt good. Like all that pain, letting it out was also a stress release.

I finished a set of ten reps, first on the right, then on the left.

"Good," Jag said. "We'll do three sets of these. One minute rest between sets."

I nodded. "Feels pretty good. I noticed you didn't make me do deprecations today."

Jag grinned. "I figured you were probably beating yourself up enough since you cheated yesterday."

I nodded. "You wouldn't believe the shit I've been through since. I think I've learned my lesson."

"Good," Jag said. "Since you've already outworked your yesterday's version of yourself."

I snorted. "Yeah, he was a pussy."

"Such a wimp," Jag said, grinning from ear to ear. "And tomorrow, you'll feel the same way about today's version of you."

I smiled. "I hope so. But I'm not going to worry about tomorrow. Tomorrow has enough worry for itself."

"Isn't that the Bible?" Jag said.

I chuckled. I hadn't even realized I'd quoted Jesus there. "Yeah, after Jesus talks about how God takes care of the lilies of the field and the birds of the air. He tells his disciples to stop worrying about what to eat and drink because if God takes care of the birds and lilies, why would they doubt that he'd also take care of them?"

Jag smiled. "Good advice. I don't know about lilies, but I do know a pansy when I see one. Stop talking and hit that next set."

"Yes, sir," I said, snickering.

All in all, I didn't lift a fraction of the weight I'd lifted the day before, but I worked the hardest I had in a long time. And it felt good. Really good.

"Make sure you're getting plenty of protein. At least one gram per day for every pound of body weight. That'll maximize your muscle development."

I nodded. "Thanks, Jag. So, what are we hitting tomorrow?"

Jag smiled. "Ever been to a gun show?"

"So, it's arm day tomorrow?" I asked.

Jag narrowed his eyes and looked at me intently. "Do you have tickets?"

"To the gun show?" I asked.

Jag nodded slowly.

"Yeah, so it's arm day tomorrow."

Jag maintained focus, staring me down, as he retrieved his credit card reader and plugged it into his phone.

"Fine," I said. "It's the gun show tomorrow."

"You still owe me fifty bucks."

CHAPTER NINETEEN

My sponsor had recommended keeping a gratitude list. It was hard to harbor resentments—a major source of problems for most alcoholics—if you focused on what you were thankful for. He suggested getting a little pad of paper, writing down everything I could think of that I was grateful for, and adding something to it every day. It didn't have to be huge. Didn't have to be particularly profound.

Maybe it was simple, like having oxygen to breathe, that the Earth keeps spinning, or the sun hasn't gone supernova yet, or something subtle and overlooked like the beauty of the trees and the sky.

Whatever. It didn't matter because a gratitude list wasn't about things.

It was about *me*. My state of mind, my attitudes, my outlook on life.

I didn't keep a pad of paper like Rusty suggested. I couldn't keep track of things like that. Instead, I kept a file on my phone. I was a twenty-first-century alcoholic, after all.

Today, I listed workouts. By that, I meant both my sparring

workout with Brag'mok and my gym training with Jag. In both situations, I had felt like a dwarf, but today wasn't like yesterday. I wasn't resentful. I didn't hate my sessions. If anything, I felt invigorated by them. I started to think that maybe, just maybe, Layla's plan to get me into shape wasn't so misguided after all.

I was actually looking forward to another yoga session at the apartment. I didn't have the time for the full hour and a half routine I usually did, but the streaming service I used to get my yoga routines had several other options.

One of them looked like it was set in Hawaii. Likewise, the title of the routine was something I couldn't pronounce. But it had Tony Horton in it, looking quite a bit younger than I was accustomed to. I figured I'd give it a go. After all, I was all about cross-cultural engagement. Yoga in Hawaii? Why the heck not?

I laid out my yoga mat and set my blocks beside me. They were helpful. With some of the poses, like half-moon, I didn't have the flexibility to reach the ground. Provided I maintained balance, that is. One foot firmly on the mat, the other in the sky, and my palm to the floor or the yoga block.

The first time I tried it, I don't think I lasted a half-second before tumbling over. But today, I was in a flow, calm of body, calm of mind. Sure, I had anxieties. I was still worried as hell about Layla. But with my attitude shift, thanks to the fairy who'd been harassing me, I felt like I could handle it.

The serenity to accept the things I could not change.

Agnus came up and nuzzled the leg that was on the floor.

"Dude, what the hell?" I asked. "I'm trying to balance here."

"And I demand love," Agnus said. "Give me love!"

I chuckled a little as I lowered my back leg, grabbed the remote, and paused the routine.

I picked up Agnus and scratched him behind the ears.

"How was your day, buddy?" I asked. "Didn't see you when I got back."

"Found a nice patch of sunlight shining through the curtains. I couldn't resist."

It was bound to be another night of more of the same, and by that, I mean my usual routine. I'd work my afternoon shift at the pub, and then, since the soup kitchen wasn't open tonight—eventually, this would be our night to run it—I'd try to catch an AA meeting. Like I said, more of the same.

Not a night from hell, like the night before. Ideally, Brag'mok's plan had worked, and I'd sufficiently pacified the trickster fairy who'd been harassing me.

So far, so good.

Part of me was irked that the little bugger had won. He hadn't liked the way I'd used my magic recklessly, and he'd succeeded in causing me to think twice the next time I was inclined to use magic for anything that wasn't necessary.

Knock, knock, knock.

I sprang to my feet. Layla had a key, but maybe she'd left it like she left her phone. I reached for the doorknob and swung open the door just in time to see a young woman with purple hair making her way back down the stairs.

I looked down. Amazon Prime.

I hadn't ordered anything. I bent over and picked up the box.

It had a little weight to it. Not a ton, but enough that it was noticeable. I didn't shake it. The box didn't say it was fragile, but why risk it? I didn't know what was in the box or who'd ordered it.

I looked at the label. It had my name on it.

Of course, I'd let Layla access my Amazon account. She must've ordered this before she left.

I closed my door and took the package over to the kitchen counter.

I sliced it open with a steak knife. There was a bag inside the box. I pulled it out.

It had a glass on the front and was filled with a green liquid.

The type said something about more than a hundred superfoods in a single serving.

"Fantastic," I said. "Now she's ordered me supplements."

The bag indicated it was a flavor called Greenberry, whatever the hell that was.

I mean, usually, green berries are the ones that aren't ripe yet. Gooseberries were green, but who would make a gooseberry shake, and if they did, why not just call it "gooseberry?" Not to mention, I'd never had a gooseberry that wasn't in a pie. I suspected they were sour.

I looked at the directions. Replace one meal per day with this shake. Mix one scoop with eight ounces of water or almond milk.

How the hell does someone milk almonds, anyway? Last I checked, they didn't have nipples.

I'd have to check the grocery store for that. For now, I'd try it with water.

I pulled my blender out from under the counter and plugged it in. I filled the pitcher to the eight-ounce marker with water from the sink. I ripped open the top of the bag carefully. It was one of those zipper bags, and I had a lousy track record of accidentally ripping through the zipper portion.

It didn't smell bad. A little sweet. Yes, it was green, but I wasn't prejudiced. Kermit the Frog taught me that it's not easy being green, and I liked Kermit just fine.

I turned on the blender.

Agnus leaped to his feet and took off into the bedroom, presumably to hide under the bed.

He did the same thing for the vacuum.

"Just a blender, Agnus," I called.

He hissed in response. "The blender from hell!"

I shook my head. "I didn't buy it from Satan, Agnus. I got it from Walmart. The blender won't hurt you."

"Tell that to the frog!" Agnus protested.

I sighed. "No one puts frogs in blenders, either."

"Then what the hell is that?" Agnus said, his head poking out of the doorway of my bedroom.

"It's a health shake," I said. "It says Greenberry."

"Frogberry, more like it!"

I laughed. "I don't think there are any frogs in this shake mix. It just says it's full of superfoods."

"Superfoods? Like, vegetables from Krypton?" Agnus asked.

"You've been watching too much television," I said. "Krypton docsn't cxist."

I took a sip from the blender.

I gagged, nearly spitting it out, but I forced myself to swallow it.

"Delicious?" Agnus asked.

I nodded, but I was sure the contorted look on my face told a different story. "Sure, if you enjoy the taste of a freshly mowed lawn."

"You have to drink it," Agnus said.

I cocked my head. "No, I don't. Layla bought this for me, and she's not here."

"That's why you have to drink it. It would be disrespectful, and therefore bad luck if you didn't."

I rolled my eyes. "Since when has refusing a health shake been a sign of bad luck?"

"Don't tempt fate!" Agnus said. "Drink! Drink! Drink!"

I took a deep breath. I stared down the grccn sludgc that fillcd the bottom half of my blender.

I grabbed the handle.

I tipped it back and choked it down. Then, I slammed the blender down on the table and released a man-roar.

Agnus stared at me blankly. "Moron."

"What?" I asked.

"You fell for the bad luck con," Agnus said.

I sighed. "Well, at least it's good for me. Hopefully, it will give me extra energy for my workouts."

Something churned in my gut. Then I heard a squeak like someone was slowly letting air out of a balloon from somewhere in my intestines.

"To the bathroom!" Agnus shouted.

I nodded and took off, slamming the door behind me.

CHAPTER TWENTY

It was a good week.

Training with Brag'mok went well. We moved from evasive measures to follow-up strikes. We'd add magic back to the equation once we knew I had my other maneuvers mastered. We moved beyond dodging punches to ducking and pivoting away from blades.

No more magic, not unless there was an emergency. Magic was like fine wine, Brag'mok told me. It was great when you used it in the right setting and savored it, but nothing would give you a worse headache than if you binged it. I knew that last part well enough, although not from experience. While I'd never been fortunate enough to drink wine properly, I understood the metaphor. And when it came to magic, at least at this point, I wasn't addicted to it.

Moderation was key, and I was determined to make sure I handled it responsibly.

Instead, Brag'mok and I sparred like two Spartan warriors in the middle of Forest Park. It had to be quite the sight.

I half-wondered if anyone would call the cops if they saw us. I mean, I was sparring with a dude who was at a bare minimum the size of Andre the Giant. We tried to stay in remote areas of the park, but there were trails nearby, and we'd garnered the stares of more than a few passersby during our morning sessions.

Now that he was swinging a broad sword at me, I was anxious about the training. I liked having my head where it belonged, firmly affixed to my shoulders, and I was also uneasy about the unwanted attention our activities might attract.

I was crushing it in the gym, too. So much about it was mind-set. Once I moved beyond the "this sucks, I don't want to be here" sentiment I'd had before I'd embraced the process, I found I'd started to enjoy my workouts. Jag was still a douche, but he was a likable douche. He also had a lot of good knowledge as long as he was limited to issues related to working out.

We only discussed his membership in the Order of the Elven Gate a couple of times, mainly because we were focused on my workouts but also because there wasn't a lot to talk about.

Fred, the Order's leader, was at a loss as to what direction they should go in since things had changed once I appeared, after the incident with the Blade of Echoes. Should the Order still prepare for an elven invasion as they had before? Originally, they'd hoped to be prepared to serve the new regime once they took over and rise to positions of prominence among whatever humans remained. But now I'd appeared, and half the order had helped Layla. At least one member had spilled the beans about our former plans to Hector before (we thought) he'd died.

Now, Jag said, they weren't sure what to do. Support Layla and me and hopefully help prevent the elven invasion? Or accept the invasion as inevitable as they had before and continue to prepare to kiss elven ass? As far as I knew, they weren't aware of the latest developments in elven politics, and I didn't tell Jag about them, either. Who knew what Layla had told him before she left? I imagined he suspected something was up, but I also doubted that he had any more insight into what was happening than I did. Even Brag'mok, who had connections to intelligence operatives on New Albion, wasn't sure.

So, we focused on what we could control.

My training.

Always be the hardest-working motherfucker in the place.

That was my goal. I wasn't going to be one of those meat-heads who lifted a set, then sat there on his phone for three minutes.

I wasn't supposed to compete with anyone else, but be my own competition.

The way I saw it, if my fitness might have something to do with whether I could save the world, I needed to push myself harder than anyone else.

"Light weight, baby!" I shouted, re-racking the Olympic bar on the bench press. I wasn't anywhere near where Jag was in terms of his bench, but it didn't matter. I was rocking two tens on each side of the bar now, and for me, that was progress. I prob-ably could have lifted it before, but now that my mind was right and I wasn't shying away from the pain, I felt stronger. I accepted the challenge.

Next chest day, I'd try three. Then maybe I'd get bold and try a forty-five plate on each side. One workout at a time.

"That's what I'm talking about!" Jag shouted back. "You're a beast!"

I roared at him. I had no idea where it came from, but if I was a beast, I figured that was the appropriate response.

"I've got more juice," I said. "Let's do a drop set."

Jag nodded, removed one of the tens from each side, and resumed his spotter's position behind me. I gripped the bar and slaughtered the set, fifteen good reps, my pectoral muscles burning.

"Damn, that felt good," I said as I re-racked the bar. "What's next?"

"That's the workout," Jag said.

"Come on," I said. "Maybe some flies. Let's do some with the cable crossover machine."

"We're out of time," Jag said. "You're only paying for one hour at a time."

I shrugged. "What's my credit score matter if the world ends? Add another thirty minutes."

Jag smiled. "All right, if you insist."

There were a lot of people who could lift more weight on a single rep than I could, but no one was sweating more than me. No one in that gym was pushing him- or herself harder than I was. We spent half the extra thirty minutes on more chest work and the other half on abs.

I hated planks. They hurt so good.

Finishing the workout, I grabbed my shaker cup, refilled it from the water fountain, and added a scoop of whey, a scoop of creatine, and a scoop of glutamine, all shit I'd charged to my card and picked up at the closest supplement store. Jag said I needed to fuel my body, make sure I was getting a complete protein with all the amino acids necessary to maximize my muscle development, so I took the word of the guy at the store. He was wearing a polo shirt and seemed to know what he was talking about, and since polo shirts convey authority, I was confident I had the right concoction. Jag agreed.

I'd had my Greenberry shake earlier that morning. No mindset would change its nastiness, but I was getting used to it. Oddly, this whey was rather delicious—a smooth vanilla flavor.

Maybe a little chalky, but I didn't notice. I would have before, but everything seemed different now. After a hard workout, knowing that my body needed protein, I craved it.

It was funny how much a shifted outlook could change one's day.

I was engaging everything I did with new vigor.

And it wasn't just so I could avoid the wrath of the trickster fairy. I didn't know for sure what I should attribute it to, but I was looking forward to my sparring sessions, even if they usually meant a giant fist or foot to my head or mid-section once or twice.

I was eagerly anticipating every workout with Jag. I even embraced my yoga videos. I still hadn't figured out crane pose, but I was trying. One foot down to maintain my balance as I shifted my body weight over my arms. I couldn't do it yet, but I could lift my toe from the ground for a split second.

Eventually, it would be a full second, then two. Before long, I'd be doing it like the great Tony Horton himself.

I'd also made some progress with Evelyn in organizing our evenings at the soup kitchen. Mondays, Wednesdays, and Fridays, I'd assist her to learn the ropes.

In a month or so, presuming we recruited enough volunteers, we'd take over Tuesdays, Thursdays, and Saturdays.

Eventually, Evelyn and I hoped we'd be able to convince the council to allow us to work together to cover Sundays. That would be an uphill battle, but maybe once we got involved, once they saw that we were able to make a difference, I'd be able to convince them to relax a little.

The week went so well that before I knew it, we'd gotten to the weekend, and I still hadn't prepared my Sunday sermon.

Thankfully, I didn't work the pub on weekends. I devoted my Saturday night to sermon prep.

This week, I knew what I was going to preach about.

Jesus said more than once that he who has eyes will see the truth. What does it take to have the proper perspective? I know I wasn't faithful to the original context of Jesus' speech, but I'd learned over the last week that much of life is about how you look at it. It was a lesson I'd learned getting sober, but somehow I'd forgotten it when it came to tackling all this fitness and saving the world stuff.

I was going to preach on the attitude of gratitude.

Jag and Layla were right. I was a sucker for clichés.

But there was a reason something became a cliché. It had to be meaningful to enough people that it was often repeated before people began to relegate it to the realm of overused platitudes.

The problem with clichés wasn't that they weren't insightful; it was the opposite. It was that we'd heard them so often that we'd forgotten why they were worth remembering.

CHAPTER TWENTY-ONE

Usually, I'd park the Mitsubishi around back and sneak in through the back door of the church, but I still hadn't gotten my tires fixed. If I'd only had one flat, that would have been one thing. I'd have put on the spare and taken it somewhere. But with four flats, I needed a tow truck, and I needed the funds to buy four new tires. I suppose, since I was running up my credit card bills with personal training and supplements, a new set of tires might make sense. But then again, since I was already running up my credit card bills, maybe not.

Not to mention, while I didn't like riding the Metro, it was a quick trip, just a few blocks. On nice days, I could walk it if I gave myself enough time. I'd done it many times. Technically speaking, there wasn't a pressing need to replace my tires.

It was a nice enough day. I would have walked, but the bus was there waiting, and I hadn't left myself enough time.

That was the thing about working out; your body needed more rest than usual. Jag said I needed to make sure I got my full eight hours. Most muscle recovery happened when you were sleeping. Therefore, I set my alarm a little later than usual. I suppose if I were a responsible human being, I'd have just gone to bed sooner.

Blame Netflix.

As I got off the bus in front of the church, I was surprised by how many people were getting off at the same stop.

And even more surprised by the small crowd that had gathered outside Holy Cross.

"That's him!" Cecil shouted as I approached. His daughter Grace stood beside him. "He's the one who healed my baby girl!"

I sighed. I wanted to cuss, but I was in pastor mode.

Beast mode was reserved for the gym.

Church folk wouldn't appreciate it if I called myself a beast. Revelation had sort of spoiled that one with the whole six-six-six thing.

I shook Cecil's hand. "Nice to see you again. How's Shanda?"

"Out spreading the word, Reverend! I hope you don't mind. We told a few people about what you were doing here."

I chuckled. "Well, they aren't all looking for healings, are they?"

"No, Reverend," Cecil said. "But any man who can do what you did for my Grace, that's the sort of man people want to hear preach."

I smiled kindly. Inside, though, I was tied in knots. I had healed Grace with magic. I suppose one could argue that it was the same sort of magic Jesus had used when he healed. The magic of creation, still coursing through the ley lines of Earth.

But it didn't feel like I was a miracle worker.

I might have been the subject of a prophecy, but I was no prophet. I was just a common preacher with a basic seminary education and a desire to make the world a better place.

At least, that had been all I'd wanted when I'd first set out to do this. Now, making the world a better place meant saving it, too.

"Well, if everyone is here to hear me preach, why is everyone outside?" I asked.

Cecil cocked his head. "Well, the doors are locked, Reverend."

I grunted. They shouldn't have been locked. There had been Sundays in the past when I was the first to arrive, but typically an elder, most likely Doris, would arrive beforehand. They'd get the thermostat set and the lights turned on.

I pulled on the door handle.

Sure enough, locked.

I shook my head and grabbed my keys from my pocket. This had to be a mistake. I hoped it was.

I unlocked the door and opened it.

"Pastor!" Jim said. "Quick, close the door behind you."

I snorted. "Why?"

"All those people, they're here looking for miracles. They're just looking for a show and probably some handouts."

I stared at Jim blankly. "Let them." I pushed the door wide and blocked it open with a wedge. "Welcome, everyone. Please come in and have a seat. The service will begin shortly."

"But Pastor," Jim started.

I raised my hand and cut him off. "Knock, the Lord said, and the door shall be opened unto you."

Jim grunted and shook his head before shuffling to his customary position in the third row from the back.

We didn't have enough bulletins for everyone. We were going to have to make a few adjustments. Unfortunately, as beautiful as the liturgy in our church could be, it was challenging for newcomers to follow. We had services printed in the front of the hymnals, but let's face it, who wanted to follow a whole order of worship from a book? Instead, I jotted down a few hymns and gave the list to our organist.

Patty had played the organ at Holy Cross since before I was born. She knew most of the hymns inside and out. Most of them, for the casual visitor, were nearly impossible to sing. I made sure to stick to the well-known tunes, *How Great Thou Art*, *Amazing Grace*, and the like. Songs people knew or, at the very least, knew the tune so they could follow along.

I also wasn't inclined to waste any time vesting up with my alb and stole. We had people here eager to hear the good word, and I didn't want to keep them waiting. I'd probably get flak for it, but truth be told, I didn't see why I needed to wear a robe. It always felt a little like getting out of the bath, and I was baptized a long time ago.

Instead, I just started speaking. I welcomed everyone to the church. We sang a few hymns, and I started to preach.

I stuck to the message I'd planned.

Gratitude.

But I supplemented it a bit.

"Gratitude is the attitude we should have when we get better than we deserve. And when that's the case, who are we to keep it to ourselves? Grateful people don't hoard their hope. They want to share it. That was why Cecil invited so many good people today; he wanted to share the hope. Hope he was grateful for, hope that for reasons I don't completely comprehend, allowed a girl who might have never walked on her own to take her first steps. A hope that sees beyond our differences, our politics, our religious views, and embraces everyone.

"After all, who are we that God should have mercy on us? What have we done to deserve God's favor? It was never about us. Gratitude isn't about getting things you deserve, it's about the cheerful heart of the giver. Having received so much from our God's generous hand, who are we to hoard His gifts for ourselves?"

The sermon wasn't supposed to be a lecture. Most of it I'd written about myself and all I'd been given that I didn't deserve. It was about learning to live life without obsessing over the shit and focusing instead on all the things I kept on my gratitude list.

But I could tell from the looks on some of our longstanding

members' faces that they didn't like it. I could have preached this topic any other Sunday, and they would have shaken my hand afterward and told me it was a good sermon. They always did that. But now, with outsiders here, people who weren't used to worshipping like they did, who didn't look like them, who came from a different walk of life, the message struck a chord—one they didn't like the sound of.

But what else could I do, turn people away? How would I be any better than my former bishop if I had done that? How could I even live with myself if I'd refused to welcome people seeking meaning in their lives, no matter their lifestyle or background?

Maybe some of these people *were* looking for a miracle worker. I was glad no one came looking for healing this week. I wasn't sure what I'd do, given the mess I'd been through with the trickster fairy. I knew, though, that despite all that, if someone was in need and I could help, I wouldn't be able to resist.

Even if it did end up with me having my bed short-sheeted or my underpants smeared with Ben Gay. But then again, maybe the fairy wouldn't mind. Healing was a good use of magic, I'd say. Certainly nobler than using it to cheat my way through my gym routine.

After nearly everyone left, Jim stayed behind. "Pastor, can I have a word?"

"Of course, Jim. What's up?" I knew what he wanted to talk about, but I didn't want to make it obvious that I had assumed.

"Is it going to be like this every week from now on?" Jim asked.

"Why do you ask, Jim?"

"If it is, Pastor, I think I might have to take my family elsewhere."

I scratched my head. "I can't force you to stay here, Jim, but I'm not going to deny anyone who wants to be here a seat."

"We only have so many seats, Pastor," Jim said.

I sighed. It was the first time that I'd seen every pew filled in all my years of preaching there. There had even been folks standing in the back. And it was the first time, in truth, that our attendance had reflected our neighborhood's diversity. It was a good thing. I hoped it lasted. I prayed it would grow.

"Jim, why don't you tell me what's really bothering you? I don't think it's having enough seats. We can always add more services if we have to."

Jim shook his head. "I grew up here. We do things a certain way, and those things mean something."

I nodded. "You've been here your whole life. Isn't your faith strong enough that you can handle a few things changing for the sake of others who are coming here for the first time?"

Jim shook his head. "I'm sorry, Pastor. I can't."

"I'm sorry to hear that, Jim. If you want to go, I won't stand in your way. But I want you to know you're always welcome here. Everyone is welcome here."

Jim snorted. "That's sort of the problem. If everyone's welcome, our ways of doing things won't be welcome anymore."

I bit my lip. I wasn't going to argue with him or anyone else about traditions, and truth be told, until now, Jim had been one of my staunchest advocates. He'd stood up for me when the former bishop had wanted to censure after my divorce. He had been one of the leading voices clamoring that I be restored once Philip took over as the new bishop in our district.

But I had to let him go. It was just as wrong to force anyone into a church where they weren't comfortable as it was to force anyone out. If only he could see the beauty that I saw when I surveyed the crowd. When I heard those unfamiliar "amens" echoing through the building. Our usual congregation didn't vocalize like that in the middle of a sermon.

Change can be scary. I knew that. I was changing. My life was changing. Everything I cared about was changing. But *growth* required change, and if this congregation didn't want to adapt, evolve, or grow, how could I force it? At the same time, how could I in good conscience prevent it? I couldn't, so I wouldn't. If they wanted me removed, the members could make it happen. Until then, I was going to do what I believed was right, no matter the consequences. After all, loving other people sometimes meant we had to accept things we weren't used to. It meant we had to go outside our comfort zones. It meant we had to be willing to take risks, and it meant we had to be ready to accept the costs.

CHAPTER TWENTY-TWO

I walked back into my apartment, and after being graced with a head butt from Agnus and scratching behind his ears in return, I quickly slipped out of my slacks and into some sweats.

I didn't like dress clothes. Part of me envied those hipster preachers who wore whatever the hell they wanted and still preached to massive crowds.

Sundays, outside of football season, were typically occupied by activities with church members, but this Sunday, after what had happened, I didn't receive any invites to lunch.

Jim was the only one who said anything to me about it. He was the only member who'd voiced his disapproval. That didn't mean others didn't have the same thoughts, but most good folks had consciences. They sensed that something had made them feel uncomfortable, and rather than retreat to bigotry or narrow-mindedness, they'd used that discomfort as an opportunity to reflect. Why did something that should be good make me feel anxious? What was it about my attitudes or beliefs, be they explicit or implicit, that was leading me to think in a way that I intuitively knew to be wrong?

That didn't mean Jim wasn't struggling with it. It didn't mean his attitude wouldn't change once he'd had a chance to reflect. Some of us struggled more internally, and others of us had to air out our struggles—wrestle with what we were feeling by putting our thoughts, even our ugliest ones, out there to be scrutinized.

I mean, hello! How many social media arguments, ultimately leading to unfriendings and unfollows, began that way? Someone shooting from the hip, airing feelings that stemmed from incomplete thoughts, from things they were sorting through, only to have the mobs descend upon them with scathing condemnations?

I'd been there and had it done to me. I mean, I'd once aired the ungodly opinion that *Toy Story 2* was better than the original, and holy hell, they'd nearly burned me alive.

It was one reason why I didn't keep social media apps on my phone anymore. I still had my accounts, and I checked in periodically to see if I had any messages from long-lost high school buddies or whatever, but I couldn't make social media a regular part of my routine. I just couldn't. Not if I wanted to be happy. Not if I wanted to stay sober.

I had an itch to go to the gym. Yeah, Jag wouldn't be there, not on a Sunday. There probably wouldn't be many folks there.

Just as I was about to grab my gym bag, my phone buzzed.

I still had the phone on vibrate, which I'd switched it to before church.

It was Philip.

Have time to talk?

I sighed. I guess I shouldn't have been surprised that someone from the church had already called him. I mean, Jesus had taught his disciples that if they ever had a problem with each other, they should deal with it themselves. Face to face. If that didn't work, bring two or three others into the discussion. But snitching? Jesus wasn't a fan.

Snitches be bitches. No, Jesus didn't say that. Call it Caspar 3:16. I typed back.

Sure. On the phone?

Figured I'd come to you. How about we do lunch at the pub under your apartment?

O'Donnell's is closed on Sundays. Applebees?

All right. Be there in thirty minutes.

Technically speaking, I'd just been reinstated. It was only my second week back in the pulpit. Well, my metaphorical pulpit. Holy Cross did have one. You had to go up a miniature staircase to preach from it. Not my style. Some of the more traditionally-minded members wished I'd used it more, but I preferred to speak in the open. People tend to put preachers on pedestals already, and I didn't deserve that. I didn't like talking down to people, either in tone or because of my elevation. Besides, our pulpit was so high that I could swear I once felt my ears pop while climbing up there.

I digress. The whole point was, I'd barely made it two weeks, and now I was having a private sit-down with the bishop. Sure, Philip wasn't Matthias. He was a much kinder and more reasonable man, but he still had a job to do.

I opened Agnus a can of tuna, and per Layla's instructions, I dumped it into a bowl rather than giving him the can. Seriously, he'd eaten from the can hundreds of times. My can opener didn't leave sharp edges. But she insisted, and I was still heeding her wishes even though she was absent.

Damn, I missed that woman. Er, elf. Elf-woman. I changed out of my sweats again, and this time, I put on jeans. It was an acceptable compromise between church attire and apartment-appropriate sweats. I half-wondered why they sold the sweats in the activewear department. Most of the time I wore them was when I was sedentary. Hell, even since I'd started training at the gym, I didn't wear sweats. I wore exercise shorts and t-shirts.

With Agnus digging into his tuna, I stepped out the door. "Be back in a few, Agnus."

"Mmmhmm," Agnus said, his mouth full of fish. He had his priorities. I was honored he acknowledged me at all.

I locked the door and headed downstairs.

Applebees was only a few blocks away. Still, I was glad I'd left early enough to account for the walk. When I arrived, I saw that Philip was already there. Of course, he was wearing a clergy shirt; you know the kind priests wear with the little white tab in the middle? I wore those in seminary. They were required back then, but I hated them. I mean, I had a good-sized Adam's apple, and that little piece of plastic sucked. Besides, I didn't like having people look at me weird everywhere I went. We weren't Catholics.

It also meant we'd likely have to endure awkward stares during the meal. And if we were unlucky, someone would approach us at some point and ask us to pray for them or exorcise a demon or whatever.

Well, they'd ask Philip. I was wearing a t-shirt with my jeans that said, Kiss Me, I'm Irish. I wasn't Irish, not really, but they were shirts we had to wear for St. Patrick's day at O'Donnell's. It's a big day when you work at an Irish pub, and the owners didn't seem to care that, at least based on the DNA test I'd sent off, I only had about one thirty-second genuine Irish blood. But if people thought I was, why the hell would someone kiss someone else just because of their ethnicity? It was a weird shirt, now that I thought about it.

It would make more sense to buy a shirt that said, Don't kiss me. I just ate a banana.

Make more sense, and generally speaking, it would avoid the

remote chance that someone might actually kiss me randomly. Unless someone liked bananas. Or they were a monkey and could read. Not likely. But then again, my cat had figured it out.

I sat down in front of Philip. He was smiling.

"Who snitched?" I asked.

"Snitched?" Philip raised an eyebrow even as he laughed. "It does sort of feel that way, now that you mention it."

I shook my head. "If people have an issue with anything I'm doing, why not just talk to me about it?"

Philip shrugged. "Fear. People are afraid of confrontation most of the time."

"Tell that to the internet trolls," I quipped.

"That's different," Philip said. "When we don't have to look someone in the face, it's easier to be the assholes we all are on the inside."

I snorted. "True enough. So I assume you more or less know what happened?"

Philip nodded. "I'm not here to reprimand you."

I nodded. "Good, because honestly, after what I just went through, if you did, I'd be just as likely to throw my hands in the air and quit as be willing to sit and listen to it."

"Understandable," Philip said. "I'm only here because I've been in situations like that. I mean, I didn't somehow heal anyone. No one ever thought I'd performed any miracles."

"Do you think I'm a miracle worker?" I asked.

"I don't know if you are or aren't," Philip said. "I tend to think there's only one real miracle worker. God just works through human beings from time to time."

"I suppose it doesn't matter what I did or didn't do," I said. "In truth, I'm not so sure I performed a miracle either."

"Doesn't matter," Philip said. "At the end of the day, a girl who couldn't walk before can now. Maybe she always could. Maybe you healed her. Either way, in my mind, give God the glory, right?"

I nodded. "Exactly. But you said you'd been through something like this before?"

"Not on this scale," Philip said. "But yes. And it wasn't because we had poor people come in."

"Black people, you mean?" I asked. "Because we have poor white members. It isn't that people are poor that made some of our members uncomfortable."

"I wouldn't say that out loud," Philip said. "People don't generally respond well to being called racist."

"I'm not saying they are, at least not hatefully so. But they have implicit biases about others like most of us do. I think it's good that they struggle with it. Maybe it will open their eyes. As long as their struggles don't run people off in the meantime."

Philip nodded. "In my situation, it was because we had a homosexual couple in our church. I was a first-year minister at the time. One of the young men had grown up there. He'd come out shortly after I arrived, fresh out of seminary, and a few weeks later, he showed up with a boyfriend. They wanted to participate. They wanted to take communion, learn the Bible with everyone else."

"I imagine there were those who thought you needed to chastise them and beat them down with God's law until they repented."

Philip nodded. "Pretty much, yes."

"So what happened in the end?" I asked.

"I tried," Philip said. "I tried to encourage people to be patient. I wanted people to see that they had giant blind spots. That they should focus on their issues rather than worry about the lifestyle of other members who were hoping to seek God the same as them."

"I'm guessing that didn't work out?" I asked.

Philip shook his head. "I was too passive about it. I was hoping people would just get over it. Eventually, they'd see that these two men were looking for God just like the rest of us. That they weren't any different from anyone else. But some of the members took it upon themselves to let them know they weren't welcome, and by the time I'd realized what had happened, the damage had been done."

"Did they find another church?" I asked.

Philip shook his head. "Last I heard, they weren't involved in any religion. They're married now. Got married by a justice of the peace. Never even asked me if I'd conduct the ceremony."

I winced. "Can you imagine? I mean, when Matthias was bishop, he'd have crucified you for that."

Philip smiled. "Probably. If he found out about it."

I snorted. "He'd have found out. That man had eyes coming out of his ass, I think. Seemed he was privy to anything that wasn't by the book."

Philip nodded. "I'm telling you all this to tell you that you can't be passive about what's happening. Believe it or not, you were called to serve the church members *and* your community. You need to find a way to unite the people. Help them see each other through God's eyes."

I nodded. "Easier said than done."

"Indeed it is," Philip said. "But you aren't going to make much progress by grandstanding or making declarations. Help them see the truth. You have a way of explaining scripture that's simple. It isn't wrapped up in seminary lingo and church dogma. Show them the heart of the message, lead them gently, and let them realize the truth for themselves."

I sighed. "That takes time. Unfortunately, with as many folks as we had today in the service, I'm not sure how long this can be allowed to fester."

"If you don't address it," Philip said, "the people will react, and it might not be pretty. This is the reason you're there: to help people see through their biases, their limited perspectives. To help them see things through God's eyes."

"You have to understand the people at Holy Cross. They

aren't bad people. But the new folks, they come from an entirely different kind of life. They have different experiences, not just because they are poor, but because they are people of color in a city and country that hasn't always treated them well."

"When we don't understand where other people are coming from," Philip said, "we become fearful. And fear is a dangerous thing. Over time, it breeds hate."

"That's what I'm afraid of," I admitted.

"*Damnant quod non intellegunt,*" Philip said.

"Latin?" I asked.

Philip raised his eyebrows. "Surely you remember enough from seminary to figure it out."

I chuckled. "I could wager a guess, but I'm pretty sure I'd be wrong."

"'They condemn because they do not understand.' That's what it means. It's a big problem with a lot of folks in our denomination, but it's also pretty universal in human nature. I don't think it was a Christian who said that originally. It was Cicero, if I'm not mistaken."

I took a deep breath and nodded. "Still, it's true. Most of the time when we condemn each other for things, we do so without understanding their perspective or comprehending their experience and viewpoint. Or only understanding a small part of the whole situation."

Philip relaxed back in his booth as he started perusing the menu. "Exactly. But how can you help people understand? How can you bring them along to the point that they might start to empathize with other folks' struggles? So they learn to embrace them?"

I huffed. "Maybe if I got them to join us at the soup kitchen."

"Not a bad idea," Philip said, looking at me over the top of his menu. "When is that starting up?"

I shrugged. "As soon as I tell Evelyn we're ready, I suppose."

Philip nodded. "In that case, I suggest you tell her it's time."

"But how am I going to get folks to volunteer?" I asked.

Philip shrugged. "Ask them. Personally."

"I've asked everyone. We'll still have a hard time getting sign-ups."

"Ask the specific people whose opinions you think hold the most sway over the rest of the members. Choose the leaders and ask them to help personally. Most people will agree if you approach them that way."

I smiled. "That's pretty smart."

"When you've been around as long as I have, you pick up a few things."

"As long as you have?" I asked. "You were only a couple of years ahead of me in seminary!"

Philip nodded. "We're getting old, Casp."

I chuckled. "Speak for yourself. By the way, is that waitress ever going to take our order?"

Philip looked around. I did the same.

I mean, you'd think she'd at least take our drink order.

"I think they might have forgotten about us," Philip said.

I snorted. "Or they're back there debating. You take the table with the priest, no, you."

Philip smiled. "Yeah, this damned collar. People behave oddly when I'm wearing it."

I nodded. "That's why I never do."

Philip pinched his chin pensively. "I've been working on a little parable. Not sure if it's sermon-illustration worthy yet, but it's getting there. I think it might fit this whole situation you're facing."

I smiled. "Storytime with Phil? Oh, goody!"

Philip rolled his eyes and cleared his throat. "Imagine being shown a great, beautiful tower and being charged to take care of it."

"Like the Sears tower?" I asked.

"Or the Eiffel Tower," Philip said. "Doesn't matter. Or make up one of your own. Just make sure it's beautiful."

I bit my lip. "All right, I've got it."

"When you saw the tower for the first time, you were taken aback," Philip said. "It was breathtaking. You'd never seen anything so magnificent."

"I don't know," I said. "I do get the swimsuit edition of Sports Illustrated every year."

Philip stared at me blankly. "Caspar, will you just shut up and let me tell the story?"

I chuckled. "Yeah. Sorry."

Philip cleared his throat again. "As you stood there, beholding the tower's wonder, a sinking feeling set into your gut. You begin to fear that someone, perhaps another architect jealous of the tower or just some common vandals might seek to defame or destroy it. So, you built a fence around it. It might not stop the vandals, but at least it would slow them down. The day you put up the fence, a few folks threw eggs at it."

"They threw eggs at my fence! How dare they!" I protested, slamming my fist on the table.

Philip nodded. "See, you knew the vandals would show up eventually. Now you feel justified. Vindicated, even. You were right to do it. I mean, what if they'd egged the tower?"

"Or spray-painted it or threw toilet paper on it."

"Unthinkable, right?" Philip asked.

I nodded.

"Then you were emboldened. You always knew the haters would target your tower."

"Haters gonna hate," I quipped.

Philip nodded. "So you built the fence taller and higher. You added a little barbed wire for good measure. Then, when people vandalized the fence again, you built a second one. You couldn't be too careful, after all. This time, you charged it with electricity.

If push came to shove, you knew you could build a moat and fill it with snakes and crocodiles. Whatever it took."

"Heaven forbid they threaten my tower. My beautiful, beautiful, tower," I made my voice a little growlier and higher than normal, "My precious!"

Philip ignored my Smeagol impression and continued. "Then, after years of reinforcing the fence, you turned around, and you were shocked to see that your once beautiful tower had fallen into disrepair. The birds had shit all over it. The weather had taken its toll. You never really appreciated its beauty because you were so focused on the fences, the barbed wire, the moat. You were so fixated on protecting the tower that you never cared for it."

"I think I see where you're going with this story," I said. "If we apply it to our religion."

Philip shrugged. "I think it applies to anything we hold dear, honestly."

I nodded. "If we don't enjoy it, if we don't relish the goodness of what we have, and in fear we fixate on the fences we've built, before we know it, we'll find we've lost what's most meaningful. We've forgotten what's good and beautiful."

"And more than that," Philip said, "we'll become hateful and resentful. That's the challenge you face right now, Caspar. You've never had much propensity for fences. You've always tested the boundaries. But trying to undermine the fence isn't the point. How can you magnify the beauty of the tower? How can you show them that the people who are coming to your church are, as Gollum might put it, precious?"

I took a deep breath and sat back in my chair. I had a lot to think about.

"Can I take your order?" a young man asked. His hair was short and his face nervous. His eyes darted back and forth between Philip's collar and my eyes.

"Do you want to touch it?" I asked.

159

"Excuse me?"

"His collar," I said. "I'm sure he'll let you touch it if you'd like."

The boy chuckled nervously. "No, thank you. Have you had a chance to look at the menu?"

Philip grabbed the little white tab in the front of his shirt and pulled it out. "See, nothing special. Just a piece of plastic."

"I didn't know that thing came out," the boy said.

I smiled. "That's because he's a cheapskate. They have other ones that go all the way around and button in the back. That's the kind I have. Don't wear it much."

"When have you ever worn your collar?" Philip asked.

I reached into my back pocket, retrieved my driver's license from my wallet, and flipped it on the table.

Philip laughed. "You wore it for your driver's license photo?"

"A lot of Catholics in St. Louis," I said with a smirk. "You wouldn't believe how often this gets me out of tickets."

CHAPTER TWENTY-THREE

The food was delicious, even though all I had was a chicken salad.

I was watching my figure, after all.

I waited for the crosswalk sign to change to walk before jogging across the road. I always tried to hurry when crossing the road. Nothing drove me nuttier than a pedestrian taking his grand 'ol time, oblivious to the fact that I was sitting there in my car, waiting.

Frickin' pedestrians. They were the worst when you weren't one.

But now that I was, the best part about having my car out of commission was that walking gave me plenty of opportunities to reflect. Even riding the Metro was a meditative experience compared to driving.

It wasn't just the food that had been a pleasant surprise. The whole interlude had gone better than I'd expected. I suppose I'd been through the wringer enough times with the various powers that be that I was preparing for the worst.

Sure, I knew Philip was more progressive than the former bishop, but I'd figured he'd feel pressure to enforce official dogma, to push me to get in line. Not to mention, when folks complained to authorities, there was a tendency to want to appease them, defuse the situation, and pacify their frustration.

Philip had taken a different approach. I was grateful for that.

People weren't usually bigots or closed-minded assholes because they were confident that they were right.

They became that way because they could not consider that they might be wrong.

Or they were afraid that if they were wrong, especially when it came to matters of religion, God would strike them down for their ignorance.

Sort of a bastardization, I thought, to the whole idea of having faith.

Faith, for me at least, wasn't about proper knowledge. It was about simple trust. The willingness to turn one's life over to a higher power and let go of the need to always be in control.

It was a freeing thing.

Because we can't control as much as we'd like to, and when we let go, at least in my experience, things tended to go to shit a lot less often than when I tried to run the show.

Not that there was anything wrong with having beliefs.

Most of us have to operate within some kind of worldview, some basic idea of what was true to move forward with a reasonable degree of confidence. We needed that to be oriented. My truth might not be the whole truth, but that didn't mean it wasn't true. And if it was sufficient to guide me through life in a way that made me a reasonably decent person and helped me avoid too many asshole moves along the way, there was nothing wrong with believing I was right, at least tentatively.

In fact, with all I'd been through—the Blade of Echoes, Layla, magic—none of my core beliefs had changed. My confidence in my core principles had been challenged. I'd had to struggle with how this new information changed the context of my worldview. It had forced me to broaden my beliefs and think outside of the box. It had even meant that about a few things, I had to admit I might have been wrong.

There was nothing wrong with being wrong.

There was the tower. And there was the fence. It was a damn good parable, I had to admit.

If we were more terrified of being wrong than loving what was true, we would never find happiness. Somehow I had to get that across to the folks at Holy Cross.

But I had to remind myself of it, too.

Unite the people. Unite all the people. That was what I was supposed to do as the chosen one.

To be, as a politician might say, a uniter, not a divider. We weren't blue states and red states. We were the United States.

Never mind. I got off track.

For me, unity couldn't be some kind of half-hearted platitude. According to the elven prophecy, I had to accomplish it.

And as hard as it might be to unite people across a political divide, I had to unite people across a divide between worlds and races: humans, elves, giants, and maybe even fairies.

Then again, that would probably be easier than trying to make Republicans and Democrats get along. I didn't identify with either political party, truth be told. There were things I liked and disliked about each side. But when you were walking a narrow path between two alternatives, you tended to be on the receiving end of judgment and hate from all around. So, as much as was possible, I kept my political views to myself.

But here I was, engaging in otherworldly politics, dealing with both elves and giants, dating one, training with the other. One loved me. Layla had given up everything because she believed in me. B'iff had died for my sake because he believed in me, too.

That was a lot of pressure, and I wasn't sure what I should do.

How much longer would Brag'mok be willing to wait for

Layla to come back? Was it fair to make him wait? He'd said he was in pain as long as his brother wasn't laid to rest.

He still wanted my help to remove B'iff's body from Earth's magical core. He still wanted to close the gate.

But how could I unite the people, all the people, if I cut them off? If I did what Brag'mok wanted and effectively killed the gate between worlds?

But he was right; it would end the possibility of an elven invasion.

However, not all the elves were bad. Not all of them deserved to languish in a world that was torn apart by perpetual war. It wasn't every elf's fault that their authorities had squandered all the magic they'd brought to the world and now their planet was dying.

Maybe I was being naïve, but perhaps the whole reason the elves hated humans was because back when our ancestors persecuted the druids, it was because they'd been focusing on fences rather than towers.

They'd used fear of the other as the driving force behind their actions.

They had never shared the beauty of their world or their culture or bothered to consider the beauty of the druids and their magic, their connection to the Earth.

So, the druids left. They found a new world and evolved into elves, and the giants with them, becoming what folklore disparagingly referred to as orcs.

Maybe this whole situation with Holy Cross, trying to unite people in my world, was meant to be practice for uniting the elves, giants, and humans if that was what the prophecy was about.

But that was the challenge. Everyone had fences. How could I get people to see beyond the others' fences and appreciate the beauty of other people's lives?

We had to start by dismantling the fence. We had to trust that the tower we cared for, be it our world, our humanity, or even our faith, was attractive and beautiful on its own.

And to do that, we had to stop comparing ourselves to others. We had to stop exaggerating other people's flaws while diminishing their virtues. We had to, as Jag put it, be our own competition, always striving to be better versions of ourselves.

It was an uneventful walk but productive nonetheless.

I climbed the stairs leading to my apartment, unlocked the door, and stepped inside.

Before I could turn on the lights, I was enveloped by two arms and a pair of lips pressed against mine. I wrapped my arms around her. It was still dark, but I knew the taste of those lips. Layla was back. Thank God

CHAPTER TWENTY-FOUR

"Thank God it's you!" I said as we briefly pulled away from each other.

"Who else would it be?" Layla asked. "Do random people sneak into your apartment and start kissing you when you come home?"

I shook my head. "You'd be surprised. It's a hard-knock life."

Layla giggled. "Sorry I had to leave so quickly."

"You seem like you're in good spirits. I'm sorry about your father."

Layla nodded. "He isn't dead after all."

"And Hector? He's back?" I asked.

Layla shook her head. "I suppose Agnus filled you in on those details."

I nodded. "I was worried. Benefits of having a cat who can talk. When your girlfriend leaves the planet without so much as a goodbye, at least I'm not totally in the dark."

Layla sighed. "I'm sorry about that."

"So, your father isn't dead?" I asked.

Layla shook her head.

"And Hector isn't back from the dead?" I asked.

"Not exactly," Layla said.

"What do you mean, not exactly?" I asked. "People believe your father is dead and that there's some kind of revolution to take over the kingdom led by Hector, claiming to be the chosen one."

Layla cocked her head. "How do you know about all that?"

I bit my lip. She didn't know about Brag'mok.

"I was going to tell you just before you disappeared."

"Tell me what?" Layla asked.

"B'iff's brother Brag'mok is here, and he wanted me to retrieve B'iff's body from the source. He said the rites needed to be completed. That as his kin, he'll be in pain until his brother is properly put to rest."

Layla sighed. "Brag'mok, you said?"

I nodded. "Yeah. He's even been training me to fight since you left. He was willing to wait until you got back because once we pulled B'iff's body from the source, there was a chance—"

"That it would close the gate forever," Layla said, finishing my thought.

I nodded. "Exactly."

"And Brag'mok showed up at your AA meeting to tell you this?" Layla asked.

I sighed. "Not exactly. He was the one who slashed the Mitsubishi's tires. He approached me on the Metro."

"That was before I left. Why didn't you tell me?" Layla asked, scratching her head.

"He told me not to," I said. "He said if I told you that you'd go back, and if you went back, you'd be killed."

Layla shook her head and sat down on the couch. "So you took some random giant's advice and kept it from me?"

"I was about to tell you!" I insisted. "I'd just gotten done processing what he'd told me. That's why I went to my meeting that night."

"You shouldn't have to go to a fucking meeting to figure out that you should be honest with me, Caspar."

I sighed. "I know. I'm sorry. But…"

"But what?" Layla asked. "I wouldn't have gone back. I would have agreed. I would have helped you do it. We could have closed the gate and ended it all."

"But Layla," I said. "The prophecy."

"But we could have saved your world," Layla said. "Prophecies have a way of coming true one way or another."

"Layla," I said, taking her hand in mine and lacing our fingers together. "What happened on New Albion when you left?"

Layla nodded. "Remember before I left, I'd told you about fairies?"

I sighed. "Yeah, about that. Since you left—"

"A fairy came after you?" Layla asked.

I nodded. "How'd you guess?"

Layla shook her head. "I figured they might. Fairies are known for trickery."

"You don't need to tell me that," I said, rolling my eyes. "My hair."

"I kind of like it," Layla said, chuckling. "I mean, I like it long, too, but you have a nicely shaped head."

"Thanks," I said. "The fairy put Nair in my shampoo bottle."

Layla laughed out loud. "Well, that's something."

"He did a lot more than that."

Layla grinned. "You can tell me all about that later. With the gate open permanently, a large contingency of fairies has traveled back and forth between the worlds. Some of those who came with us when our ancestors left Earth came here. Some of the fairies who'd hidden here on Earth went to New Albion. They reunited, and with more power, they've become emboldened. I think they're looking for revenge."

"On elves?" I asked.

"And humans," Layla said. "It wasn't Hector who attempted to assassinate my father. It was a fairy impersonating Hector. He'd apparently showed up a few days before claiming to be the chosen one, but my father knew Hector had stabbed himself."

"But it wasn't with the Blade of Echoes," I said. "Your father should have known that even if Hector had survived, as it seemed he had, he hadn't fulfilled the prophecy. He didn't survive a stab by the Blade of Echoes."

"I'm sure he realized that," Layla said. "But the fact that Hector had survived a stab by a blade that looked like the Blade of Echoes and other legionnaires witnessed it when they were on Earth was an opportunity to try to force the hand of the prophecy. To raise who he thought was Hector up as the chosen one and use him as a general to lead the legions to Earth."

"But it wasn't Hector. You said it was a fairy impersonating him?"

Layla nodded. "And that wasn't the only fairy. There were hundreds of them. They didn't kill my father. They wouldn't do that. But they abducted him. One fairy impersonated him, and the one pretending to be Hector faked an assassination."

I furrowed my brow. "Why would they do that?"

"To cause upheaval in the kingdom," Layla said. "Fairies manipulate their enemies by creating chaos. In this case, they knew if word came that my father had been killed, I'd have no choice but to return to New Albion."

"Why would they want you to go back?" I asked.

"Because I was teaching you how to use magic," Layla said. "If I left and they closed the gate, we'd be stuck on a hostile planet without much magic left. And you'd be here, the only one who can use magic. All they'd need to do was convince you not to use it."

I sighed. "Which was exactly what they did."

"How did you get back?" I asked. "If they were hoping to close the gate?"

Layla shook her head. "They wouldn't close the gate now. I

think it's because Brag'mok is still here. They were looking for a way to get him back to New Albion."

"For the same reason they wanted you to leave Earth?" I asked.

"I think so," Layla said. "Because he could teach humans how to use magic, as I did. You said he was already teaching you."

I sighed. "He told me I had to embarrass myself. If I made enough of a fool of myself, they'd stop their pranks."

"He said what?" Layla asked. "That makes no sense unless he was trying to distract you. To get you off their scent."

"He told me that if I embarrassed myself, I'd appease the fairies, and if I stopped using magic, they'd leave me alone."

"Of course he did," Layla said. "Do you know where Brag'mok is now?"

I shook my head. "He usually meets me in the park in the morning."

Layla nodded. "Then we need to kill him."

"What?" I asked. "He's not our enemy."

"No, he's not," Layla said. "And I'm sure it was originally him who appeared to you. But the one who told you to embarrass yourself? That sounds like fairy trickery. I don't know why he'd tell you that."

"Brag'mok, or the person I thought was Brag'mok, was a fairy?" I asked, raising my eyebrow.

Layla nodded. "Which means B'iff's brother is in trouble. The fairies must have abducted him, just like they did my father."

CHAPTER TWENTY-FIVE

"What happened to your father?" I asked.

Layla shook her head. "I had to make sure he was still alive, and he was. The fairies had surrounded him, trapping him in a cave. I couldn't get him out, but they weren't hurting him. At least I didn't hear any cries. I only got one glimpse of him, but he looked fine. Healthy. Even happy if you could believe it."

"Why didn't they just kill him?" I asked.

"Fairies aren't opposed to killing for the greater good, but it isn't their way since magic is part of the source of life."

"And since they see themselves as the protectors of magic, killing would be, like, heresy or something?" I asked.

Layla nodded. "Don't get me wrong. Fairies can wreak all kinds of havoc, but given any other choice, they won't kill. At least not directly. Not intentionally."

"And you didn't try to rescue your dad?" I asked.

Layla shook her head. "I couldn't even if I wanted to. There were just too many fairies. I'd never seen so many on New Albion. Most of them must've come from Earth. Not to mention, even if I did save him and he reaffirmed his claim on the throne, he'd know I was back on New Albion. Remember, I am still suspected of treason on account of siding with you."

I nodded. "It would have been too great a risk."

"So is allowing the fairy impersonating Brag'mok to continue doing so. I don't trust it. They're up to something."

"I'm not sure your theory about him adds up," I said. "Brag'mok continued training me. Do fairies know fighting skills?"

Layla stared at me. "Of course they do."

"But the one that was hassling me, it was so small, like Tinkerbell."

"First," Layla said. "Tink isn't a fairy. She's a pixie."

I shrugged. "What's the difference?"

"About two inches," Layla said. "Fairies are two inches taller than pixies on average."

I cocked my head. "Brag'mok is at least seven feet tall, probably closer to eight. There's no way."

"A fairy can alter its size or shape through magic. They aren't particularly good at it unless they've captured the person whose appearance they intend to copy. Sort of like how an artist might require a model when painting or sculpting a figure."

I took a deep breath. "Which was how they impersonated your father."

Layla nodded. "All I saw was the corpse at the funeral. Not sure if it was dead. I mean, a fairy doesn't have the usual vital signs that elves and humans do. Even without a heartbeat or not breathing, the fairy could still be very much alive, just waiting until they buried the body to resume its normal shape and disappear."

I scratched my head. "Well, if fairies can shift so convincingly, how do I know for sure that anyone is who they say they are?"

"Including me?" Layla asked. "I mean, that's what you're wanting to ask me, isn't it?"

I sighed. "Not that I don't believe you."

"Would a fairy kiss you the way I did before?" Layla asked, smirking in a mildly seductive way.

"I don't know," I said. "I've never kissed a fairy before."

"Sure you haven't," Layla said. "It's okay if you did. I mean, everyone experiments in college, right?"

I snorted. "I didn't even know fairies existed back then. Besides, how would you even know what college is like?"

"I've studied human college," Layla said.

"Is there a college for that?" I asked. "Majoring in college studies?"

Layla chuckled. "No. And even if I went to college, I'd never major in anything ending with the word 'studies.' Not unless I was independently wealthy and had no career aspirations."

"Heaven forbid, a useless college degree. Why would anyone get one of those?" I coughed into my hand.

"Didn't you major in philosophy before you went to seminary?" Layla asked.

I sighed. "Yeah, but philosophy is useful—if you ever want to sound smart in a crowd or confuse the hell out of people. Besides, I had a second major in history."

"Right," Layla said. "Because history is an incredibly lucrative field."

"Hey," I said. "History is important. If you don't know your history, you're doomed to repeat it."

"You're missing the point," Layla continued. "If I was a fairy, would I know about your college majors?"

I shook my head. "Still isn't proof. I mean, you could probably find out what my college major was by finding one of my old resumes or transcripts or looking it up on the internet. And I assume modern-day fairies could access a computer if they wanted to."

Layla scratched the back of her head. "Agnus!"

My cat came running and jumped into her lap and purred.

"If I was a fairy," Layla continued, "Agnus would know it. Cats can't stand the smell of fairies."

I narrowed my eyes. "But if you were a fairy, you could just lie to me about that."

"It's true," Agnus piped up. "That whole time that fairy was screwing with you, this apartment smelled like ass."

"Fairies smell like ass?" I asked. "Don't cats smell butts sometimes?"

"Please!" Agnus protested. "Dogs sniff ass, and some of them eat shit. We're more refined than that."

"Bullshit, Agnus," I said. "I've seen you sniff butts before."

"Only if it's another cat," Agnus said. "I'd never sniff a human butt. And that fairy smelled like human ass."

I scratched my head. "How do you even know that if you've never sniffed human butts before?"

Agnus stared at me blankly. "Your flatulence."

"Not the same," I said. "Sniffing the source is completely different."

"I doubt it's *completely* different. It's close enough, and I have an imagination."

"Sure you do," I said. "Agnus, do you sniff my drawers when I'm sleeping?"

"No!" Agnus said. "Not yours. Layla's maybe, but not yours."

"You what?" Layla asked.

"Kitty likes the smell of kitty, what can I say?"

Layla quickly tossed Agnus off her lap onto the floor. "If he couldn't talk, I wouldn't think anything of it. But after what he just said, having him on my lap..."

"It's okay," Agnus said. "I understand. You have to pretend you aren't into me when he's around. We'll have our fun later."

Layla just shook her head, then looked at me. "He doesn't know when to quit, does he?"

"No, he doesn't," I said. "Put on Animal Planet or something. Channel his passions toward something more appropriate."

Layla grabbed the remote and navigated to the proper channel.

"Oh, my God!" Agnus shouted. "Elephants! Change the channel. I don't know why they even show this. I mean, honestly! Who the hell is into elephants?"

"I don't think the producers at Animal Planet consider the sexiness of a species when making programming choices," I said, rolling my eyes. "Besides, Agnus, you're seriously not into trunks?"

"Are you?" Agnus asked.

"Not really," I said. "Fair point. But I know what you *do* like. I bet I can get *Lion King* on Disney Plus."

"*Lion King*?" Agnus asked. "The cartoon or the newer movie version?"

I shrugged. "There's a movie version?"

"Much hotter than the original," Agnus replied with a nod.

"I had no idea," I said, chuckling. "But doesn't the cartoon work for you?"

"Do cartoon women do it for you, Caspar?" Agnus asked.

I bit my lip. "Not usually, unless it's anime."

"Seriously?" Layla asked.

"No, not really." I cleared my throat. "I mean, not that I'd admit, anyway."

Layla giggled and shook her head. "Men are so weird."

"So, what's the plan with Brag'mok?" I asked. "I want to make sure that your theory is correct before we even consider you shooting an arrow through his heart."

Layla shrugged. "Then we bring Agnus with us."

"If he is a fairy, do you think he's going to let us bring our cat along?" I asked.

Layla shook her head. "He'll avoid Agnus at all costs, which is exactly how we'll know."

"Unless he just doesn't like cats," I said.

"Who doesn't like cats?" Agnus asked with a hint of shock in his voice.

"Dog people," I said. "Believe it or not, a lot of people don't like cats."

"Savages," Agnus quipped, leaping off the couch.

"Dog people are savages?" I asked as Agnus walked the other way.

"Barbarians works, too," Agnus continued.

"Where are you going?" I asked. "We're trying to formulate a plan."

"I have to take a shit, Caspar. Do I need to announce my every intention?"

I snorted. "No. Sorry. I guess not."

Agnus huffed and continued walking into the laundry room where I kept his litter box. Not the most ideal place for it, but in a small apartment, I was lucky to have a room dedicated to laundry, and I didn't have a better option. I wasn't going to put it in my room or in the kitchen. Gross. Not the living room either. So his box went into the laundry room. I remembered to tidy up his box from time to time. He had a self-cleaning affair that worked with clumping litter; it sifted through the litter after it sensed he'd been in there and dumped the crumbs into a little chamber I kept lined with a bag. All I had to do was replace the bag every couple of days. Then I didn't have to change the litter as much as make sure he had enough and top it off regularly. Once a month, give or take, I'd change it all for good measure, but for the most part, the high-tech cat box worked pretty well. As long as he didn't have diarrhea. Then the whole system went to shit.

So he ate tuna fish, which was his treat, and Science Diet. As long as we didn't change his food too much, we were good. Anyone who ever owned a cat knows this. Add variety to a cat's diet, and it will start coming out of both ends.

"So, why do you think that killing him is the right move?" I asked. "Say he is a fairy. So what? Aren't they trying to protect the Earth in their way?"

"You squish spiders when they show up in your apartment," Layla pointed out. "Why?"

"Because spiders are creepy!"

"And fairies aren't?" Layla asked.

"That's different. I mean, from my few encounters with them, the fairies are intelligent and self-aware."

"So, is it okay to squish humans if they have low intelligence or perhaps, lose their memories?"

"Of course not," I said. "Killing is never okay."

"Unless it's spiders."

I sighed. "Okay, maybe I shouldn't kill spiders either. But if I'm inconsistent about that, it doesn't mean I should resolve that inconsistency by agreeing to kill other things, like fairies."

"If this fairy is masquerading at Brag'mok," Layla said, "it means it kidnapped the real Brag'mok. And with the shenanigans they pulled on New Albion with my dad and pretending to be Hector, you wouldn't believe the kind of havoc they can cause."

I shrugged. "Well, considering the instability in the elven kingdom, it gave you a chance to go back there without being immediately executed."

Layla shook her head. "Doesn't mean anything."

"And you don't think sparking a revolution in a kingdom that would see its own princess killed because she fell in love with a human might be a good thing in the long run?" I asked.

"People die in revolutions, Caspar."

"I know," I said. "Most of the time, that's true. But that doesn't mean it needs to be. What if you *did* take over your father's throne? That could fix everything."

Layla sighed. "Not possible, as long as he's still alive."

I nodded. "But it sounds like that was the fairies' plan all along. Lure you back to New Albion, spark a revolution that leads to a regime change."

"Me inheriting my father's throne wouldn't be a regime change," Layla said. "That's how hereditary monarchies work."

"I don't know," I said. "I mean, Bloody Mary and Queen Elizabeth were sisters, and their visions for England were completely different. Mary used force to try to undo her own father's Protestant reforms. Elizabeth took over and re-instituted his reforms but more effectively. They were family, part of a hereditary monarchy."

"What's the point?" Layla asked. "Even if I could make some radical changes for the better, it doesn't mean the people would ever accept me. They're brainwashed by the elven dogma."

I snorted. "Sort of like medieval people on Earth were, due to their religious assumptions?"

Layla sighed. "You're not going to prove to me that majoring in history was any more worthwhile than majoring in philosophy."

I shrugged. "I could have majored in women's studies. I hear that's a great way to meet chicks."

Layla rolled her eyes. "Another major that is, perhaps, important for a lot of reasons. But not exactly great for making a career."

"When have you ever been so career-oriented, anyway?" I asked. "I mean, isn't it noble for some people to study things that might allow them to have a voice in making social changes without thinking about their career prospects later on?"

"I don't know," Layla said. "If you can't eat or provide for yourself at all, how much change can you effect?"

"A lot," I said. "Gandhi pulled it off."

"Gandhi was a lawyer, Caspar," Layla said. "He starved himself to make a point."

"See," I said. "Knowing history is useful."

"Then show me an example of a peaceful revolution," Layla said. "Where a regime change happened without massive loss of life."

"Well," I said. "There was the Bloodless Revolution in the United Kingdom in the late sixteen hundreds. In the nineteen-eighties, they had a peaceful revolution in the Philippines. Another one in Germany."

Layla folded her arms. "How do I know you're not making that up?"

"I was a history major!" I said. "And like I said, it's useful when trying to convince an elven princess to take over her father's throne."

"Was that on the college brochure when you chose your major?" Layla asked. "Come and major in history, save an elven kingdom!"

I laughed. "Not exactly. But that's the point, Layla. Maybe the fairies are on to something. I mean, they didn't kill your dad, right?"

"Still," Layla said. "They were trying to deceive everyone. Force a revolution by luring me back to New Albion, putting me into conflict with their false Hector."

I scratched my head. "And you didn't play along with that? If that was their plan, they were handing your kingdom to you. Giving you a chance to claim it and end the war. Why wouldn't you do that?"

Layla sighed. "They also had a plan to close the elven gate, Caspar."

I nodded. "To prevent a war, I'm guessing, that would have brought elves to Earth because the elves would have misused Earth's magic to conquer humans."

"And if I went along with that, I'd never see you again."

I sighed. "So you turned down a chance to save the world, a chance to take over your kingdom for love?"

A tear fell down Layla's cheek. "For love, and because I still believe in the prophecy. I don't know how it's supposed to work out, Caspar. I really don't. But what the fairies are doing, that's not what was foretold. Their plan isn't the only way to achieve peace."

"And because New Albion is failing," I said. "The magic that's left can only last you so long."

Layla nodded. "But it wasn't to save New Albion that I came back. That's part of it, of course, but it was you, Caspar. My love for you and my faith in you."

CHAPTER TWENTY-SIX

Faith is only as good as the object it trusts. You can have faith in a doorknob all day long, but insofar as your spiritual desires involve little more than opening and closing doors, it will likely betray you if you ask it to do much of anything else for you. It won't do much good if you're trusting it to save you when you jump out of a plane. You need to put a little faith in a parachute for that.

This was a part of the problem with Layla's decision to come back to Earth.

Don't get me wrong. I was *glad* she was back, but she'd effectively thwarted a plan enacted by fairies to do what I was busting my ass in the gym trying to do—to save the world. I mean, yeah, I'd made some progress. Training with Brag'mok, or the fairy who was pretending to be Brag'mok, had given me a few moves. Even Jag was impressed with how much progress I was making in the gym.

But let's be real.

A lifetime of training wasn't going to be enough to stand against a whole legion, especially one that could take over the world. I mean, even if I was a badass, the James Bond of ministers, I was still one man. Sure, I might have some latent and untapped magical abilities, but I hadn't progressed much in that domain, especially not since Layla left. One strike against Brag'mok in the park. It was a David-versus-Goliath moment for me.

Except that Brag'mok didn't actually want to kill me.

That had to be the real Brag'mok. But the next time we met, when he didn't want me to use magic, maybe that was the fairy? It made sense, I suppose.

But he'd still trained me, even after he convinced me that we'd gotten rid of the fairy. He taught me how to evade a strike and use my opponent's momentum against him.

It was pretty slick. How could that *not* be Brag'mok? Why would a fairy who had a plan that involved having me give up magic bother teaching me fighting moves?

A lyric popped in my head that summarized my feelings— revised, of course, to fit my dilemma.

Won't the real Brag'mok please stand up?

Two trailer park girls go 'round the outside, 'round the outside, 'round the outside...

Sorry, I got carried away.

Not sure what females who lived in a mobile home exploring the perimeter had to do with anything, either in my situation or in the context of the Eminem song.

But it was catchy. Not the first time I'd co-opted the rapper's lyrics for my purposes.

I'd once created a flier for a missions festival at the church where we were talking about the return of Christ and how Jesus coming back should motivate us to go out and tell the world. You know, before it's too late. Fear tactics sucked when it came to evangelism, so I tried to lighten the mood a bit.

The caption on the flier: *Guess who's back. JC's back. Tell a friend.*

I had a photoshopped picture of Jesus standing there with his arms folded over his chest.

I mean, Jesus was something of a rebel. Stood up against the man. It was brilliant, I thought, totally meme-worthy.

Matthias, my bishop at the time, hadn't seen the humor in it. I wondered how he'd react to the Punk Rock Jesus comic books. I had the whole collection.

I just couldn't accept the idea that Brag'mok was the enemy. Sure, he'd told me to lie to Layla, which was sort of a dick move. But he'd had his reasons for it. And he was willing to live with the pain of his brother's loss, without his brother receiving his death rites, just to give Layla a chance to return.

But here was the dilemma.

If Layla was back and he knew it, and he was really Brag'mok, not a fairy, he'd want to retrieve B'iff's body and close the gate.

But if he was a fairy, he might want to do the same thing. Only, he'd probably try to find a reason to get Layla through the gate. The fairies didn't want her here. They didn't want anyone here who could show humanity how to use magic again.

"I don't think you can come with us," I said.

Layla was standing at the counter, polishing her bow. "Like hell, I can't."

"Think about it, Layla. If it is a fairy and they know you're back, they're going to do whatever they can to send you back again before we seal the gate. If it is Brag'mok, he's going to want us to retrieve B'iff's body, which would also seal the gate immediately."

"With the elves in disarray, divided against themselves, the giants will surely conquer us," Layla said before taking a deep breath. "Maybe it would be for the best."

I shook my head. "Maybe. Maybe not. But with the gate shut, we'll never know."

Layla sighed. "But there's still the prophecy. That's not how this is supposed to go down. You aren't supposed to forever divide the people."

"I'm supposed to unite them."

Layla nodded. "I know it doesn't make sense to put blind faith in a prophecy, especially when two of the seals haven't even opened yet. When there's still so much we don't know."

"If you have faith," I said, "it doesn't matter what the other two seals reveal. You know the endgame, right? You know what the chosen one, what *I*, am supposed to do, don't you?"

"That part is clear. How it comes about? Those details are subject to interpretation. But we know that all division is supposed to end."

I nodded. "Same goes for how different denominations interpret the Bible. Everyone agrees that Jesus is supposed to come back and defeat death and sin, but people disagree about tribulations, raptures, and whether Jesus is going to rule over some kind of kingdom for a thousand years, or believe those verses are symbolic. Some people believe the bulk of Revelation was fulfilled in the first century, while others believe that almost none of it has happened yet and obsess over finding parallels between the prophecy and what they're seeing on the nightly news."

"What view do you hold?" Layla asked.

I shrugged. "My view is that it doesn't matter. I don't think John wrote Revelation in order to help us predict the future. I think he wrote it to encourage people during persecution, people going through trials and tribulations, to know that the end is already decided. It's sort of like when you're watching a movie or a television show and the hero is in peril, but you know there are sequels or three more seasons, so despite how perilous it seems, you have faith that the hero is going to prevail."

"And when it comes to the elven prophecy, I have to believe that somehow you are going to prevail, too. But what do we do in the meantime?"

I shrugged. "I guess we act as if."

"What does that mean?" Layla asked.

"Act as if everything is going according to plan. Don't panic. Don't do anything rash. You know, like kill a giant who has been helping us just because we have a suspicion he might be a fairy. Or kill a fairy at all. If we're acting as if we believe I'm going to unite all people, then we need to act like it now. That includes respecting the fairies."

Layla sighed. "Then what can we do?"

"First thing, how about we eliminate killing anyone as an option?"

"You're no fun." Layla huffed and tossed her bow on the couch.

"This is supposed to be fun?" I asked.

Layla shrugged. "Elves just wanna have fun."

"It's trolls," I said. "Trolls just wanna have fun."

"Actually," Layla said, "it was girls originally."

I chuckled. "Yes, it was. But I don't think however you sing it, having fun entails shooting arrows at people."

"Just fairies."

"Still people," I said. "Not humans, but people. I mean, they have individual will, right? I think that makes them people."

"So what do you suggest we do?" Layla asked. "If killing things is off the table."

I shrugged. "We confront Brag'mok. If he isn't a fairy, he surely knows more about what's going on than he's letting on. And we try to talk to the fairies."

"You don't talk to fairies," Layla said. "Did the one who was messing with you while I was gone strike you as the conversational type?"

I bit my lip. "No, he just squirted ketchup on my butt cheeks."

Layla furrowed her brow. "How did he do that?"

"Packets under the toilet seat."

Layla laughed. "That's fantastic!"

"If my butt was made out of French fries, maybe."

"Well, before you started working out, I'd say it might as well have been."

I smiled. "That's a fair point."

"I'll tell you what," Layla said. "We'll try this your way. You go, bring Agnus along, and try to talk to the fairy."

"To Brag'mok, you mean?" I asked.

"Whoever it is," Layla said. "And I'll be waiting with my bow in case the fairy gets anxious. Once Agnus figures it out, the fairy is likely to get violent."

CHAPTER TWENTY-SEVEN

I didn't like the compromise. I mean, nothing says ill will more than having someone lurking in the bushes, waiting to snipe you if you make the wrong move. I know I wouldn't react well to that.

But I just couldn't get on board with the theory that Brag'mok was a fairy. Sure, Layla had more experience with the creatures than I did. And yeah, it would be one hell of a prank for a fairy to pull, especially since he was the one who convinced me to embarrass myself with shoddy pick-up lines directed toward random strangers.

But to be a fairy pretending to be a giant?

I trusted Layla, of course. I didn't want to doubt her, but I'd spent a lot of time with Brag'mok. Something in my gut told me she was wrong.

Sorting that out was the second biggest challenge of the day.

The first was trying to figure out how to bring Agnus to the park. Forest Park wasn't a quick walk. I had to take the Metro. Getting him to ride in the car was challenging enough, a feat that had become a lot easier once Layla was in the picture. He'd sit on her lap and remain mostly content.

Not to mention, I was reasonably certain that you weren't

THEOPHILUS MONROE & MICHAEL ANDERLE

allowed to bring pets with you on public transit. Not unless it was a service dog or something, and I don't think they have such a thing as service cats. Cats don't serve. They are served. I was Agnus' service human.

"You could fly," Layla suggested.

I raised one eyebrow. "Seriously? Use magic? The fairy made it clear—"

"You're going to be intimidated by a fairy?" Layla interrupted.

"You're the one who wants to kill it, and you're telling me I shouldn't be intimidated by it?"

Layla laughed. "It's not like it wants you dead. From what you said, all it did was pull a series of mostly harmless pranks."

I sighed. "True. But if I come flying into the park in all my magical glory, if he is a fairy, he'll know it. He'll realize something's up because as far as he knows, I'm committed to not using magic unless it's necessary."

"He's going to realize something's up the second you show up with a cat anyway," Layla said. "What's important is to get Agnus near him so we can determine for certain that it is a fairy. If it is, we can try to convince it to tell us where the real Brag'mok is."

"How exactly are we going to do that?" I asked.

"We'll play it by ear," Layla said.

I smirked, glancing at Layla's pointy ears. "That's funny."

"That's rude," Layla said. "To make a joke at the expense of my superior ears."

"Whatever," I said. "You know I think they're hot."

Layla smiled slightly. "So it's decided. You fly to the park. I'll take the Metro and meet you there."

"I'll have to fly slow or give you a thirty-minute head start or something. But what if people see me? I mean, if I'm Superman-ning it across the city, someone is bound to notice."

"Well, you can't perform multiple spells at once," Layla said. "Otherwise, I'd suggest cloaking yourself while you do it."

"I can cloak myself?" I asked.

"It's Earth magic. It's not like a cloak, not like a starship would on *Star Trek*. It's more like a chameleon. You can use magic to blend into the world around you."

"Well, even if I could visualize that, like you said, I can't do it while flying."

"Technically," Layla said, "you probably could, given your level-five abilities."

"Not going to figure it out now. The only way I can see pulling this off at all is if we go while it's still dark. If people see me, it'll be too dark for them to tell what it is as long as the magic glow around me isn't too obvious."

Layla nodded. "I'd wear black just in case."

I nodded and went to my closet. I had a few dark-colored polos, but my arms were so white that I figured long sleeves were best for cloaking purposes. The only long-sleeved black shirt I had was my clergy shirt, the one that was supposed to have the ring-neck clergy collar affixed to it. Without that, it just looked like one of those collarless dress shirts from the nineties. You know, the ones that just buttoned to a ring-neck and, back then, had some kind of stud or something to fasten it together at the Adam's apple. Of course, it wasn't like I was hip on the latest fashion. For all I knew, it was back in style again.

Last I'd tried it on, it hadn't fit. I had been thinner back in my seminary days. But I put it on, and I was pleasantly surprised.

"Wow," I said. "I don't think I've worn this in five or six years. Surprised it fits."

Layla winked. "Looking good, hottie. You must work out."

I smiled. "I do. By the way, thanks for siccing Jag on me."

"He's a douchebag, right?" Layla asked.

"Yeah," I said. "In a good way, if that's a thing. But fifty bucks a session?"

Layla shrugged. "End of the world money. I figured it was worth it."

"Except saving the world doesn't pay well. If we succeed, I'm going to have to pay it off."

Layla shrugged. "I'd say those are first-world problems. You know, they're the sort of problems you have when there's a world to have problems in."

"True," I said. "Here's hoping I get to pay off my credit cards."

I finished buttoning my shirt and slid into a pair of black slacks. "How do I look?"

"Sexy," Layla said. "You look really good in black."

I nodded. "Yeah, better than I thought. Still not putting the clergy collar on the shirt, though."

Layla giggled. "Flying priests!"

"Except I'm not a priest. I'm a pastor."

"I know," Layla said. "But that's what people would think if they saw you."

I chuckled at the idea. I mean, there are a disproportionate number of superhero and *Star Wars* fanboys who go into the ministry, Catholic, Protestant, whatever. Most of us had superhero fantasies when we were children, and once we realized saving the world through powers wasn't a viable career path, we figured we'd try to save people with religion instead.

At least, that was my working theory about why so many geeky fanboys ended up as ministers.

The rest of them, I suppose, became urban fantasy authors.

CHAPTER TWENTY-EIGHT

Part of me wanted to put on my collar. The whole "Super Priest" alias tickled my funny bone.

But I hated wearing that thing because breathing was one of those habits I'd rather not shake.

Layla got a head start. We figured a good thirty-minute delay on the Metro, but we'd left enough time that I figured I'd be able to make it to the park while still enjoying the cover of night.

I don't know if I was hoping Layla was right or not. I mean, if she was wrong, using my magic to fly across the city was sure to get the attention of the fairies again.

Then again, I didn't want her to be right, either.

Brag'mok, or the giant I'd assumed was Brag'mok, had become a friend. I'd learned a lot from him.

How would he feel about me siccing Agnus on him?

I'd worry about that later.

"I'm not flying with you," Agnus said as I tried to push him into his carrier.

"You have to," I said. "It's the only way to pull this off. They won't let me bring you on the Metro."

"Haven't you ever heard of Uber?"

I bit my lip. "Dude, why didn't you speak up earlier?"

"Look it up," Agnus said.

I pulled out my phone. Sure enough, Uber offered pet-friendly rides.

I shook my head. "Layla already left. We have to stick to the plan."

"You probably could have called a regular taxi too, dumb ass," Agnus said.

I snorted. "Again, we can't change our plans. Layla is expecting us."

"Text her," Agnus ordered.

I sighed. "Dude, I was looking forward to this."

"Don't call me 'dude,'" Agnus said. "It's irreverent."

"Irreverent?" I asked. "You're a cat."

"Precisely."

I rolled my eyes, then pulled out my phone and texted Layla. I suggested an Uber. She responded with a laughing emoji.

"What the hell does that mean?" I asked, showing it to Agnus.

A few seconds later, she responded, **Just fly. Tell Agnus to get over it. If I'm wrong, we need to deal with the fairies anyway.**

"Sorry," I said. "The boss has spoken. Air Caspar, it is."

Agnus stared at me. "Fuck."

I laughed out loud. "They say flying is the safest way to travel."

"On a plane!" Agnus protested. "Not in a cat carrier in some wannabe superhero's hands!"

"Wannabe?" I asked. "I'm seriously trying to save the world here. What's wannabe about that?"

"You don't even have a cape," Agnus said. "At least get a cape."

"I'll have to put that on my to-do list," I said. "But not a bad idea."

"Just hold me," Agnus snorted. "Don't make me go into the box of death."

"It will be easier if you go in the box," I said. "And won't you feel safer?"

"Safer?" Agnus asked. "Because if you drop me in the box, my chances of survival are exponentially increased? Just carry me, Caspar."

"Fine," I said. "But don't wiggle."

"Why would I wiggle?" Agnus asked, "You just better not drop me. If you do, I'll haunt you with my lost life and terrorize you indefinitely with the eight I have left."

I shrugged. "At least if I did drop you, you'd land on your feet. They say cats always land on their feet."

"That's a myth, asshole."

"We could test it. I mean, you've seen *Mythbusters*, right?"

"No need for experiments," Agnus said. "I have experience. If I can't fall off the back of the couch and land on my feet…"

"Good point," I said, chuckling. "Don't worry, I won't drop you. I have a strong grip, you know, since I've been working out."

"How many times have you done this now, anyway?" Agnus asked.

I shrugged. "This is, like, my fourth time."

"Not much of a sample size to prove it is safe."

"It will be fine. Just don't wiggle. You're harder to hold onto that way. Consider this payback for clawing up my couch," I said as I scooped up Agnus.

"Payback?" Agnus asked. "You can't put a perfectly good piece of furniture in our place and expect me not to claw the fuck out of it. That would be unthinkable."

I smiled. "Now hush. I have to focus my mind to do this."

Agnus started singing, "*I'm a little teapot, short and stout.*"

"Shut up," I said.

"If you can't focus, you can't fly."

I sighed. "Whatever. I can tune you out."

"*This is the song that never ends,*" Agnus continued singing. "*It just goes on and on, my friend. Some people started singing it, not knowing what it was.*"

"Yeah," I said. "*And they'll continue singing it forever just because.*"

"This is the song that never ends!"

I rolled my eyes and took a deep breath while Agnus started his second round of what very well might be the most annoying song ever. Thankfully, he lost interest after the second time through. If there was such a thing as an annoying knob, he'd turned it up to max.

"Mmm bop, a doobie doo wop, mmm bop."

I should never have doubted that he might be able to find something more irritating.

"Hey, Barbie," Agnus said, lowering his voice as much as I imagined he could. *"Wanna go for a ride?"*

Then, in full falsetto, he continued, *"Sure, Ken!"*

"Agnus," I said, holding him in front of my face. "Shut up!"

"Come on, Barbie!" Agnus shouted into my face. *"Don't you want to party?"*

I tucked him under my arm. If I could focus through yoga and could get through that whole routine while ignoring his sarcastic remarks, surely I could focus now despite his tone-deaf attempt at a mash-up of the worst songs ever recorded. At least before the turn of the millennium.

I inhaled deeply and focused on the air as it entered my lungs. I was standing right next to my Mitsubishi. If only Brag'mok hadn't slashed my tires.

I released my breath.

Not the cleanest air in the city, but it did feel cleaner when it was dark and still cool. Before the sun came out and cooked the smog that coursed through the air.

Breathe in, breathe out.

Machinehead by Bush came to mind. I loved that song.

With a song I liked on my mind, I could more easily tune out Agnus, who was now who-who-who-ing his way through *Who Let the Dogs Out.*

Breathe in, Breathe out.

I visualized myself hovering over my apartment, then taking off into the skies.

Based on my limited experience wielding magic, I knew when I visualized it and felt the tingle of magic around me, it was happening.

I tightened my grip on Agnus. I couldn't let him distract me mid-flight.

He got the clue. No sooner did I feel the breeze against my face than he stopped singing, his body curled up and shaking in my arms.

I felt bad for him. He'd been through more than his share of traumatic experiences, being kidnapped (or catnapped) by Hector, accidentally turning on the bathtub faucet full-stream while pawing at the knob, hoping to get a drink, having his anal glands expressed by the vet, or anything that had to do with going to the vet.

Hopefully, he'd get used to this. For me, it was a thrill.

I maintained my focus. While I was connected to magic, it was better to use my mind's eye than my actual eyes to navigate. It was like the magic of the world, what some folks referred to as the spirits of the place, all coalesced in my mind, giving me a picture of everything around me, more than I could normally see. I could see through things, around things. I could visualize the whole path between my apartment and Forest Park.

I fixed my mind on my destination, and the wind against my face intensified. I'd say it blew my hair back, but since I'd had that encounter with the fairy and Nair-tainted shampoo, all I had was a little stubble.

It would grow back sooner or later, but for now, I wouldn't have a wind-blown mop of ridiculousness atop my head when I landed.

CHAPTER TWENTY-NINE

I landed in the clearing where I'd been practicing with Brag'mok. I figured he'd be here soon. I'd never arrived before he did, so I didn't know how early he usually was for our training appointments.

I pulled out my phone. **Almost here?**

Layla responded a few seconds later. **Yes. I see u. Just looking for a place to hide**.

She was there in case the shit hit the fan once Agnus revealed Brag'mok to be a fairy. Giant or fairy, either way, the Brag'mok I'd been training with was pretty strong. If he wanted to, he could rip me apart. Layla was waiting, probably with her bow drawn.

"How was the flight, Agnus?" I asked, scratching my cat behind the ears.

"And they say flying coach is bad."

I laughed. "I wouldn't know. I've never flown anything other than coach."

"Think they have a sandbox around here?" Agnus asked.

"I don't think so," I said. "Maybe a playground. Sometimes they fill the play areas with sand."

"Or mulch," Agnus said. "I'm not pissing in mulch."

"Just go anywhere," I said. "We're outside. No one cares."

"If I can't bury it, I'll hold it," Agnus said. "Or I'll go when you're holding me for the flight back."

"Yeah, the flight back." I chuckled. With the sun coming up, we hadn't thought about a flight back. "I think we'll be taking an Uber back home."

"Brilliant idea," Agnus said with more than a little sarcasm in his voice. "Wish I'd thought of that the first time."

I rolled my eyes.

Then I heard a scream.

Brag'mok had caught Layla in the bushes on his way in, and he had her pinned to the ground.

"Agnus!" I shouted. "Now!"

"Get off of me!" Layla shouted and she kicked hard, catching Brag'mok in the nuts.

I winced.

Brag'mok rolled off her, clinging to his family jewels.

"Now show us who you really are," Layla said, standing over him, drawing her bow, and pointing it at him.

Agnus leaped onto Brag'mok's chest just in time.

"Honey," Agnus said. "This is no fairy."

Layla cocked her head. "What?"

"You thought I was a fairy?" Brag'mok asked. "Seriously?"

"Sorry," I said before looking at Layla. She just shrugged as if to say, "Welp, I must've been wrong about that one." I reached down to grab Brag'mok's hand. He grabbed mine.

"You think you can help me up? Your whole body weighs not much more than one of my legs."

I smiled. "It would be rude not to try."

"And a cat? You thought I was a fairy too, Caspar?"

I shrugged. "Care to explain your theory, Layla?"

Layla took a deep breath. "Sorry, Brag'mok. And my condolences on your loss."

Brag'mok nodded. "Thank you. But now that you're here, we

really must retrieve my brother's body and hopefully close the gate."

"About that," Layla said. "What do you know about what's happening in my father's kingdom?"

"Same as anyone," Brag'mok said. "Hector, seemingly back from the dead, assassinated your father. He's making a play for the throne. I figured when you went back, you'd be challenging his claim."

Layla shook her head and proceeded to explain what she'd told me about how neither Hector nor her father being who they appeared to be. How they'd abducted her father and were holding him in a cave.

Brag'mok grunted. "Everything makes sense now. Come, we must hurry. Before it's too late."

"Too late?" I asked. "What's happening?"

Brag'mok shook his head. "The fairies didn't abduct King Brightborn. He *invited* them to New Albion. They are carrying out his plan."

Layla cocked her head. "You're certain of this? How can you know? And why would he fake his death?"

"So he could return from the dead," I said. "Nothing inspires people more than a resurrection. Trust me, people have been following the faith I preach for centuries on the basis that someone rose from the dead. If he wants to rally the elves, if he wants to do something big..."

Brag'mok nodded. "And if he gets to the source and he retrieves B'iff's body before I can conclude his death rites..."

Layla sighed. "B'iff was attuned to the Blade of Echoes. When he stabbed himself—"

"He became the new Blade of Echoes," Brag'mok said. "Everything the blade was meant to do, to bring magic back to New Albion, his body can do that."

"So, when you were going to commit his body to the ley lines on New Albion," I said, "you were planning to save your planet at the same time?"

Brag'mok nodded. "It's not the only reason. What I told you before was true. A pain languishes in my soul until he is put to rest. But it has always been the giants' position that we should make New Albion our home, while the elves wanted to return to the Earth."

"They wanted that with a vengeance," Layla said, shaking her head. "Not what I'd been taught growing up."

"But a fact no less," Brag'mok said. "It's why the elves and giants have been fighting nearly since the day we arrived on New Albion."

"And if King Brightborn acquires B'iff's body first?" I said. "I mean, the gate is open now. Wasn't the original plan to use the Blade of Echoes to create a permanent gate?"

"It was," Brag'mok said. "And he'll be able to do that, only with the power contained in my brother's body, he'll be able to control the gate. And he won't use the magic contained in B'iff's body to save New Albion. He'll use it to assault Earth."

Layla shook her head. "I don't understand. Why would the fairies do that? From what I saw, most of the fairies who had come to New Albion were from Earth. If my father invited them, why would they come? Don't they hate those who misuse magic?"

Brag'mok nodded. "But the fairies of old were honored by the druids, your ancestors. The Earth-born fairies know nothing of your father's taste for blood or the way he's used magic before."

"What if the Earth fairies meet any from New Albion?"

Brag'mok shook his head. "Before he invited the Earth-born fairies, he killed them all, Layla."

"Every one of them?" Layla asked.

Brag'mok nodded. "There weren't many, as you know. But I suspect he's known where they were hiding for years. A hollow in the hinterlands."

I shook my head. "So he's allied with the fairies to inspire the elves to attack the Earth?"

"But if I can recover B'iff's body and complete the rites, we might be able to close the gate before he has a chance."

"Then we'd best get going," I said. "Too bad someone slashed my tires."

Brag'mok coughed into his hand. "Just a way to get your attention."

"We can travel the ley lines," I said. "But we'd have to go to the gateway to do that, where the ley lines intersect."

"You'd better fly," Layla said.

"Oh, hell, no!" Agnus protested.

Layla smiled. "You can come with me if you'd like. We'll take an Uber."

"No need for that," Brag'mok said. "I have an eighteen-wheeler."

"How'd you get that?" I asked, raising my eyebrow.

Brag'mok shrugged. "Intimidated some guy at a truck stop."

"So it's a stolen rig?" I asked.

"Just borrowed," Brag'mok said. "Don't worry, the trucker won't be telling anyone. And I've removed the tracking devices his company had on the vehicle."

"He won't be telling anyone?" I asked. "Don't tell me—"

"I didn't kill him," Brag'mok said. "I have him in a cage in the back. I feed him a couple of times a day. Make sure he has plenty of water and a bottle to pee in."

"First, where the hell did you get a cage?" I asked.

Brag'mok shrugged. "Took it from some pet store."

"Took it?" I asked. "As in, you stole it?"

Brag'mok shrugged. "No one tried to stop me."

"Well, at your size, I doubt anyone would," I said, shaking my head. "But all that's beside the point. You're going to have to let that guy go. He's not some animal you can cage. He's a human being."

"What's the difference?" Brag'mok asked.

I huffed. "Excuse me?"

"No offense," Brag'mok said.

"See how it feels?" Agnus piped up. "When you put us in cages?"

CHAPTER THIRTY

I couldn't believe Brag'mok had been keeping a human like a pet in the back of a stolen rig. Thankfully, it was springtime. Not so cold or hot that the poor guy would either freeze or bake to death.

"We're going to the gate," I said. "After we let this guy go."

"But Caspar," Layla said. "If we do that, he might go to the police."

I shook my head. "Probably not before you get to the elven gate. By the time he gets there and tells his story, the police would have to mobilize. And without any idea where we're going, it's not like they'd find the rig immediately. Besides, I have an idea."

"We need to hurry," Brag'mok said. "No time for this."

"I'm not letting some poor guy stay in a cage any longer. It's not okay, Brag'mok."

"But he's right," Layla said. "The fate of the world might be in the balance."

I sighed. "It's been how long now since B'iff died, and King Brightborn hasn't sent anyone for the body yet. I think we can spare five minutes. What good is it to save the world if we lose our humanity in the process?"

Brag'mok shrugged. "I'm not human."

"Technically, I'm not either," Layla said.

"But you're good," I said. "Both of you. That's what I mean by humanity. It isn't a question of DNA. It's a matter of basic decency. Besides, I have an idea, and if you two insist on arguing with me about this, it'll only delay us further."

"Fine," Brag'mok said. "Release the human, but make it fast."

I nodded.

Brag'mok showed us where he had the eighteen-wheeler he'd stolen stashed. Thankfully, it didn't have any notable markings that would make it easy for the police to quickly identify it.

"When we go back there," I said, "show yourselves to him."

"You mean," Brag'mok said, "without covering my face?"

I nodded. "And Layla, make sure he sees your ears. I'll bust in, throw some light magic around. You two act like it hurts."

"Why do you get the play the hero?" Layla asked.

"Because I'm human," I said. "It makes sense."

Brag'mok shrugged. "Why not just let him go?"

"From his perspective, it'll look like an elf and an orc were in there, and some wizard came and rescued him. Fat chance the police will buy his story even if he's bold enough to tell anyone about it. And if I appear as a hero and ask him not to tell anyone, tell him I'm handling it."

"You're betting he'll choose to take your word for it over appearing delusional to the police," Layla said.

I nodded. "If the cops think he's crazy enough to be a danger to anyone, they could have him committed. Probably not something he'd like to risk. Particularly not if his hero asks him to stay quiet."

"Ok," Brag'mok said. "Let's do this, but we need to make it quick. Layla, we'll show ourselves. Act like we're about to put him to sleep."

"What about me?" Agnus asked, snuggled into Layla's arms.

I shrugged. "Layla, pet Agnus maniacally. Totally cliché villain shit."

Layla raised her eyebrow. "How do you pet something maniacally?"

"No cutesy-poos or I love yous. Just long, casual strokes down his back. You know, like Blofeld from the James Bond movies."

"I don't know the reference," Layla said.

I sighed. "Like Doctor Evil and Mister Bigglesworth from *Austin Powers*."

By the look in her eyes, I could see a light bulb went on. Go figure, she hadn't seen any of the older Bond movies, but she had seen *Austin Powers*. "Just stand in the back. Make sure that the light makes you a silhouette and the guy back there can see your ears. Totally creepy, but it'll look like you're the mastermind and Brag'mok is your henchman."

"Who happens to be an orc?" Layla asked.

"A giant," Brag'mok corrected.

"He won't know the difference," I said. "Doesn't matter what he thinks you are, he'll be scared as hell. Presuming he hasn't seen your face yet."

Brag'mok shook his head. "He hasn't."

"All right," I said. "Let's do this. Layla, start talking about how it's time to eliminate the humans, yadda yadda. Then I'll show up and start throwing light around. Act like it burns and take off running. Both of you."

The charade went off as planned. Brag'mok busted into the back of the tractor-trailer and Layla stood toward the back in silhouette, petting Agnus.

"Kill the human," Layla ordered. "We can't leave any loose ends."

Brag'mok grunted. "Gladly."

Then I heard a girlish scream. The trucker, whoever he was, had probably pissed his pants by now.

The shriek was my cue.

I focused and drew in a little magic, visualizing it forming as a golden light in the palm of my hand.

I opened my eyes and it was there. Pretty cool, actually. Couldn't feel anything other than a slight tingle and a subtle warmth.

I leaped into the back of the rig and charged Brag'mok, waving my light at him.

He screamed, sort of. It sounded more like a cow in heat, but it was enough to get the idea across.

I turned and looked at Layla. "I'm coming for you next!" I shouted.

Layla took off running, Brag'mok behind her. His steps shook the rig as he ran out the back.

I held the magic in my hand and looked at the man, who was still stuck inside what looked like a dog cage.

At least a dozen packets of ramen noodles sat around him. All Brag'mok had given him was uncooked ramen? Reminded me of college.

"I'm getting you out of there," I said.

"Thank you!" the man said, tears in his eyes. "What the hell were they?"

"Not from this world," I said. "But don't worry. I'll handle them."

"And what are you?" the man asked. "*Who* are you?"

"Just a friend," I said. "They won't bother you again. I'll make sure of that. Mind telling me your name?"

"Dwight," the man said.

I smirked.

Dwight sighed. "You're picturing Rainn Wilson's character from *The Office*, aren't you?"

I had to admit I was. "Sorry, I couldn't help it."

"That fucking show ruined my life. 'Dwight' was a perfectly decent name until that show made a total joke of it."

I shrugged. "If it means anything, Dwight was my favorite character."

"Never mind," Dwight said, crawling out after I unlatched the hatch on his cage. He stretched as he struggled to his feet.

I took him by the arm. "You okay, Dwight?"

"Yeah, it's just my legs are cramped. A little bit asleep. I'll be fine."

I nodded. "You'd best get out of here. Mind if I borrow the truck so I can chase down the ones who took you?"

"I need my rig back."

"There's a truck stop two miles down the road," I said. "Go there, get yourself a shower and something decent to eat. I'll bring it back to you in a few hours. Deal?"

"Yes," Dwight said. "I can do that."

"One more thing," I said.

"What's that?" Dwight asked.

"Don't tell the police about this," I said. "They won't believe you anyway, and they'd only get in the way of me stopping that elf and orc."

Dwight shook his head. "I suppose that makes sense. *I* don't believe it!"

"That elves and orcs exist?" I asked.

"And wizards! You're like Gandalf!" Dwight said. "What are they after?"

I looked at Dwight as seriously as I could. "One ring to rule them all."

"Holy shit," Dwight said. "Are there hobbits, too?"

I nodded. I didn't know that there were hobbits, but at this point, I couldn't rule out the possibility. It seemed like I was learning about a new mythic species every month, so it wasn't a total lie. If he wanted to think the plot of *The Lord of the Rings* was playing out in the real world, I could roll with it.

Dwight made his way to the end of the tractor-trailer. I hoped Layla and Brag'mok had had enough sense to hide somewhere. If they were just hanging out and waiting, it would spoil the ruse.

"Like I said," I continued, "wait at the truck stop. I promise I'll return your rig in a few hours."

"Go get 'em, Gandalf!" Dwight shouted as he leaped from the back of the rig.

I jumped out behind him and headed for the cab. "Thanks," I said, smiling. "I might have to start working on that beard, though, if people are going to start calling me that."

"Would you prefer Harry Potter?" Dwight asked. "Or Merlin?"

"Merlin is cool," I said. "But not Harry Potter. Or Dumbledore."

"Doctor Strange!" Dwight exclaimed.

I nodded. "That works for me. Either way, but like I said, don't tell anyone. Especially not the police. Let me handle this, okay?"

"You got it!" Dwight said. "See you in a few hours?"

I nodded. I reached into my pocket and handed Dwight a twenty-dollar bill. "I don't know if you have any money on you, but help yourself to a decent meal while you wait."

"Thank you," Dwight said. "I think I still have my wallet in my back pocket."

"But no phone?" I asked.

Dwight shook his head. "Left it in the cab before that ogre grabbed me."

I chuckled. "Ogre."

"Was that Shrek?" Dwight asked. "Like, the real Shrek?"

I shook my head. "Not exactly. But don't worry. I've got this."

CHAPTER THIRTY-ONE

I'd never driven a semi. Thankfully, this one had an automatic transmission. I'd driven a stick before. My dad had gotten me a manual transmission for my first car, said it was important I learned how to drive it. One of those old-school ideas. You know, like learning to do math with pen and paper instead of using a calculator or a calculator app as was more often the case these days.

Thankfully, I didn't have to drive too far. Just far enough to keep up the charade and ensure I was out of sight of Dwight.

I texted Layla and let her know where to meet me—about a half-mile down the road from where we were parked.

Thankfully, that was the direction they'd gone anyway, so we regained a little of the time our lack of foresight when I cocked up my half-baked plan to free Dwight might have cost us. But I was rushed. I hadn't had much time to think through the after.

It worked out anyway.

"I think you should ride with us," Layla said. "If you fly there, what if you run into elves at the gate?"

"He can handle it," Brag'mok said.

I raised my eyebrow. "One or two, maybe. If I use magic."

"And your training," Brag'mok said. "Remember your training."

"Still," Layla said. "I think it's best we arrive together. In case there are elves, and you're wrong and they stop Caspar."

"Not to mention," I interjected, "the morning rush-hour traffic is going the opposite direction right now. We can probably make it there in fifteen or twenty minutes. Not sure I could fly there much faster."

"I see your point," Brag'mok said. "I can't retrieve B'iff's body without your help, Caspar. Maybe we should show up together."

Layla nodded. "Right."

"Okay," Brag'mok said. "But I'm driving."

"No arguments here," I said. "This isn't at all like driving my Eclipse."

"Yes," Brag'mok said. "Even if this truck lost four tires, it would probably be okay."

"Not the point," I said. "But thanks for reminding me of that."

"You're welcome," Brag'mok said, apparently failing to detect the sarcasm in my voice. Despite how much I appreciated what he'd done, I was still mildly resentful about the whole tire situation. I mean, really? It had been completely unnecessary.

Brag'mok drove like a bat out of hell. Not especially smart, I thought, because if we got pulled over for speeding, he didn't have a driver's license. Also, the police would probably freak the fuck out if they stared my giant of a friend in the face. I mean, I'd been exposed to all this stuff gradually. My first encounter with a giant, with B'iff, had been in a dark alley. I had been stabbed. Layla had healed me, and elf ears weren't so shocking, especially after the Order of the Elven Gate was established. In short, exposing me to the realities of the other world had been like boiling a lobster in water. They say that when you put a lobster in a pot and start turning up the heat, the change happens so gradually that the lobster doesn't even realize it should try to escape. It boils to death before realizing it was ever in jeopardy.

Not that being here had killed me or anything, but it came at me slowly and gradually enough that I didn't notice until I was consumed by my new reality. Some random cop comes face to face with Brag'mok? I couldn't imagine how he would react. Not to mention, if I was caught riding in a stolen rig, I'd probably be arrested. If that happened, so much for being available for any world-saving activities.

"Dude," I said. "Try to stay no more than five over the speed limit. You don't want to get pulled over."

Brag'mok shrugged. "If the police pull us over, I will handle it. I still have the cage in the back."

I snorted. "Yeah, probably not the best idea."

"Did the other human finish all his soups?" Brag'mok asked.

I chuckled. "First, they weren't soups. Without boiling water, they're barely edible. And even when they're cooked, ramen is devoid of any real nutritional value. But second, feeding the cop isn't my concern. It's well, the whole *idea* of trying to put a cop in a cage. It wouldn't end well even if you got away with it."

"Relax," Layla said. "We're almost there anyway. The cops are more focused on the other side of the highway where all the traffic is."

I sighed. "You're probably right, but it's just not worth the risk."

"Neither is wasting any more time," Brag'mok said.

Thankfully, we made it without any intrusions by law enforcement.

I released a sigh of relief.

Then we climbed out of the truck and onto the ground.

The last time we'd been at the confluence of the Meramec and the Mississippi, we'd faced off against Hector, along with King Brightborn and his legions.

At least, the last time we'd been there together.

Layla had passed through the gate recently, and Brag'mok had too since the last time I'd been there.

And Layla had checked on the gate periodically ever since.

I hadn't had any reason to come back. I had no plans to journey off-world, and still lacking real combat expertise, I wasn't going to go there alone in case I ran into any elven legions on their way to assault the world.

So far, they hadn't tried that.

When I was there before, I could see the magic swirling in the water where the gate was.

It was not visible to everyone, but anyone who had any experience wielding magic or had a sensitivity to it could see it: elves, giants, me, probably the fairies.

"I don't understand," I said. "I don't see the gate."

Layla sighed. Brag'mok grunted.

"I told you," Brag'mok said. "We needed to hurry."

"What happened?" I asked. "Why is the gate gone?"

"Because they've already retrieved B'iff's body."

"If you couldn't do it without my help, how could they?" I asked.

"Fairies," Layla said. "Remember, my father is allied with the fairies."

"Well, shit," I said. "What the hell do we do now?"

Brag'mok stared blankly at the water. "With B'iff's body, the elven king will be able to open the gate himself when he's ready. There's nothing we *can* do."

CHAPTER THIRTY-TWO

Agnus piped up. "That's what you get for worrying about saving a human."

I rolled my eyes. "We did the right thing."

"At what cost?" Brag'mok asked.

"At less of a cost than it would have been if we'd allowed that man to linger in the cage any longer," I replied.

"One man at the cost of your world?" Brag'mok asked. He released a massive roar and slammed his fists on the ground. It was hard enough I suspected it might have registered on any nearby Richter scales.

Layla put her hand on my shoulder. "I still believe in you."

I shook my head. "Maybe you shouldn't. Maybe it's time I start doing what you tell me to."

"There's a reason you are the chosen one," Layla said.

"Because I got fucking stabbed and happened to survive?" I shrugged her hand off my shoulder. "A bunch of bullshit. Your prophecy, or whoever the asshole was who made the prophecy, chose wrong."

Layla bit her lip. "Wait, Caspar. That's brilliant."

I chuckled. "What is? That your prophet was an asshole? I

have to admit, it might be the smartest thing I've come up with since all this shit started."

"No," Layla said. "I mean, he might have been an asshole. Who knows? But the prophet was the one who opened the first gate to the world we now call New Albion. If he could do it, you should be able to do it, too. You have level-five magic."

I chuckled. "Aside from flying, I haven't been able to do a whole lot."

"He can't do it," Brag'mok said. "But there might be a way."

"With enough magic drawn from the source?" Layla asked.

"And with the help of the fairies," Brag'mok said. "At least one stayed behind, and based on the way he was harassing Caspar, I think he's a loner."

Layla cocked her head. "Fairies don't travel alone. They're always in herds or flocks or whatever the hell you call a swarm of fairies."

"Unless he's an exile," Brag'mok said. "A fairy who opposed the will of the collective."

"Still," I interjected. "Say we do open the gate from our end. King Brightborn has your brother's body. He has the magic. He's accomplished what he originally hoped to do with the Blade of Echoes."

"Again," Brag'mok said, "the fairy might be key. If the original prophet used the fairies to help create the gate to the new world, perhaps it was also with the fairies that he created the original Blade of Echoes."

"What would be the point of doing that?" I asked.

"To recharge the ley lines on New Albion," Layla said. "It would give the giants magic they could use."

"For more war?" I asked, raising my eyebrows.

"Yes," Brag'mok said. "But necessary to thwart King Brightborn. If we can deliver magic to New Albion, at the very least, our hordes should be able to slow down the elven legions. We might not be able to stop them indefinitely, but we could buy time for the rest of the prophecy to unfold."

I sighed. "Again, you're putting faith in my ability to unite all the people. I'm sorry, but I think your prophecy is crap."

"Doesn't matter what you think of it," Layla said. "You've still been chosen, and you've been preparing for this."

"I've been working out and learning basic fighting maneuvers in the park," I said. "That's not going to be helpful when it comes to unifying races that are at war."

"I'm not talking about that training," Layla said. "Your other training."

I cocked my head. I'd had the thought already, but really, I wasn't ready for that either. "You mean, with the church? The people at Holy Cross just got me back, and now they're fixing to run me out of town."

"But they haven't yet," Agnus piped up. "Don't you have a plan?"

"Well, sort of," I said. "From when I met with my bishop the other day. But I don't know how that plan could work now. That's different."

"Is it?" Agnus asked. "You told me the people at the church condemn because they don't understand. That they need to walk in the shoes of the people who are flocking to the church so they can understand and learn to embrace them."

I sighed. "I was hoping the soup kitchen would help with that. I don't know that soup is going to help this situation."

"Let's focus on the issue at hand," Brag'mok said. "The path forward to fulfill the prophecy will be revealed soon enough. When the time is right, the final two seals will open, and you'll know what to do."

I sighed. "All right. What do we need to do?"

"First," Brag'mok said, "we need to get your pesky fairy's attention again."

I sighed. "In other words, I need to use more magic."

"As often as you have the chance," Brag'mok said. "And even better if you use it around humans. The fairy won't be able to resist intervening."

"And when he does," Layla said, "we'll be waiting to catch him."

CHAPTER THIRTY-THREE

Tonight was one of the nights Evelyn was running the soup kitchen. It was my best chance, and I hoped the fairy would be there. So far, every time I'd been, he was.

I walked through the door, Layla at my side, with her hood pulled up to hide her ears. Not that people at the soup kitchen, not even the Methodist volunteers, would have cared much. All sorts were welcome as long as they were hungry. But she didn't want to cause a distraction.

I saw a lot of familiar faces. Many of them were part of the crowd who'd joined us at Holy Cross the Sunday before.

I scanned the crowd and saw Cecil, his wife Shanda, and their daughter Grace. They were seated at one of the cafeteria tables, the sort they have at schools that fold up with little stool-like seats attached.

I approached them.

"Cecil and Shanda?" I asked.

"Reverend!" Cecil exclaimed, smiling as he hurried to his feet and extended his hand.

"This is my girlfriend Layla," I said.

Cecil nodded. "It's a pleasure to meet you!"

"I've heard a lot about you," Layla said. "And this must be Grace?"

"Yes, ma'am."

"How are you, sweetie?" Layla asked, kneeling to talk to Grace.

I'd let them have their moment. Layla and Shanda were laughing as they looked at Grace, who was saying something. Not sure what, but I'm sure it was cute, whatever it was, based on the response she was getting.

"Cecil, do you have a moment?" I asked.

"Sure, Reverend. Of course." Cecil straightened his shirt.

"When Grace was being treated before she was healed, where did you take her?"

"Cardinal Glennon Children's Hospital," Cecil said. "Very generous people. They took care of everything. I mean, they didn't heal her. Not like you did."

"And were there support communities? Other parents with children who had similar conditions, or other groups you were part of?" I asked. Cardinal Glennon was, as you might guess, a Catholic children's hospital. I hadn't had many chances to visit anyone there. We didn't have a lot of children at Holy Cross, and of the few we did have, none of them had been unfortunate enough to fall seriously ill or require hospitalization since I'd been the pastor there. But since I'd also attended the local seminary, I had made a few rounds at Cardinal Glennon as part of my training. If things hadn't changed over the last several years, they had pretty extensive support systems for the parents who brought their children there—the sort of support system that becomes like family.

"Of course," Cecil said. "I was meaning to talk to you about that, but I didn't want to cause any more problems than I already did."

"What problems?" I asked. "You haven't caused any."

"You don't think I couldn't sense that we weren't welcome last Sunday?" Cecil asked.

"You're always welcome," I said. "The members there are fairly set in their ways. I think it was just a shock to see so many people."

"So many black people, you mean?" Cecil asked.

I bit my lip. "Yeah. I hate to say it. Don't get me wrong. They aren't hateful people. They're just…"

"I get it," Cecil said. "Trust me, I've lived with that sort of treatment from white folks my whole life. You get used to it."

"I'm so sorry about that," I said. "I'm hoping to bring some of them here. Give them a chance to get to know some of the folks who live in the community."

"I think that would be really nice, Reverend," Cecil said. "But you were asking about the support community at Cardinal Glennon?"

I nodded. "How many of them could you get hold of on short notice?"

"All of them," Cecil said. "There's a Facebook group."

"Tell any who'd like, any who want to know how your daughter was healed, to come to Holy Cross tonight at seven o'clock. I think it's high time I used this gift I've been given to do some good."

Cecil smiled even more broadly than usual, which was saying something because I don't know if I'd ever talked to someone whose face was happier than Cecil's, at least since his daughter was healed. "I can do that, Reverend. But aren't you worried that if you do something like that, you might get into trouble? With your church, I mean?"

I sighed. "People condemn because they don't understand, but I won't be hindered by their ignorance."

Cecil nodded. "I can respect that, Reverend."

"I don't think most people intend to be hateful. They're just afraid. They fear change."

"Hate is the secondary emotion, Reverend. Fear is more often than not, at least in my experience, the primary emotion hiding behind it."

"Well, you know what they say about dealing with fears, right?" I asked.

"There's nothing to fear but fear itself?" Cecil asked.

"That, too. But I was thinking more along the lines that the only way to overcome fear is to face it. Once people see that the change they fear is beautiful, that it's at the heart of what they've always valued even though they never realized it, whatever hate or discomfort they have will fade, too."

"Perhaps you're a bit naïve, Reverend," Cecil said. "But I hope you're right. Not just for our sake, but for theirs. That kind of fear; that's no way to live."

I smiled. "No, it isn't, Cecil. Not at all."

"Seven o'clock, you said?" he asked.

I nodded. "As many who are willing to come are welcome."

CHAPTER THIRTY-FOUR

I'd be lying if I said I wasn't nervous. Not because I'd probably face repercussions from the church. I knew Philip had my back, but if push came to shove, the elders could vote me out of there, go over Philip's head, and have me censured. And the denomination's archbishop, basically the president, the one to whom Philip had to report, was cut from the same cloth as my former bishop Matthias Flacius. If he found out I was holding healing services in our church, he'd blackball me in a second. As far as I knew, that would make me the only minister in the history of our denomination to be blackballed twice. It was not something you generally came back from. The fact that I did the first time was a small miracle. And technically speaking, while it was only a formality since Flacius' recommendation hadn't been processed by the bureaucracy yet before he got himself ousted, I'd never been excommunicated. But for all intents and purposes, this would cause a second blackballing if it ever got reported.

Technically, I wasn't inviting anyone from the church, so there was a chance they wouldn't find out. But who was I kidding? If I healed that many people in one service, the crowd that had come before would be nothing compared to the numbers who'd show if I pulled this off.

There would be no hiding this or getting away with it. I'd have to face the music one way or another. All I could hope for was that either the folks of Holy Cross would come to embrace it, at least a majority of them, or Philip's support would shield me from official heresy charges. Not likely, but it was possible. I didn't expect him to support me publicly, either. I mean, if you defend a supposed heretic, you're generally considered to be part of the problem. I didn't expect or want Philip to sacrifice his career on my account. He could do a lot of good and make a lot of changes over time if he remained in his position.

I wouldn't allow him to shield me. Not if, or rather, when, things got nasty. This was my doing, and if push came to shove, I could testify to the church authorities that he'd recommended a different approach. That he'd only suggested I bring volunteers from Holy Cross to the soup kitchen. This healing service had been my idea and mine alone.

I wouldn't allow anyone else to take a hit for it.

Layla and I went to the church and waited. Cecil had used his phone to post a message for the other Cardinal Glennon parents while we were at the soup kitchen. I hoped it would work, but there was no telling.

You'd think that given an opportunity to have their children healed of irreversible conditions, parents would jump at the chance.

But I also knew that people were by and large cynical about claims that involved the miraculous. And many of these parents had been jaded by treatments that didn't work, surgeries that failed, and medications that only had a marginal impact on their children's conditions. They probably wouldn't be willing to listen to some preacher who thought he could do what the doctors couldn't.

I was beginning to think my plan was destined to fail. I'd have to resort to using my magic to fake my way through more workouts or to do other random shit in hopes of eliciting the fairy's attention. But if it was true that allowing humans to learn of magic or how to use it was the thing the fairies were the most afraid of, this was the most effective way to welcome the little trickster back into my life.

I mean, last time, it hadn't been faking my workout with magic that did it. It was that I did it in front of someone. And I'd healed Grace a few days before.

I looked at my phone to check the time. Fifteen more minutes.

"Getting anxious?" Layla asked.

I sighed. "I am."

Layla looked around the sanctuary. "You know, this place is very pretty."

I smiled. "It is, isn't it? Not a lot of newer churches have this kind of aesthetic. When they built churches like this one, it was all about creating a space that fostered reverence. Today, in a lot of other churches, while I wouldn't say it's wrong, the focus is less on a transcendent God who has to be feared and revered and more on an imminent deity who walks among us, who embraces technology, even the music of the day, to speak to people's hearts here and now."

"Sounds like that's the sort of church you'd rather minister in," Layla said.

I shrugged. "I don't know. There's something to be said for both styles. I mean, if God isn't transcendent and holy and whatnot, that can't by definition be God. On the other hand, if God is so other, so transcendent, that we can't relate to Him and we always hold Him at a distance—if we revere Him but don't allow Him to embrace us in our lives—what's the point? That's how religion becomes religion. It becomes reduced to a set of practices you do just because, without any real relevance to people's lives."

"Again," Layla said, "sounds like you have a pretty good idea of the sort of church you'd prefer to serve."

I chuckled. "Fantasizing about the ideal church is sort of like having a child and trying to imagine them being something they aren't. In truth, all children can be a pain in the ass in their way, but we love them because they're ours. I think that's how I view this church. There are some warts here, even some serious closed-mindedness, but it's still my church. It's the place where I've been called to preach, and I'll keep doing that as long as they'll allow it."

The front door of the church clicked and swung open. The evening sun shone through, illuminating the whole sanctuary as one family after another came through the doors. It wasn't like a crowd trying to get in or out of a concert or anything. We didn't have that many people to invite, only those who were members of Cecil's and Grace's support community.

Still, there were probably twenty families there with their children.

So many children. So many *sick* children.

Some of them, like Grace had been, were in wheelchairs. Others were on crutches or wearing oxygen masks. There were more than a few without hair on their heads. It was heartbreaking.

There was a sense of nervousness over the crowd. It wasn't like one of those healing services you could catch on public access television. These people were anxious. They were tired. They were distraught. And they were desperate.

I glanced at Layla, who smiled at me and nodded.

"I believe I've been given a gift," I started. "And I think it's my responsibility to share it. I'm not going to preach at you tonight. If you want to hear that, I'm here every Sunday. At least, for now, I am."

One family, sitting in the back row, stood out from the rest. The mother had her head covered with a scarf, but the father had his hand raised.

"Yes, sir," I said.

"We are Muslim. Are we welcome, too?"

I nodded. "Of course. As I said, I'm not going to preach, and I believe that God, however we conceive of him, loves each one of us. He made each one of us, and he isn't so petty as to wait for you to sign on to a bunch of doctrines before he'll deign to have compassion on you. I'm not here to tell anyone what to believe. Whatever happens tonight, if this goes as I hope it will, just be grateful. Not to me, but to the God you know and worship."

"Thank you, sir," the man said.

"Would you like to come forward?" I asked. "I presume you have a child who is ill?"

"My son," the man said. "He was diagnosed with leukemia just yesterday."

I nodded. "Come here, young man."

The man came forward with his son. Looking at him, aside from his being slightly emaciated, you wouldn't realize he was sick. He just looked like a thin kid. Not uncommon, but he'd barely been diagnosed. They caught it early, and hopefully, he'd be able to beat it, but I knew enough about what he'd have to go through. Chemo. Radiation. Bone marrow transplants.

"How old are you, son?" I asked.

"I'm ten," the boy said.

I nodded. Too young to have to go through all that. This wasn't going to be a sensational healing, but it didn't need to be. I wasn't doing it to get the attention of humans. I wasn't even doing it solely to get the attention of the fairy. I genuinely wanted to help. Still, I needed the fairy. If I didn't get his attention, if we couldn't catch him and convince him to help, we'd all be screwed sooner or later.

I placed my hand on the boy's head.

"Your name?" I asked.

"Salim," the boy said.

"I love that name," I said, then closed my eyes and focused. I imagined the boy well, his blood pure, his hair full. I pictured him receiving a clean bill of health from the doctors. I felt the tingle from my hand into the boy's body. In my mind's eye, I saw his body enveloped in a golden hue.

I opened my eyes and what I had seen in my mind's eye was right in front of my face. Based on the look on the rest of the people's faces, they could see it too. This wasn't one of those magical things like the elven gate that only a magically attuned person could see. Everyone witnessed it.

I heard a few gasps.

"That kind of tickles," Salim said.

I smiled. "You're well, Salim."

"Thank you!" Salim's father said. His mother was in tears.

"Bring him to the doctor as soon as possible. Get medical confirmation and continue to follow their advice and prescriptions."

"Of course! Again, thank you! Praise Allah!"

I smiled, then I walked up to a child in a wheelchair. His chair was in the center aisle, and his parents were in the pew beside him.

"A spinal injury," the boy's mother said. "From a car accident. The doctors said he would never walk."

I didn't have children, but I could imagine how painful it must've been to hear that news. How awful it was to imagine a boy who wasn't even a teenager yet, who could have played sports, who could have danced, and find out he couldn't do any of those things if he wanted to.

I touched his back and healed him like I'd healed the first boy.

He didn't stand up. That might take time. By the looks of his legs, he'd been paralyzed for a while, and they were thin and weak. But his foot moved, then his other foot moved a little, too.

"Oh, my God!" the boy's mother cried as she embraced her son. He was giggling with delight. So much joy for a small movement of the foot.

"Again," I said. "Bring him to the doctors. They'll recommend whatever therapy he needs to learn to walk again."

The whole evening was like that. One heart-wrenching tragedy after another, each one alleviated as I seemed to heal them. Of course, the cancers weren't immediately obvious, but they had the glow, as the young Muslim boy had had when I healed him. I was as certain as I could be that it had worked.

Truthfully, I'd never believed in faith healing. I used to make fun of the preachers who conducted fake healing services on television. People with psychosomatic conditions receiving psychosomatic cures—that was my explanation. From what I could tell from my sporadic internet research, very few of those healings lasted long-term, and some of the folks involved had admitted they had not been sick or injured to begin with. In other words, there was enough evidence to question the legitimacy of most of the purported miracles. Perhaps some of them were genuine, but when there were questions surrounding so many of them, you doubted them all.

But this, what was happening here and now, was different.

Yes, it was magic. It wasn't the sort of miracle you'd expect a genuine prophet to perform. But then again, if I wielded the Earth's magic, a magic that had been part of primordial creation, which had been responsible for making everything that exists, something powerful enough to vivify a dead planet to give the elves and the giants a home, who was to say that God couldn't be credited for it? It was all a matter of perspective and faith. Was this magic part of God's world from the beginning that had been latent within the Earth he had called into existence? Or was it an undiscovered material substance? Something as natural as oxygen, only not understood by science. Was it magic at all?

I couldn't answer any of those questions for certain, but I

knew it worked. I also knew things couldn't go back to the way they had been. Not for me. Not for Holy Cross. And certainly not for these dozens of children who had gotten their lives back.

Even if I couldn't save the world, it was worth it.

CHAPTER THIRTY-FIVE

"Good work tonight," Layla said. "It was something to see you healing. To see the looks on people's faces. The feeling of hope was in the air. It was palpable."

I smiled slightly. "It was, wasn't it? Let's hope it worked."

I nodded, retrieved my set of keys from my pocket, and locked the church door.

"You did magic, a lot of it, in front of humans. I don't know how a fairy could resist."

We turned to go down the set of steps in the front of the church, and I stepped on something squishy. I barely got a look at it before my foot slipped out from beneath my body.

It happened in slow motion. My leg kicked into the air. My body fell to the ground.

My back cracked as I hit the ground. I winced in pain. It wasn't broken, but I was sure I was going to need a chiropractic adjustment and a solid dose of ibuprofen.

"Are you okay, Caspar?" Layla asked as she knelt beside me.

I laughed out loud. "Well, I think it worked."

"Are you sure you didn't just slip and fall?" Layla asked.

I'd seen it on my way down—the cause of my tumble. I

reached down to where my foot had stepped and retrieved a banana peel. "Seriously? Slipping on banana peels is a real thing? I thought it was something that only happened in cartoons and Mario Kart." Layla giggled. "Classic. That had to be the fairy's work."

"Do you see him anywhere?" I asked.

"Not yet," Layla said, surveying our surroundings, her hand extended with magic aglow on her fingertips. I wasn't sure what spell she had in mind. She knew a bunch because she had been raised on a magical world, but since I'd met her, I'd only seen her use magic a handful of times.

You'd think if you could wield mystical powers, you'd be constantly doing spells like enchanting household objects to do your chores, teleporting, or flying to and fro. Truth be told, though, magic was exhausting. Not paralyzingly so. I hadn't done anything yet, not even my flight across the city, that had completely drained me of energy. But every spell left me feeling like I'd just completed a marathon. No, not just after finishing it, when the endorphins were still pumping. More like a couple of hours later, after my body had cooled down.

Or after eating Chinese food. That was a similar kind of tiredness.

In other words, I'd come to learn through my limited experience that magic could be taxing on the body. Like anything else, I supposed, I'd have to build up endurance for it and a keen sense of when to use it and when not to.

Layla, not a level-five sorcerer but powerful nonetheless, had more trained endurance than I did. But let's face it, even professional athletes crashed after their games. Layla was careful about when she used her magic, and since we'd been living in the perpetual expectation of some kind of mystical shit hitting the fan pretty much since we met, she'd wanted to stay alert and ready. Yes, she and I both had to sleep, and I needed to work out and train. But if magic wasn't strictly necessary, she avoided using it.

All things considered, I wasn't tired. Despite the massive amount of mystical energy I'd channeled to heal twenty or more children, and despite just landing on my back in front of my church, I was invigorated.

Maybe I'd crash later. Maybe not. But right now, I needed to help Layla find the fairy.

I stood up, not too quickly. By the feel of my back, I'd thrown at least one of my lumbar disks out of whack. In my experience, the worst of that sort of back pain sets in later. For the time being, I could press on. And I needed to.

I pushed my hand into my lower back.

"Here," Layla said, putting her hand where it hurt. I felt a quick jolt and the mild stiffness that was destined to become a lot more if untreated went away. The muscles in my lower back immediately relaxed.

"Thanks!" I said. "You could put the chiropractors out of business with that touch."

Layla winked at me. "I think I'll focus on helping you save the world first."

A buzz startled my attention. Not the sort you heard if a gnat flew into your ear, more like the sound a hummingbird's wings made when it was feeding nearby.

I turned and saw the green glow I'd noticed when he'd terrorized me.

Before I could respond, Layla shot a jolt of energy at the fairy.

He dodged her strike.

I swung my arm at him, trying to catch him. It was not like I had much of a chance. I'd caught a few fireflies that way, but catching a fairy in mid-air was more challenging. Not only could he move faster than lightning bugs, but he was guided by his intelligence.

The creature giggled annoyingly as he buzzed around my hand. He hovered two inches in front of my face for a moment.

I swiped at him again.

The fairy made a quick spin around my hand, then threw himself against the tip of my nose.

"Ouch!" I said.

"Nice haircut, human!" The fairy cackled as he buzzed around my head. Now I knew he could communicate, but I half wished he couldn't. The thing had a voice that was comparable to Gilbert Gottfried's on the annoying scale.

I was getting a little tired of non-human creatures referring to me as "human." I had a name, after all.

Layla took another shot, green chains of magic flying from her fingertips.

Again, the fairy dodged the blast, buzzed around her, and grabbed her by the back of her pants.

"Ouch! Wedgie!" I shouted, trying my best not to laugh.

Layla shrieked.

The fairy buzzed off with a swath of frilly pink cloth in his hands.

Just in time to meet a giant paw—Brag'mok's hand, swiping through the air and catching him by the wings.

"Let me go, you brute!" the fairy shouted.

"No can do," Brag'mok said.

"Nice work, buddy," I said.

Layla was still rubbing her ass. I mean, a wedgie strong enough to rip her panties off was brutal.

Brag'mok held the little guy in front of my face.

He wasn't as ugly as I'd imagined. In fact, he was kind of cute, human-like in terms of shape, with greenish-brown skin and two semi-translucent wings. His hair, though, was bright blue and frizzled on his head in a way that would resemble Bob Ross's if he'd ever dunked his head in his paint.

"Sorry," I said. "We did all this because we had to catch you. We need your help."

The fairy spat in my face.

A creature that small doesn't produce much saliva. It was only a small spritz.

I wiped it off my cheek.

"I'm serious," I said. "Don't your kind travel in swarms?"

The fairy huffed.

"It seems you've been exiled," I said. "So I'm guessing you aren't entirely on board with what the rest of the fairies are up to."

"They're morons!" the fairy said. "They think the elves from the other world are friends. Allies. But they're worse than the humans!"

"I agree," I said.

"But you humans aren't any picnic either. You might not use magic, but you've created your own. Your smog. Your pollution. You destroy the Earth too! The rest of us are trying to stop you!"

"But allying with those who've used magic to wage wars for centuries?" I asked.

"At least it's on another planet. Once they use up their magic, they're done!"

"True," I said. "But do you think they'll do any better if they come here and defeat humanity?"

The fairy snorted. "That's why I'm alone."

"Then will you help us stop them?" I asked.

"For a price," the fairy said. "Only if you can meet my price."

I shrugged. "What do you want?"

"Silly string."

I raised my eyebrow. "Silly string?"

"The stuff is hilarious!" the fairy exclaimed. "If you get me silly string, lots of it, I'll talk to you about helping."

I snorted. "It's a deal. I'm Caspar, by the way."

"I know who you are, dummy," the fairy said. "I'm Ensley."

"Please to meet you, Ensley," Layla said.

Ensley smiled wide. "Sorry about your butt crack. I couldn't resist."

Layla chuckled. "I think I'll be fine."

"'Sorry about your butt crack,'" I said, laughing as I repeated Ensley's apology. "That's not something someone has to tell you every day."

CHAPTER THIRTY-SIX

"Holy shit!" Agnus screamed as we walked through the door. "Who farted?"

I tossed four Walmart bags full of silly string on the couch. "No one did. We caught the fairy."

"Disgusting!" Agnus said. "It smells like you after one of your Taco Bell binges."

"Or after my Greenberry shake."

"Oh, did that come?" Layla asked. "That stuff is supposed to be incredible."

I scratched the back of my head. "If incredibly nauseating was what you were thinking, then sure."

By the loud thuds coming from outside the apartment, I ascertained that Brag'mok and Ensley were nearly at the top of the stairs.

"I want my silly string!" Ensley insisted.

"If we give it to you, you'll help us?" I asked. "You won't just buzz off and show back up later to short-sheet my bed?"

"I can't promise no pranks," Ensley said. "I am what I am. But I will help if I can."

"We're looking for how to wield fairy power," Layla said. "Like the ancient druid who took our people to New Albion did when he forged the gate and created the Blade of Echoes."

"Give me a can of silly string," Ensley said.

"Can you help or not?" I asked.

"Give me the can and we'll talk."

I opened one of the cans and handed it to Ensley. He pointed it at Agnus and shot him right in the face.

Agnus meowed loudly and hissed, taking off after Ensley, who simply flew over him.

Agnus leaped up and down, trying to snag the fairy with his claws. "Get down here, you little shit!"

Ensley pointed the can at Agnus and hit him in the face a second time.

Agnus shook it off and stared at me.

"Screw you guys. I'm going home." Agnus sauntered to the back bedroom.

"Can you two behave?" I asked. "We don't have time for your antics."

"He's the one who compared my natural aroma to Taco Bell farts," Ensley protested. "Believe it or not, the ancients hunted us, not to kill us, but that they might bathe in our scent."

"They hunted you for your body odor?" I asked.

"They found it intoxicating."

"Gross!" Layla protested. "Not that I can tell. You don't smell like much as far as I can tell."

"Oh, honey," Ensley said. "If I poofed in your face, you'd be begging me for more."

"Poofed?" I asked.

"We don't fart," Ensley said. "We poof. It's glittery and smells of lavender."

I chuckled. "Makes sense. Cats can't stand the smell of lavender."

Layla cocked her head. "Really? I had no idea."

I nodded. "Lavender, geranium, most citrus. We like the smells, but as Agnus would say, to cats, it reeks like ass."

"Can we stay on topic?" Brag'mok interrupted. "My brother's body is in the hands of elves. They're dishonoring his memory, his sacrifice."

I bit my lip. I hadn't thought about the pain Brag'mok must be experiencing. Not just because his brother was being disrespected, but because of the bond giants felt to their kin, a bond that required a particular death rite to sever. He was in anguish, and we were making comparisons between fairy body odor and taco farts.

"I'm sorry, Brag'mok," I said. "We weren't being sensitive."

"I don't care if you're sensitive," Brag'mok said. "Just focus on what must be done."

I nodded. "Ensley, is what we describe possible? Could I wield fairy magic to re-open the gate between worlds? Could I create something like a new Blade of Echoes?"

Ensley buzzed around me. "What you ask is possible, but it is not something that is often permitted. Fairies and humans…"

"I know," I said. "You can't stand us."

"It's not that," Ensley said. "We used to get along beautifully, we and the druids of old. With the new religion, the new world, then human machines and industry, humanity lost its need for us, and instead of turning to magic to preserve the world, created their own magic to destroy it."

"Magic?" I asked.

"What is that little glowing square in your pocket?" Ensley asked.

"It's a phone," I said.

"How does it work?" Ensley asked. "If you woke up on a deserted island, could you make one for yourself?"

"I have no clue how it works," I said. "And there's no way I could."

"But there are some who could. They understand the magic,

what you humans call science, that works together in a complex way to transmit images and sounds through the air from one device to the next."

"I can see why you'd call that magic," I said. "I guess in a way it is."

"It is precisely a kind of magic," Ensley said. "Nothing you humans invent is original. You don't make things out of nothing. You rely on the Earth's energies and elements. You harness the Earth's power to do your bidding. You call it technology, but that's what magic is."

"But what we ask is possible, right?" I asked.

"Of course it is," Ensley said. "Give me another can of silly string."

I reached into one of the Walmart bags and tossed him another can. Impressively, he grabbed it out of thin air. Since the can was nearly his height, the fact that he could hold it, much less stay in the air with it, was more than a little impressive.

He turned the can toward his face and squirted it into his mouth.

Then he exhaled it out his nose.

"Disgusting!" Layla said.

"Feels incredible," Ensley said. "Clears the sinuses."

I cleared my throat. "So, you were saying we can access fairy power?"

"Definitely," Ensley said. "You said that there are some humans, a rare few, who might know how to make one of those devices you carry around from scratch. They have all the knowledge necessary. If the world ended tomorrow, eventually they could find a way to manufacture them again."

I took a deep breath. "I suppose there *are* some folks who have that knowledge."

"But they'd also need the right materials," Ensley said. "The world ended tomorrow, they'd have to start with basic materials. They'd have to first learn to harness electricity again. They'd have to acquire all the necessary materials. They'd have to refine the metals and wires. The world blows up tomorrow and one scientist survives with all the knowledge, he isn't going to start churning out smartphones a day later."

"Of course not," I said. "Are you trying to say that you can or can't teach us how to wield fairy magic?"

"I can give you the knowledge," Ensley explained. "But you have to start with the basics. You can't just make portals or supercharged artifacts overnight."

"We don't have time for that," Brag'mok said. "Surely there's another way. A shortcut?"

Ensley shook his head. "There aren't any desirable short-cuts. Not any you'd want to pursue, anyway."

"How do you know what I'd be willing to pursue?" I asked.

"It would change you, human. I'd have to wield it through you."

"Wield your magic through me?" I asked.

"Think of it as a possession," Ensley said. "I'd burrow beneath your skin and join our minds."

"How would you do that?" I asked.

"I'd have to tap into your spine."

"How would that change him?" Layla asked.

Ensley shrugged. "When minds meld and are then separated again, something of each person is left with the other."

"So it would change you, too?" I asked.

Ensley nodded. "Anything you're hiding, any secrets you have, I'd learn them. Any beliefs you hold, I'd understand them. The same would occur to you in reverse, and that's not even accounting for the potential side-effects."

"Side-effects?" I asked.

"Headaches. Blurred vision. Slight memory loss. Hard to say for sure."

"How has it impacted other people you've done this to?" I asked.

Ensley shrugged. "Well, you'd be my first, so I can't say."

"Caspar," Layla said. "You don't have to do this. We can find another way."

"You might be able to wield enough power to open the gate to New Albion," Brag'mok said. "But to recharge our planet's ley lines?"

I shook my head. "Just opening the gate isn't enough. We need full fairy power. We need to save your planet and give the giants a shot at thwarting your father, Layla."

"But your mind, Caspar. If you aren't yourself when this is over…"

"Layla," I said. "You're the one who told me you have faith in me. You had faith in me from the beginning because you believed in the prophecy. If you still think I am the chosen one and I still have at least two seals of the prophecy to complete, you have to believe."

"I do. It's just terrifying."

I smiled. "You're not the one letting a fairy inside your head. Trust me, I'm not thrilled by it either."

"No pranks while you're in there, Ensley," Layla said.

"I would never!" Ensley said, feigning indignation at the suggestion.

"You're sure, Ensley, that you know how to do the two spells we need?" Layla asked. "To open the gate and charge an item with enough magic to heal New Albion?"

Ensley shook his head. "It's all theory. There's a reason the fairies haven't traveled freely between the worlds. The kind of magic we'll be using isn't just fairy magic, it's the magic the ancients wielded when fairy magic combined with the power humans wield naturally in communion with the Earth. By our powers combined…"

"I am Captain Planet!" I interjected.

Everyone looked at me with raised eyebrows and cocked heads.

"Sorry," I said. "Reference to an old-school cartoon."

"As I was saying," Ensley said. "It is a combination of our powers. The ancient druids wielded our power, which they learned to control when we offered it to them. In this case, I'd be possessing Caspar so I could wield his power together with mine."

"You're sure that approach will work?" Layla asked. "With you pulling the strings instead of him?"

"It should," Ensley said. "But like I said, never done this before."

CHAPTER THIRTY-SEVEN

Having a fairy burrow under your skin isn't a painless experience. It was what I imagined it must've felt like when people got taken by the Goa'uld in *Stargate*. Except, in this instance, I didn't immediately lose my free will or have any universe-conquering aspirations. On the contrary, my desire was still firmly fixed on saving the world.

But I did suddenly have access to a wealth of practical joke ideas. Ensley's mind was like an encyclopedia of ways to annoy your friends and piss off others.

So many memories. So much knowledge. I couldn't begin to absorb it all. Maybe it would take time. It was just too much, so I accessed whatever was on the forefront of his mind.

Mostly pranks.

Ketchup packets weren't the only thing that could go under a toilet seat. Snap-pops were on Ensley's list of similar pranks. Injecting donuts with Miracle Whip. Replacing the filling of someone's Oreos with toothpaste. Painting the bar of soap with clear nail polish. The possibilities were endless. I felt fortunate at the moment that I'd only experienced a handful of them and that he had never put scorpions in my underpants. It could have been worse.

"You in there?" I asked, touching over the place at the base of my spine where he'd burrowed inside me. It was smooth. Surprisingly, his entry hadn't left so much as a mark.

I was still a little sore, though. Tender, like the skin was chafed. All in all, though, it had been relatively painless.

I heard a giggle in my head.

"What are you laughing about?" I asked.

Layla was looking at me curiously. She could only hear what I was saying, of course, and was oblivious to everything going on inside my head.

There's no way your sixth-grade teacher's boobs were that big! Ensley exclaimed.

"It's just how I remember it," I said, shaking my head. This was going to be awkward. I'd had my share of embarrassing situations and thoughts. Things I'd never told anyone. And now, the trickster fairy who'd been wreaking havoc on my life not long ago was privy to it all.

"Can we just focus on what we need to do?" I asked.

"What's he saying?" Layla asked.

I sighed. "Nothing. He's going through my memories and bringing up embarrassing moments from my past."

Layla shrugged. "We all have things we're embarrassed about. No biggie."

"Yeah," I said. "But most of us are allowed to keep those things secret."

You had a crush on Lisa Simpson? Ensley asked. *She isn't even real. And her hair!*

"Shut up, Ensley," I snapped. "I was only, like, ten at the time."

Layla smirked. "What is he saying?"

"He's making fun of me for having a cartoon crush when I was a kid."

Layla shrugged. "You were a kid. So what?"

"First things first," Brag'mok interjected. "We need an item we can enchant. Ideally, a dense metal that can hold significant quantities of magic."

"The Blade of Echoes was made of bronze," Layla said as she scrolled through her phone. "The densest metal is osmium."

I shrugged. "I don't even know what the hell that is, so I don't know how we'd find it."

"How about platinum?" Layla asked. "It's up there too."

I shook my head. "I hate to use it. I don't want to look at it, to be honest. I was actually thinking about trying to sell the thing to help pay for all that personal training."

"What is it?" Layla asked.

I scratched the back of my head. "My wedding ring was made of platinum. I have it in my underwear drawer."

"That could work!" Brag'mok exclaimed.

I chuckled.

"What is it?" Layla asked.

"Just something someone said to me earlier. That guy Dwight," I said.

"The guy from *The Office*?" Layla asked.

"Right!" I said. "I had the same thought. Felt like an ass for mentioning it since probably everyone he meets thinks the same thing."

"How couldn't I make that connection?" Layla asked. "I love Dwight!"

I shook my head. "I don't know how you find the time to watch so many shows on streaming."

"Did you know," Layla asked, "that Pam from *The Office* is from St. Louis?"

I nodded. "Everyone in St. Louis knows that. She's, like, the most famous person from here. Anything big happens, she's always there. I mean, if this was LA or New York, no one would pay her one bit of attention. But here, she's a superstar."

Brag'mok cleared his throat. "Who is this Dwight? Not the one from this office you speak of. The other one."

"The guy you kidnapped, Brag'mok. He's the trucker whose rig you commandeered. One ring to rule them all. That was what he said, and that was why I brought him up just now."

"What does that mean?" Brag'mok asked.

"It's a quote from *The Lord of the Rings*," I said. "I just find it humorous that we're about to enchant a ring and take it to another world so we can throw it into a pit."

"A ley line," Brag'mok corrected me.

"And that presumes we're able to do it and that we can make the gate to New Albion," Layla said.

Tell the elf to get back on the shelf and stop doubting me! Ensley shouted inside my head. *I've got this!*

I snorted.

"What?" Layla asked.

My eyes darted back and forth. I wasn't sure if I should say anything, but if I didn't, it would probably be worse. "He just called you an elf on the shelf."

"That little fucker!" Layla exclaimed.

Come on, elf! Don't you have any original insults?

I smiled.

"What did he just say? Tell me, Caspar."

"He said calling him a fucker isn't all that creative. He's challenging you to do better than that."

"All right, buttface!"

I shook my head. "Seriously, Layla?"

"It's creative!" Layla stood there, her eyes wide and her hands out.

I bit my cheek. "Not really."

"Think about it! Buttface! It's saying you have a face that looks like a butt!"

"That's the sort of name you call someone in the third grade, Layla. Hardly original."

Layla huffed. "Well, how should I know? I didn't grow up on this world!"

"Or we could stop worrying about whose insults are better," Brag'mok said. "And stick to the task."

I nodded. "Yeah. Sorry. Again. First things first. We have to go back to Meramec Springs to charge the ring."

Brag'mok nodded. "I'll drive."

"Drive?" Ensley asked. "Who needs to drive anywhere?"

A warm sensation, more tingly than when I wielded magic, flowed through my body. It started in my chest and spread, first through my torso, then down my legs and arms.

I extended my arms. I assumed that whatever magic Ensley was summoning would be released from my hand.

A golden glow filled my eyes, and almost like if I had Superman's heat vision, streams of energy burst from them.

I could barely see. It was one thing when a light was being shined into your eyes, but when it was coming out of your eyes, there was no squinting or shielding your face to block it. It was blinding.

When the energy faded and my eyesight returned to normal, a giant circle swirling with glittery gold mana was suspended about a foot off the floor in the middle of my apartment. It extended nearly to the ceiling. "A portal?" Layla asked.

To the springs, Ensley said. *Basic fairy shit.*

I chuckled.

Just wait, Ensley continued. *If you thought that was impressive, even I can't wait to see what happens when we combine our powers to create a gate between the worlds.*

I smiled. "This will take us to Meramec Springs."

As we were about to go through, I heard a meow.

"Hey, buddy," I said. "What's up?"

"Nothing," Agnus said. "I guess I'll just stay here. Have fun saving the world without me."

I felt bad for him. Why was he so upset? Was he jealous of Ensley? Did he seriously think the fairy had taken his place?

I knelt and scratched Agnus behind the ears. "It's okay, buddy. You know we wouldn't be here to do this if not for you."

Agnus looked at me blankly and nodded. "Caspar, I'm fine. But you smell horrible with that thing inside you."

That thing? Enley protested. *You realize that cats don't smell much better to us? Get over it! We need him to come along.*

"Ensley says you are needed, Agnus. No time for Animal Planet."

Agnus huffed. "Why do you need me?"

Because where we're going, there will be a lot of other fairies, and I can't sense their presence from inside you. As much as I hate to say it, we need the cat.

"You're the only one who can detect fairies, and there are swarms of them on New Albion. We're going to need your help, Agnus."

"Swarms of ass," he quipped. "Delightful."

I smiled as I patted the cat on the head on the way to my bedroom. "You'll manage."

I opened my underwear drawer. I had a few layers. First, there were the regulars, the pairs I wore frequently. Beneath that were the pairs I could wear if I got lazy and hadn't done laundry for a while, but they weren't my favorites. Not as comfortable but wearable. Then there was the bottom layer, the undies I hardly ever wore. The ones that were too tight, or they had been before I'd started working out. While I was thinking about it, I took the bottom layer, about five pairs, and put them on top. I'd have to try those on later. They'd probably fit again.

Beneath those sat my old wedding ring.

I hadn't worn it in a few years. For a while, even after the divorce, I didn't take it off. I was in denial about it all.

Good thing I hadn't sold the thing. For the first time in years, I had a reason to use it.

I couldn't bring myself to put it on my finger. In some odd way, it felt that if I allowed my finger to break the plane that was the center of the ring, all my old emotions and pain would somehow come back. I knew it was dumb. Maybe I was just superstitious, but I wasn't going to wear it, even if putting it on my finger was the best way to ensure I didn't lose it. I tucked the ring into my front pocket instead.

CHAPTER THIRTY-EIGHT

Travel by fairy gate was interesting. I mean, I didn't know the physics of it, but like Ensley said, I didn't understand how my smartphone worked either.

When I stepped through the gate, it was like participating in a trust fall. I couldn't see where I stepped as I put my foot over the threshold, and I didn't feel a good place to secure my footing.

There were two ways to tackle something like this. It was like trying to get into a cold pool. You either waded in slowly, prolonging the anxiety, or you jumped in and trusted you'd adjust to the temperature shock. After taking the first approach, initially, Ensley advised that I take a step back and dive in head-first.

Truth be told, I didn't dive into pools either. Not that I hadn't tried. Every dive I'd ever attempted had turned into a belly flop.

My preference was the cannonball, and that was the way I jumped into the gate.

I tucked my legs as I jumped through it and heard a splash, then it was cold.

The gate let me out over the spring where I needed to take the ring to charge it.

I mean, the season didn't matter. Spring water was freezing-cold, even in the heat of the summer.

I did wish that Ensley had warned me. I'd assumed the gate would open on the shore, not into the pool.

I'd been here before. I could use my magic to help me through it.

I've got this, Ensley said. Warmth quickly spread over my body.

Brilliant, I thought. I mean, I was underwater, so I couldn't respond, but this might have been the first time the fairy had ever done something to make me more comfortable.

No magic gills. I'd done it with an oxygen tank the first time I swam into the source. When I went into it with B'iff, the magic we were tapping into took away my urge to breathe. I wasn't exactly holding my breath. I mean, I did when I realized I was in the water, but it was a matter of instinct.

Now that I was closer to the source, it was like my body was feeding off the magic around me. I didn't need oxygen. I was bathing in the source of life.

I supposed this magic was akin to the breath of life that God breathed into Adam's nostrils after forming him from the clay of the Earth. I wasn't a strict literalist when it came to the events recounted in Genesis. My denomination was, but in my mind, the message of the creation account mattered more than the details. It was a compelling narrative that detailed the selfless act of a God who lacked nothing choosing to make a world and human beings because it was his nature to love, and love requires an object. Humanity was the product of God's eternal and selfless love. That was much more significant than debating the length of a day or who the serpent was or who Cain's wife was.

Maybe it had something to do with my faith, maybe it didn't. But as the magic swirled around me, the thought was comforting.

I didn't know what to do. Not exactly.

Before, the only way I could speak to Ensley was out loud.

Underwater, for obvious reasons, that didn't work. Despite my attempts to try to communicate with him via telepathy, none of my thoughts were getting through, at least not clearly. He could read my memories, and I could draw on his mind, so there had to be a way, but tapping into another mind was a surreal experience. You had to silence some of it. Otherwise, you were overwhelmed by new and strange information. But if he did hear me, he wasn't responding.

I'd charged a fake bronze blade. I'd assumed charging my ring would be similar, but with the advantage of fairy magic, it would happen on a more powerful scale. I couldn't explain why, but the way I understood it, based on what I was able to pick up from Ensley's mind, it was like how you compress files on a computer and send complex files using fewer bytes than they held. Somehow, with his fairy power combined with mine, the magic the ring was absorbing was dense, compressed, and nearly boundless.

Unlike the Blade of Echoes, of course, the Ring of Power (I know, the name wasn't original, but the New Albion elves wouldn't know that unless they read Tolkien) wouldn't be able to stab anyone.

I mean, if a cut from a magically enhanced blade would kill anyone except me, apparently, why use a blade? Unless the ancient druid who had done to the blade what I was doing to the ring had known about the prophecy.

Ensley's thoughts were all over the place. Complex. I'd tried to ignore most of what my mind had gained from our melding.

As I held the ring in the source and Ensley combined his magic with mine, Earth magic spun around me like a tornado, coalescing on the ring.

Still, I couldn't shake the thought. What if being connected to a fairy mind was how the ancient prophet had gleaned the information integral to the prophecy?

Maybe he hadn't been a prophet; he just had access to fairy

knowledge. Could fairies tell the future? No clue. I'd ask Ensley once we got out of here.

That's it! Ensley said. *Enough magic to bring a dead planet to life!*

I held the ring in my hand. I still couldn't bring myself to put it on. When Bilbo Baggins had put on his Ring of Power, he'd disappeared. The same thing had happened to Frodo. I was not sure what *this* Ring of Power would do. I just hoped it wouldn't turn me into Gollum.

No, I couldn't put it on, and not just because it had once been my wedding ring. I couldn't help but wonder, like in *The Lord of the Rings*, if it might do something to me if I dared put it on.

I quickly slipped it back into my pocket, then kicked my way to the surface. I couldn't talk to Ensley. Did he know what I wanted? I still wasn't sure he could hear my thoughts. He hadn't indicated that he understood me.

Maybe he did?

As I kicked up, my eyes glowed again and another portal formed just above us, a few feet before the surface.

Sure, we could have just traveled the ley lines to where we needed to forge the gate, but not without Layla and Brag'mok.

I kicked my way through the gate, then gravity shifted, and I crashed face-first into my apartment floor.

I peered up, and Agnus was looking me in the eye.

"I'd slow-clap right now, but you know, paws suck for that."

I rubbed my nose. It had taken the brunt of my fall, and touching it was causing my eyes to water. I hoped it wasn't broken.

"Did you do it?" Brag'mok asked, his gravelly voice taking my attention from my aching snot locker.

I nodded, reached into my pocket, and held the ring in my hand as I stood up.

Then I threw my voice a few octaves higher. "My precious!"

"Can I see it?" Brag'mok asked.

I closed my hand around it and clutched it to my chest. "Nasty giantses wants to takes it from us!"

Brag'mok looked confused. Layla cocked her head to the side. They didn't get it.

Agnus was cracking up, rolling on the floor. I nearly forgot he'd been there watching those movies alongside me. I was glad I wasn't the only one who found the situation amusing.

CHAPTER THIRTY-NINE

Another fairy gate, this time to the intersection of the ley lines at the confluence of the Meramec and the Mississippi. That was where the gate would be formed.

The original druids hadn't traveled from the middle of Missouri. They had left from somewhere around Wales in what had once been called Albion. There, the intersection of ley lines was marked by stone circles. In North America, there were probably other ley lines I wasn't aware of, but two of them corresponded with these two rivers.

The magical phenomenon that occurred where the ley lines intersected made a portal between worlds feasible. While no one knew for sure who had formed it, there was a gateway here that had previously opened only during full moons.

But we had fucked with the magic that coalesced at the gate by destroying the Blade of Echoes at the deepest part of the spring, where we had direct access to the source of Earth's magic. We'd supercharged the ley line and blown the gate open. When B'iff's body was removed from the spring, the source went into a temporary brownout. The gate closed, and we weren't sure when or if it would open again.

But with a little fairy magic and some happy thoughts, we were confident we could open it. The fairies, in fact, in conjunction with ancient druids, had done it before. We could do it now.

At least, that was the hope.

This time, thanks be to God, Ensley's gate set us onshore.

So much had happened here just a few months earlier. It seemed like yesterday when Hector had stabbed himself with the fake blade. When I destroyed it and thereby killed him.

Part of me felt bad about that. I mean, while all I did was overcharge a fake blade, since Hector's soul had attuned to it, I'd killed him.

Didn't matter how evil someone was. That was the sort of burden that would weigh on someone's conscience. So far, I'd mostly avoided dealing with it—out of sight, out of mind. But coming back here flooded me with all the emotion of the incident.

To be honest, when I'd heard that Hector was back and alive on New Albion, part of me was relieved—until I'd heard he'd assassinated the king. Then I had been conflicted. After hearing that all of the above had been a ruse conducted by fairies, I wasn't sure what I felt. Human emotions were fickle that way, and I'd never been particularly attuned to mine. Sure, I felt things. I got happy and sad like anyone else. Give me ice cream, I get happy. I finish the ice cream, I am sad it's gone.

See, real emotion.

But when feelings get complex, when they deal with matters of life and death, I have a hard time defining what I feel. Maybe it was because I'd done so many funerals, I became jaded about death. I'd so often had to be the one comforting those mourning that it had become mundane.

Or perhaps it was because I'd lost a close friend when I was eighteen. We had been college roommates. When that happened, I took comfort from my religion. It was what ultimately led me to decide to become a minister. That was before I knew squat about my denomination, the politics behind it all, the infighting, and the dogmatism. Now I wasn't sure how I felt about much.

I was just numb most of the time when it came to emotions.

I think that was one reason I used to drink. I couldn't handle emotions I didn't understand and couldn't control. Alcohol gave me an out. I didn't have to deal with my feelings when I was shit-faced. But it became a vicious cycle to drown those feelings, then they came back like a flood later, which meant more drinking, more forgetting.

AA had helped me come to grips with my emotions. My sponsor'd had me read a letter to my old roommate at his gravesite. It had been a healing experience.

I still didn't have a full grip on my emotions, but I was at peace with the loss of my friend. I forgave him. Yes, that was something I had to do. I'd built up resentment through the years because he'd left me. I know it sounds selfish, but it was real.

But this with Hector and Layla's father and all the world-saving I was supposed to do, it wasn't just testing my resolve, it was testing my sobriety.

I didn't want to drink. I didn't think I would be at risk of that ever again, but there is something they call a dry drunk when you're acting self-centered and cold, practicing escapism rather than confronting the truth of any given situation. I was close to that, and I didn't like it.

Layla put her hand on my shoulder. "A lot happened here."

I nodded. "I think that's why I haven't been able to come back. Better to pretend none of that happened than have to deal with the fact that I killed someone."

Layla nodded. "Killing isn't easy to deal with. You never really get over it."

"You've killed?" I asked.

Layla nodded. "When you grow up in a kingdom that has been in a perpetual state of war for generations, it's par for the course."

"But you are a princess," I said. "Why would the king's daughter have to kill anyone?"

Layla shrugged. "I was also trained as a warrior. Not all women are, but I was. I insisted."

"We've all done it," Brag'mok said. "She's killed giants. I've killed elves. It's surreal that we're standing here together, all fighting for the same thing."

Layla nodded and chuckled under her breath. "It is."

"Are we ready to do this?" I asked. "Ensley is chomping at the bit."

I think he was as eager to try it as I was to see him do it. He'd never forged a gate between worlds, combining human and fairy magic. I mean, fairies and humans haven't mixed well for centuries, not since the druids left. Hell, there weren't a lot of humans who believed fairies existed now or ever had, much less those who worked with fairy magic.

I suppose there was the occasional pagan or druid revivalist who has dabbled with things like that, but I didn't know anything about it. From what I could glean from Ensley's memories, he'd never worked with anyone like that either.

"Where will this gate take us?" I asked. I wasn't sure if I was asking Ensley since he was the one manipulating the magic needed to create the gate or if I was asking Layla and Brag'mok, who'd been through the old gate. I suppose I was just throwing the question out there so one of them could answer. I didn't want to be taken off-guard this time and end up emerging from the gate underwater again without being prepared for it.

"The previous gate opened deep in a cave on New Albion, one you could only access from the top of a mountain."

Brag'mok grunted. "That was why neither the elves nor the giants could claim the gate for themselves. Accessing the gate meant nearly a day's journey since it was removed from civilization."

"We placed outposts out there to guard the gate, but it was not feasible. There just isn't any room for legions to remain up there for a long period. To take a legion through, they'd have to march through narrow paths and caverns single-file."

"And if it's difficult for elves to maneuver, imagine how hard it is for us since some of us are twice their size."

I nodded. "Makes sense, I suppose."

"It's for the best," Brag'mok said. "It is not right that either race should own the gate. Of course, now that it closed on the other side, the chances of us finding anyone near the gate when we go through are slim to none."

I nodded. "Well, I suppose that's good news, all things considered. If we have to fight, we'll be ready."

"*You'll* be ready," Brag'mok said.

I rolled my eyes. "You've taught me fewer moves than I can count on my fingers and toes. How can I hold my own against warrior elves who've trained their whole lives?"

"Remember who you are," Layla said. "The magic you wield is powerful."

"On Earth," I said. "But on New Albion? I don't know."

"It's a good point," Brag'mok said. "Which is why we need to bring the ring to the ley lines as soon as possible, and we need to hope we'll avoid any confrontations with the elves along the way."

Layla nodded. "Sounds like a plan."

Agnus was curled up in Layla's arms. "A plan? To hope we avoid elves? That's a matter of luck. Good fortune is your plan?"

"Would you rather we had bad luck?" I asked.

"Of course not," Agnus said. "But you should have a plan in case things don't go according to plan."

"If you must," Brag'mok said, "draw on your fairy's magic but do not use the magic contained in the ring. Not until it's been committed to the ley lines."

I nodded. "I'll try to remember that."

I was the only one who didn't have any weapons. Layla had

her bow and a full quiver of arrows. Brag'mok had a giant hammer—think sledgehammer but five times larger. In his hands, the thing would be devastating.

Images of the Gallagher sledge-o-matic came to mind, except with heads rather than watermelons.

All I had were a couple of guns: my right and my left. Okay, maybe "guns" was overstating it. I'd only been working out for a few weeks, but I was now wearing tighter shirts to show them off. As Jag had pointed out, my triceps were starting to pop. Since I didn't have a concealed carry license, I was going to have to start wearing tank tops exclusively. Sure, maybe they were just peashooters at the moment, but they were M-16s in the making.

Still, being the only one of the bunch without a lifetime's worth of combat training, it seemed I should have something more. You know, just in case.

Hopefully, I wouldn't need any weapons anyway.

We'd cast the Ring of Power into New Albion's ley lines and, ideally, let Brag'mok and the other giants take over. They'd worry about trying to get B'iff's body back. They'd fight the elven legions and hopefully prevent them from coming to Earth.

My stomach was in knots, but not in a bad way. I was excited to see New Albion, truth be told.

As far as I knew, I'd be the first human to set foot on another planet since the ancient druids had come to New Albion.

"All right," I said. "You ready to do this, Ensley?"

I'm as ready as I'll ever be!

"Is there anything I need to do?" I asked.

Pull your left earlobe.

"What?" I asked.

Just do it.

I pulled my left earlobe.

"All right, now what?"

Nothing! Did you think that would do something?

I grunted. "Then, why?"

Just seeing how compliant you'll be. Silly human.

"Seriously," I said. "What do you need me to do?"

Just focus on where the gate was the last time you saw it. I'll do the rest.

I took a deep breath and tried to visualize the portal. If I focused, I could sense the magic coursing through the ley lines. I imagined the magic swirling in golden hues deep beneath the muddy rivers' waters as it had before.

Then blinding light flashed from my eyes, like before but brighter. The tingle coursing through my body was even more intense. I had to admit the feeling was addictive, even more so than the buzz I'd spent years chasing after my first drunk. But this was different. I felt more alive, more in control of not only my body but the world around me. I wasn't oblivious to my surroundings; I was hyper-aware as if every tree near us was speaking to me, encouraging me. I felt emotions, real emotions, the kind I used alcohol to drown out, but when my magic aligned with Ensley's, I was at peace with everything I sensed.

So much was going on in my mind. Sensations consumed me, Ensley's memories and knowledge now readily accessible but not, in this state of mind, overwhelming.

It wasn't that the fairies hated humans. Or elves. They mourned for us. They lamented our isolation. Isolated from the Earth, the ground from which we were made, from the magic that had vivified us as creatures bearing the divine image. At least, that was how I understood Ensley's thoughts once I'd filtered them through my worldview.

More plainly, we humans had potential we wasted, a capacity for good we too often neglected, and a connection to the Earth envied by every other species that we ignored.

So much was going on in my mind that I was almost oblivious to the luminescent gateway that Ensley was blasting open in the water.

It was more marvelous than before, even after we'd over-charged the gate and blasted it open.

Woot! Ensley exclaimed.

I laughed out loud. "Woot?"

Layla and Brag'mok shot me confused stares.

"Is it done?" the giant asked.

I nodded. "Who wants to go first?"

"Not me!" Agnus protested.

"Sorry, buddy," I said. "I know you don't dig baths."

"I promise," Layla said. "Once we hit the water, you won't even realize it. The gate will pull us through, and we'll be dry on the other side."

"Dry?" I asked. "How does that work?"

"No clue," Layla said. "But I never get wet going back through the gate. Coming through on this side? That's another story."

"See?" I said, scratching Agnus behind the ears while Layla held him. "You won't even get wet."

"You weren't listening!" Agnus shouted. "She said we would on the way back."

I shrugged. "One problem at a time, right?"

Agnus hissed. "I prefer to exercise foresight, and the fortunes tell me if I go through, there will be a bath in my future."

"You'll survive," I said, making eye contact with Layla. I nodded.

She nodded back.

And dove head-first into the gate, clinging to Agnus.

Agnus meowed loudly, but his hissy-fit was muted the second they struck the water.

Brag'mok followed, making a much larger splash.

I'd never been much for cliff-jumping. I didn't like heights.

But the flying I'd done lately seemed to have helped me conquer that fear.

I jumped, tucked my legs, and cannonballed my way into the portal.

CHAPTER FORTY

Layla had been right. After falling through the gateway, I found myself on dry ground.

It was dark. Layla put Agnus in my arms.

He was surprisingly quiet. I'd expected he'd be bitching about the trip. I think he was in a mild state of shock, but he'd made it through okay.

With my cat in my arms and her hands free, Layla channeled light from her fingers. The gateway illuminated the cave a little, but with her spell, we could make out the path ahead.

From what I could see, the cave was fairly dull. No stalactites or stalagmites. Nothing remarkable, just a hole. Layla had said it was on the top of a mountain.

I followed Layla and Brag'mok through the cave until light was visible at the opposite end of one of the caverns.

Layla released her spell. Given the literal light at the end of the tunnel, we didn't need it anymore.

I followed my friends through the corridor and stepped into the light.

I was underwhelmed. I'd imagined an exotic place, something like Pandora from *Avatar*.

However, knowing that the place was barely habitable apart from magic, I shouldn't have been shocked to find that it more closely resembled the photographs I'd seen of Mars. There *was* evidence that plant life had thrived here before the magic that had sustained the place had faltered.

Now, as I emerged from the cave atop a mountain and looked down on the planet, it was nothing but miles of reddish-brown sandy soil and death as far as the eye could see.

Dead trees, most of them standing but barren of foliage. Dead grasses ground into the soil. Withered bushes.

And it was quiet except for a slight breeze, unusually warm, that whistled around us.

I could imagine that when the planet had been invigorated by Earth magic, the place had been a sight to behold. Now it was desolate and depressing.

"This is your home?" I asked.

Layla nodded. "Nothing like it used to be. Not like I remember it being when I was a girl."

I looked up at the sky.

The sun here was bluer than the one that warmed the Earth. From the little I knew of astronomy, that meant it was a younger star.

It also cast a slightly different hue over the world than the yellow light that warmed the Earth. Layla's skin, I noticed, looked a little gray under New Albion's sun. I probably looked the same since my skin tone wasn't much darker than hers.

"What a shithole!" Agnus exclaimed.

I laughed. "Be nice, Agnus."

"He's right," Brag'mok said. "It is a shithole now. Wasn't always."

"You'd be shocked if you had seen how beautiful this place was back when magic still vivified it."

I nodded as I checked my pocket to be sure the ring hadn't

fallen out in the portal. It was still there. "Well, hopefully, we can fix that soon."

"I'll be right behind you," Brag'mok said, pressing his finger to his ear. "Just checking with my contacts here to make sure nothing is going on that might take us by surprise."

I nodded. "Well, I don't think we're going to get too far ahead of you regardless."

The hike down the mountain was arduous.

The air was thin, hot, and dry.

If I'd known it was going to be this way, I'd have brought water.

"How far are we from where we need to drop this ring?" I asked.

"Not far," Layla said. "The gate always takes us to the cave. The actual ley line, though, is deep in the mountain. You can't access it except from a river that used to run around it."

"Used to?" I asked.

"It dried up," Brag'mok said, having caught up with us from behind. "This whole place dried up. The cave used to flow with water drawn from Earth. Over time, the cave formed, and the water from your rivers flowed from the mountain into the valley below."

"Our muddy river water?" I asked.

"It was filtered," Layla said. "All the impurities lost in the portal."

"So, does it purge impurities from our bodies, too?" I asked. "I mean, I've heard of detox."

"It would," Layla said. "If magic was still here. The magic here drew water through the gate to nourish the land all around, but there's not enough magic left. Even with the gate open again, until the ley lines are recharged, no water will flow through."

"And we can't just travel the ley lines from the gate to where we need to go like I did on Earth?"

"That won't work," Brag'mok said. "Not as long as the ley lines are devoid of magic. We have to take your ring to something like your spring."

"Any news?" I asked.

"Huh?" Brag'mok asked.

"You were using your earpiece. Checking in," I said.

Brag'mok paused for a moment. "Nothing that will impact our plans at this juncture. We just need to hurry."

"There's a valley about a mile from here," Layla said. "Not far at all. In it, there's a deep pit. That was where the ancient druid brought the Blade of Echoes to invest our world with magic."

"A mile doesn't sound bad, except that we're on top of a mountain and have to climb down the rest of the way."

"Right," Brag'mok said. "When she says a mile, that distance starts from the base of the mountain."

"With nothing to drink," I quipped.

Brag'mok reached into his pocket and retrieved a flask. "You're welcome to a sip."

I shook my head. "I don't do alcohol."

Brag'mok extended it to me again. "I know. This isn't alcohol."

I took a sip. "It tastes like…is this Sunny Delight?"

"I can't get enough of it!" Brag'mok said. "It's the nectar of the gods!"

I chuckled. "I don't think there's any real juice in it. Mostly water, sugar, and artificially produced vitamins."

"Whatever," Brag'mok said. "If you don't want any…"

"No," I said. "I appreciate it."

"Have as much as you like," Brag'mok said. "I have three more flasks full."

I laughed. "Thanks. I'm glad at least one of us was prepared."

"Once we recharge the ley lines," Brag'mok said, "I will be leaving you."

"We could use your help to get back," I said.

Brag'mok nodded. "I must retrieve my brother's body. He must be properly laid to rest. "

"I understand," I said. "Thank you for your help so far."

"It has been an honor," Brag'mok said, "to aid the chosen vessel of the prophecy."

CHAPTER FORTY-ONE

Despite trekking through a desolate wasteland, I felt oddly invigorated. Either the fairy magic I'd accessed via Ensley to get here or Brag'mok's Sunny Delight was to blame.

I hoped for the former rather than the latter. A sugar high would lead to an inevitable crash, and I needed to preserve my energy for the trek back to the gate.

After all, once we'd recharged the ley lines, it would only be a matter of time before the elves would know what happened. He'd have his legions on us in no time, with more than whatever magic they'd hoarded for themselves via B'iff's corpse. A recharged planet gave them a second chance, but it was one they were likely to squander on more war. If they caught me here, not to mention Layla, there'd be nothing better to confirm King Brightborn's defiance of the prophecy than to have the chosen one's head on the end of a spear, or on a platter, or however elf kings liked to display severed craniums.

My preference was to keep my head firmly affixed to my shoulders.

Were my feet already blistering? This wasn't a long walk, but the hike down the mountain was more challenging than you'd think. While going up hills is hard, the trek down was so steep that it took a lot of strength to make sure I didn't fall and end up sliding the rest of the way on my ass.

Might have been more fun, but the heat radiating off the dirt would probably have chapped my hiney.

My feet were burning too, both from the work of trekking down the mountain and the heat of the ground.

One mile was like thirty when it was that hot, and the warm breeze I had felt on the mountain seemed more like a sandstorm when we were on the ground.

Nothing like sun-scorched sand striking your face.

"This sucks the balls I don't have," Agnus complained.

"I agree," I said. "I mean, not that I'd know what sucking those is like."

"In your dreams, Casp. In your dreams."

"My dreams?" I asked. "As if it isn't your dream to have balls again."

"Let it be known for the record that I hold you responsible for my lack of testicles."

"I accept that responsibility," I said.

"Can you give me back to Layla?" Agnus asked.

"Why? Don't tell me you're holding a grudge now that we brought up the subject of your neutering."

"It's the smell of the fairy. It gets stronger every second."

Stronger? Ensley asked. *I don't think it's me he's smelling.*

"Hey, Layla, Brag'mok, there might be other fairies around," I said. "Agnus smells something."

Layla nocked an arrow. A precautionary measure, perhaps, but I was glad she was on top of things.

"I don't see any other fairies," Brag'mok said. "Let's keep going."

Doesn't mean they aren't here, Ensley said.

"Just keep an eye out," I said. "Ensley thinks there might be some hiding."

"We're almost there," Brag'mok said. "Hopefully, if there are any lurking around here, we'll accomplish what needs to be done before it becomes an issue."

I nodded. "I don't see anything up ahead. It's just red sand as far as I can see."

"It's there," Layla said. "I can't draw enough magic here to do it, but if you and Ensley can do something, maybe create some wind blowing the other way? There's a well up ahead, but I'm guessing it's covered in sand."

"A well?" I asked. "The source is accessed through a well?"

"No one ever had to use it," Layla said. "It's considered a holy site."

"Because the ancient druid dug a well to charge the ley lines here?" I asked.

"Exactly," Layla said. "It should be around here, just covered up. Can you and Ensley blow the sand around?"

"Can you, Ensley?" I asked.

Can I? What sort of question is that? Open your mouth, human.

I cocked my head. Open my mouth? Really? This was going to be interesting.

I opened my mouth as wide as I could.

Now just breathe, then blow.

I inhaled deeply and then exhaled, but the wind kept coming. My eyes glowed at the same time. Apparently, the golden eye wasn't just a James Bond film. It happened to me every time Ensley cast magic through me.

The wind, pouring out of my mouth, blew harder. It was like I was vomiting a hurricane over the desert.

On the checklist of Superman powers I'd always prayed that God would give me when I was a kid, so far I'd mastered flight, something similar to his heat vision when we'd cast the gate, and super breath? Now I just needed indestructibility. Then again, I'd survived a stab by the Blade of Echoes.

I just kept exhaling. Where was all this wind coming from? I mean, I was a preacher; I was supposed to be full of hot air. A blow-hard, I supposed, but this was on a whole other level.

"There it is!" Brag'mok shouted.

I could hardly see through all the sand, but I also didn't know what I was looking for. Then Layla pointed at it, and I saw it. Barely.

There was a small circle of stones, old-looking stones well weathered by the centuries. The well was at the center, I supposed.

I stopped exhaling, and the sandstorm I'd created calmed down.

We stepped toward the well and looked inside.

"Do you smell that?" Layla asked.

"See? What have I been telling you!" Agnus interjected.

"No, not that."

"I was able to draw enough magic before. Maybe I still can." Layla held her hand over the well, and light began glowing from her fingers again.

I set Agnus down on the ground as I leaned over and looked into the hole. Brag'mok stood beside me.

B'iff's body, his corpse rotting. That was what we smelled, but the ley line wasn't charged.

"I don't understand," I said. "I thought his body was filled with magic? That he'd become the Blade of Echoes."

"He had," Brag'mok said. "But the king used too much of it, and I suspect he thought he'd try to use the rest to charge the lines."

"My God," Agnus said. "The smell, not the body. It's awful."

"Hello, daughter," a deep voice said from behind us. We turned, and there stood King Brightborn, except his eyes were aglow with golden magic. Just like mine were when Ensley channeled magic through me.

"Good work, Ensley," King Brightborn said. "You can leave him now."

A sharp pain struck me at the base of my neck, and Ensley flew out of the wound. This time, it didn't heal as easily.

I grasped the gouge in my neck, my blood covering my hand.

"Ensley!" I shouted.

"Sorry, human," Ensley said. "I wasn't disowned by my kind. I am the fairy king, and we have an alliance with the elves."

"You shit!" I screamed.

"Told you so," Agnus interjected.

"Shut up, Agnus!" Layla and I replied in concert.

"Just saying," Agnus said. "Should have listened to me from the start."

"Father," Layla said, "what have you done?"

"Fucking fairies," I muttered under my breath.

Brag'mok was breathing heavily behind me. He was even angrier than I was. I turned, and he gripped his hammer tightly. He was going to go after the king.

"You don't want to do that, orc," the king said.

The king waved his hand, and in a semi-circle around us appeared two dozen elves, their eyes aglow like the king's. They were all possessed by fairies and enhanced by the magic they'd taken from B'iff's body.

"Now, human, why don't you give me the blade?"

"I don't have a blade," I said.

"You brought something to recharge the ley lines."

"It's a ring," Ensley said. "In his front pocket."

"Don't give it to him," Brag'mok said. "He'll kill you either way."

I sighed. "Like you said, he'll kill me either way."

"Father!" Layla protested. "You've seen that he fulfilled the prophecy! How could you?"

King Brightborn raised his hand. "The prophecy? A prophecy dictated when a man, a druid, united with a fairy? So I have, daughter, and I am rewriting it."

"You can't rewrite the prophecy!" Brag'mok said. "We have our own scrolls!"

"Your scrolls mean nothing to me," King Brightborn told him.

"Now, human, give me the ring, or I'll have no choice but to take it by force."

"Casper," Brag'mok said, "I should have told you sooner, but the sixth seal has broken. Another part of the prophecy has been revealed. Do you trust me?"

I nodded.

"Put the ring on," Brag'mok said.

"Are you sure?" I asked.

"Just do it."

"*Now, human!*" King Brightborn shouted. "Or I'll kill you where you stand!"

I took a deep breath, then reached into my pocket and grabbed the ring. I held it in the air.

"This is what you want, Your Highness?" I asked.

"Ensley," the king said, "retrieve the ring for me."

The fairy flew at me.

But before he got to me, I slipped it on. Not my left hand. That was where I'd worn it when I was married, but this ring had a different meaning now. I put it on the ring finger of my right hand.

And my whole body filled with magic. All the magic, enough to charge a planet.

My skin was about to burst.

The power! So much power!

"No!" King Brightborn shouted.

"Strike the ground," Ensley said. "After I go back inside you."

I looked at Ensley curiously. "Why would I do what you say?"

"I've read your mind and your memories, human. You are not like the rest. I am sorry I didn't tell you the truth before. I had to hide certain things from you, so I thought about tricks and pranks. Anything I could lift to the surface of my mind in hopes you wouldn't go much deeper. Thankfully, it worked. Trust me, Caspar."

"Ensley!" King Brightborn shouted. "Take the ring from him!"

"All right, here goes nothing," I said.

Ensley dove back through the wound on my neck. This time, he healed me as he went.

He added his magic to mine.

My eyes glowed with fairy magic, even as the rest of my body was overwhelmed with enough magic to power a planet.

Then the king came after me with a large blade.

"Pivot!" Brag'mok shouted.

I remembered my training. I swung my foot to the side, evading the king's strike, then used my hand, my left one that didn't have the ring on it, to shove the king out of the way, forcing him to stumble.

My eyes glowed brighter and, looking at the ground, a portal formed, glittering gold, just the size of my fist.

A target.

Strike it! Ensley said.

I slammed my right fist into the target Ensley had made, and all the magic that filled my body poured into the small portal.

A shock wave sent everyone around me flying.

Not only Brag'mok and Layla but the king and all his soldiers, too.

The king and his men screamed in pain as they picked up their bodies off the ground, holding their necks.

Green orbs floated out from behind them.

The other fairies had left the elves.

And in a split second, new grasses grew from the soil.

A cool breeze struck the side of my face.

We'd done it. We'd recharged New Albion.

"Back to the gate," Brag'mok said. "I'll try to hold them off."

"Come with us," I said. "I can't leave you to fight a whole legion."

"He isn't alone," Ensley said, climbing out of my skin again. This time, he healed me on the way out. "We're here to help him fight them. Be yourself, Caspar. We're depending on you. Both worlds depend on you."

I nodded at Ensley, then at Brag'mok. "Thank you. Both of you."

"Now that the ley lines are charged," Brag'mok said, "the gate will likely go back to how it behaved before, opening only on full moons. And only a few can go through at a time. You have to hurry."

I nodded and scooped up Agnus. "Layla," I said, "come on!"

"One second," Layla said, pulling an arrow from her quiver. She aimed and shot it through her father's leg.

"Layla!" the king shouted as he screamed in pain.

"That'll slow him down," Layla said. She fired another arrow, then another and several more in rapid succession, striking the elf soldiers in their legs.

"Damn!" I said. "Impressive."

Layla shrugged. "I've had practice. Wanted to give Brag'mok and Ensley every advantage I could."

I smiled.

"Come on, Casp!" Agnus said. "I can't stand this smell. Too much fairy!"

I laughed and took off running.

Running through fields with freshly sprouted grass, with trees growing all around us, almost like watching them take shape through time-lapse photography. It was surreal.

And beautiful.

"It's been years," Layla said as we ran side by side. "I never thought I'd see our world like this again."

I smiled. "I'd talk, but I'm out of breath."

Layla chuckled. "I think we need to add more cardio to your routine."

CHAPTER FORTY-TWO

Agnus was freaking the fuck out.

When we came back through the portal to Earth, just as Layla had said, we appeared in the middle of the river.

The gateway dissipated behind us the moment we passed through.

Agnus squirmed and released a drawn-out nasal meow.

I could barely hold onto him.

"I'm going to die! I'm going to drown!"

"You'll be fine," I said, kicking toward the shore as I tried to swim with the current, holding him above the water as best I could. "But if you keep wiggling in my arms, I won't be able to hold you out of the water."

Layla made it to shore before I did. Because of the current, Agnus and I were probably twenty yards farther downstream by the time we reached dry land.

"I will *never* forgive you," Agnus snarled.

I rolled my eyes. "You forgave me for neutering you. You'll get over this."

"I never forgave you for that. I just chose not to think about it.

Too traumatic. Some things you don't talk about, not with anyone. Only those who've been through the same thing."

"Well," I said, "I don't know many eunuchs, and even if I did, they wouldn't be able to talk to cats."

"Little boxes. I put my feelings in little boxes. *Dry* boxes."

I snorted. "Well, if it's any consolation, I'm drenched, too."

"We could fly back," Layla suggested.

"Like hell!" Agnus protested.

I cocked my head as I felt something I hadn't noticed before.

I bit my lip. "Just a second. I have an idea."

A tingle spread across my brow as my eyes started to glow gold and green. The fairy magic combined with my own.

"That little bugger," I laughed out loud. "He left something of himself behind, more than his knowledge. Some of his magic, too."

I focused my eyes in front of me, and with a beam of light, formed a circle large enough for us to pass through.

"Are you sure you know what you're doing with that magic?" Layla asked.

"Not at all," I said. "But if I visualized this correctly, it should take us to the apartment."

I gestured at the gate I'd made.

"Ladies first," I said.

Layla rolled her eyes. "I'm not sure if you're being gentlemanly or you just want me to test this thing first. You know, in case it drops us into the middle of traffic somewhere."

I smirked. "Ensley gave me some of his powers—and a great knowledge of his many pranks, so you never know."

"I'm trusting you, Caspar," Layla said as she jumped through my makeshift portal.

Holding Agnus tightly, I jumped through behind her.

We crashed on the bed. I landed on top of Layla.

She rolled her eyes. "Convenient."

"I want nothing to do with this!" Agnus protested. "I'm going to go watch Animal Planet."

I laughed as Agnus jumped off the bed and headed for the living room.

"I can't believe we did that," I said, smiling at Layla.

"I never doubted you," Layla said. A single tear fell from her eye and trickled down her cheek.

"Are you okay?" I asked.

"So many mixed emotions."

"Want to talk about it?"

"Maybe later," Layla said. "Have any energy left?"

I smiled sheepishly. "I think I do."

Layla wrapped her arms around me and pulled me in for a kiss.

I felt a tingle, but it wasn't across my brow this time. This was a whole different kind of magic.

Layla and I lay there, out of breath. We'd been through a lot. I wasn't sure how we'd found the energy.

I'd lasted a full ten minutes this time.

I think that was twice my record.

I might be nearly forty, but when it came to some things, my skill wasn't that much better than an eighteen-year-old's.

"You saved our world, Caspar," Layla said. "I knew you could do it."

"For now," I said.

Layla choked up.

"What is it?" I asked.

"My dad. I can't believe it came to that."

"Having to fight your dad?" I asked. "That must've been hard."

"I shot him in the leg, Caspar," Layla said. "I mean, it might as well have been a shot through his heart."

"You Give Love a Bad Name," I said.

Layla raised her eyebrow. "Isn't that a song?"

I chuckled. "Bon Jovi."

Layla laughed. "I should be angry that you're making light of my pain, but you know, it felt good to laugh."

I took a deep breath. "I'm not making light of it. In my experience, we sometimes have to find a reason to laugh about the things that hurt the most. There's no other way to get through it."

"Tell that to Agnus," Layla said. "I don't think he'll ever get over that little swim."

I laughed. "I've never seen him quite like that. I mean, there's the car freak out, but this was on a whole other level."

"Well, hopefully, he found some lions or tigers on the television."

"Fucking giraffes!" Agnus shouted from the next room. "Seriously?"

I laughed. "Can you imagine if it was Shark Week?"

"Oh, he'd be livid," Layla said. "I mean, who's into sharks anyway?"

"I know, right?"

My phone dinged from my nightstand—a text message.

I reached over and picked it up.

Caspar, what the hell?

The text from Philip could only mean one thing. News of the healing service had gotten out.

I responded with an action-based text, demarcated by the inclusion of dual asterisks:

shrugs

He sent a link.

The event had made the news.

Not just in the St. Louis Post-Dispatch or one of the local television stations. This was a national news site.

The headline: *Dozens Healed and Cured: Miracle or Fraud?*

"Well, shit," I said.

"What is it?" Layla asked.

I showed her my phone. Layla shrugged. "People were bound to find out."

"Yeah, but the national news?"

Layla smiled. "You're shocked that people are skeptical?"

"Not at all," I said. "I mean, they crucified Jesus. Not saying I'm Jesus."

My phone buzzed again.

Already got a call from the AB.

He was talking about Dr. Schmidt, the archbishop of our denomination. That was what "AB" was short for. No, he wasn't a medical doctor; Schmidt had a D.Min, which stood for "Doctor of Ministry." I always got a chuckle that when you read someone's name followed by that particular academic credential, it wasn't all that flattering. Schmidt: Demon. Since he represented the hyper-conservative right-wing of the denomination, those like my former hard-nosed bishop, I wasn't entirely certain if in this instance, the label didn't fit.

And?

Have a second to talk?

I sent a thumbs-up emoji in response.

I was exhausted after, you know, traveling between worlds, being possessed by a fairy, and saving another planet. I wasn't in the mood to deal with church politics, but I also knew that if I didn't talk to Philip now, I'd be tossing and turning, wondering what his conversation with Dr. Schmidt had involved.

I went out to the living room and sat down on the couch. Then I stood up again.

I can't ever sit down when I'm on the phone. I'm a pacer.

D.C. Talk's *Jesus Freak* sounded from my pocket. That was Philip. I picked up the phone.

"Hey, Phil."

"Caspar," Philip said. "Please tell me this is fake news."

"Nope," I said. "All of that happened pretty much the way the article described it."

"It's not the healings Schmidt is concerned about it. It's that you confirmed the validity of a Muslim family's beliefs."

I rolled my eyes. "Of course, that would be the issue. They had a kid with leukemia, Philip. Arguing with them about the identity of God wasn't the point."

"But you used our church to deceive them."

"I didn't deceive anyone," I said. "Their kid is cancer-free, is he not?"

"According to the article."

"That's what it says. The doctors said their boy had no trace of cancer. Isn't that what's important?"

"Just between us," Philip said, "are you claiming you healed those people?"

I shrugged. "Does it matter? Schmidt is going to want my head either way."

"Not necessarily," Philip said. "At least, not yet."

I huffed. "Not yet?"

"It wouldn't be great press for the denomination to excommunicate a minister in the wake of healing a bunch of children. I mean, can you imagine what the media would say?"

I laughed. "So, let me get this straight. Schmidt believes, like Matthias did, that I'm a heretic?"

"He does," Philip said.

"But he won't do anything about it because it might be a bad PR move?" I asked.

"Exactly," Philip said.

"That's priceless," I said. "These guys, they pretend to be God's knights defending pure doctrine, but they cower in the light of what might be bad press?"

"You know as well as I do that our denomination is shrinking," Philip said. "At the rate of more than two percent every year."

I snorted. "So, you're telling me the president who said when he was elected that what was required was a bold confession, not pragmatically inspired compromise, is now bowing to pragmatism?"

"Well, if I were you, I wouldn't point that out to him," Philip said. "Not to mention, even if he's on your side, albeit with mixed motives, you still have to survive the voters of your congregation."

"I'm still hoping they'll volunteer at the soup kitchen."

"Might be too little, too late, Caspar."

I shrugged. "If it is, it is, but I'm not going to apologize for healing people's children. I didn't deceive anyone. You saw the article. So far, several physicians have confirmed the results."

"Just be careful," Philip said. "Schmidt has his eyes on you. When the news cycle turns over, if he has a good reason, he'll act. He believes you healed those people using a demon."

I laughed. "I wouldn't be the first one to be accused of that."

"I know," Philip said. "They accused Jesus of the same."

"Again, I'm no Jesus."

"I know you aren't, Caspar. But for whatever reason, you have been given a gift. I'll do what I can to help, but I wanted you to know this is over my head now."

"Don't sacrifice your career for my sake," I said. "Even if they blackball me again, you can still do some good. I don't want to bring you down with me."

"I appreciate that," Philip said. "But I have a conscience, and if I let them come after you with false accusations and I said nothing in your defense? I don't know if I could live with that."

"Just don't do it for my sake."

"I won't," Philip said. "But this is bigger than you. It has to do with the whole ethos of our church. How can we survive if we continue addressing any sort of dissent by silencing people? What are we saying about how secure we are in our beliefs if a difference of opinion is such a threat that we can't tolerate listening to it or considering it?"

After a few more minutes of conversation, I shut off the phone and set it next to the bed.

"Layla?" I asked.

I leaned over. She was breathing heavily. She'd fallen asleep.

"Hey, Agnus!" I said. "Going to sleep now."

"Sure it's safe for me to come in?" Agnus asked.

"I promise," I said.

A few seconds later, I saw the doorknob turn. He'd figured out how to reach up, grip it with both paws, and swing his body until it opened.

Clever cat.

Then he came waddling through the doorway before leaping on the bed and taking his place between us.

"Goodnight, buddy," I said.

"Yeah, night, Casp."

It took me a while to fall asleep. So much had happened. If we hadn't had to leave so soon, I could have talked to Brag'mok. He'd said the sixth seal had been broken. Somehow, it seemed, my recharging New Albion with the Ring of Power was tied to that, but I still didn't know what the new section of the prophecy said. It was too late now to find out. Was there anything more to it than that? We might be able to find out eventually if Brag'mok outlasted the elves.

I rolled over and took a deep breath. I had to clear my mind. My body was exhausted, but my mind was still churning. The sixth seal of the prophecy. All the bullshit going on with the church and the archbishop. I put my arm around Layla, and she spooned into me.

Her touch was comforting. Quieting.

I closed my eyes and fell asleep.

CHAPTER FORTY-THREE

Bang! Bang! Bang!

"What the hell!" I said, sitting up. If it was some frickin' fairy screwing with us after all we'd been through, after all the fairies had put us through and then saved us from... After saving a whole planet, you'd think a guy deserved a little sleep.

Bang! Bang!

"Just go see who it is," Agnus said, rolling over between my legs and Layla's. "I'm trying to get my beauty sleep here."

Layla rubbed her eyes and looked at me. "Never know. Could be important."

I groaned as I rolled over and retrieved my phone from my nightstand. It was nine p.m. It felt like three in the morning.

I stumbled out of bed and threw on a t-shirt and sweatpants. I doubted whoever it was wanted to be greeted at the door by me in a pair of Star Wars boxer shorts that said Dark Side across the ass. I'd had them for years. It was one of those pairs that never seemed to wear out.

As proud as I was of them, only a select few people got to see me in them. My mysterious evening door knocker wasn't one of them.

Bang! Bang! Bang!

"Just a second!" I shouted. I flipped on the light switch, squinting as my eyes adjusted to the brightness.

I checked the peephole at the door.

What the hell was Jag doing at my house?

I sighed. Probably a late-night training tactic.

I opened the door.

"Dude, what are you doing here? We were all asleep."

Jag looked at me dumbly. "It's nine o'clock, Caspar. Don't be a pussy."

"Yeah, well, I've had a crazy last twenty-four hours, and being a pussy had nothing to do with it."

Jag nodded. "I need to talk to you. Can I come in for a minute?"

I groaned. I was surprised; mohawk notwithstanding, the guy cleaned up pretty well. I was used to seeing him in gym shorts and tank tops that were two sizes too small, but he was standing there in a nice pair of slacks and a button-up shirt.

"Yeah." I gestured at the couch. "Let me just let Layla know so she doesn't come out half-naked."

Jag shrugged. "I won't complain if she does."

I snorted. "I know you won't. I mean, honestly, who would? But *she* might not appreciate it."

"Fine," Jag said. "She should probably hear this too."

"Layla!" I shouted. "Jag is here. He says he has something important to tell us."

Layla came out. She had thrown on a t-shirt, my favorite one —the one that commemorated the Chiefs' last victory in the Superbowl. I had to admit, she looked extra-sexy wearing my team's apparel over her nightgown. She'd also slipped into a pair of jeans.

"Hey, Jag," Layla said. "Thanks for training Caspar while I was gone, by the way."

"Don't mention it," he said.

"I'm sure he appreciates my money," I quipped back.

"Hey, you get what you pay for," Jag said. "Show me those triceps. I swear, when you opened the door for me, I could see a little definition."

"I'm not flexing for you, Jag."

"Just do it. Come on. You should be proud."

I sighed and extended my arm to flex my right-side triceps.

"See, look at that!" Jag said.

Layla reached over and touched it. "Damn, Caspar! You're really getting toned."

I nodded. "Thanks. So, I don't think you came over here just to feel me up."

"No," Jag said. "I'm not into dudes like that."

"Didn't suspect you were." I smirked.

"So, we had a meeting tonight."

"The gym did?" I asked.

Jag shook his head. "The Order of the Elven Gate."

"Oh, yeah," I said. "I guess that makes sense. What's going on?"

"We had some strange visitors, Caspar. Elves, but not like you Layla, Their skin was darker, almost purple. Their ears even more pronounced."

Layla bit her lip. "Drow?"

"I think that's what they said. That's right, they were drow."

"What the hell is a drow?" I asked.

Layla sighed. "I didn't believe they existed, to tell the truth."

"Are they elves?" I asked.

Layla nodded. "Of a sort. They evolved differently because they didn't come with us to New Albion."

"Wait," I said. "These are elves who've been on Earth the whole time?"

Layla nodded. "There are legends, stories, that centuries ago, they sent emissaries to New Albion in hopes of luring us back, not to fight but to peaceably stand up to the Empire that had persecuted us."

"I'm taking it the elves on New Albion didn't dig that idea?" I asked.

Layla shook her head. "We'd all be burned for what they wanted to do. It's the whole reason our people fled to begin with. If they'd had their way, we'd all have been martyrs. We assumed they'd all been killed for doing exactly what they wanted us to do because after a while, according to our histories, they stopped sending emissaries."

"Well," Jag said, "I can assure you, they didn't all die. Three of them showed up at our meeting tonight. They said they'd sensed a new magic, a human in tune with the Earth's energies. They wanted to come to see this chosen one for themselves."

"So they want to meet me?" I asked.

"And they came with gifts, I think," Jag said.

I laughed. "Please tell me it isn't gold, frankincense, and myrrh."

"Those would be shitty gifts," Jag said. "But one of them had a bag from the Apple Store. Maybe he got you an iPad."

"Awesome!" I said. "I could use one of those!"

"Did you tell them where they could find us?" Layla asked.

Jag shook his head. "We didn't, but I told them I see you frequently and that I'd speak to you. Said maybe you'd come to meet them."

I sighed. "All right. When is your next meeting?"

"It's going on right now," Jag said. "I told them I'd come and get you tonight."

I sighed. "Can't they wait until morning?"

Jag shrugged. "They traveled a long way to meet you, and I don't think they've checked into a hotel or anything."

"We should go," Layla said. "I'm pretty excited. I mean, a real drow? How awesome is that?"

I shrugged. "All right. I suppose until the world's been saved, sleep is out of the question."

Jag snorted. "Sleep is for pussies."

"You told me I needed eight full hours every night for muscle recovery!" I protested.

Jag smiled. "I was just looking for a reason to call you a pussy again."

I chuckled. "All right, well, let's go meet these drow."

"One more thing," Jag said. "Some guy showed up at our meeting the other night. Said an orc had kidnapped him, and some hot elf boss-chick was behind it. Told us a wizard he referred to as Gandalf the White saved him."

I laughed. "Dwight? I thought he'd decided to refer to me as Doctor Strange?"

Jag nodded. "Well, it's Gandalf now. You're saying you had something to do with that?"

I smiled. "Didn't expect he'd join your order. And he said he wouldn't tell anyone. But I guess after what happened, it makes sense. And yes, we borrowed his truck."

Jag shook his head. "He has a lot of crazy ideas. Something about one ring to rule them all, and how our whole world is doomed if you don't save us."

I chuckled. "Well, he's half-right, I suppose. Not about the ring."

Jag nodded. "Can you straighten out his story? He's all worked up about it."

I chuckled. "Yeah, I'll talk to him."

AUTHOR NOTES - THEOPHILUS MONROE

MAY 3, 2021

Like *Who Let the Dogma Out*, this book is largely the product of a number of my own experiences. First, I am something of a workout addict. I used to be a trainer and still, even in my early forties, do some amateur bodybuilding. I can be obsessive at times. Jag is, oddly enough, a bit of a parody of myself, I suppose, combined with other gym rats I know. As I wrote this, in fact, I even had a mohawk. Thank you, "Carona Cuts" (my wife's bathroom hair salon... since social distancing from the barber is virtually impossible).

Speaking of my wife—she inspired the whole "deprecations" thing. She's currently really into "affirmations," and has a number of positive, self-affirming statements plastered all over our walls. It's really powerful, actually. Makes a difference. Jag's "deprecations" were something of a parody of that. Because... yes... as powerful as these affirmations are, they can be a little silly, too. My wife doesn't know I did this yet... I'm anxiously awaiting her reaction. I've been practicing my "ducking" skills. Or, perhaps taking Caspar's lead, a back-foot, turn-and-pivot would be a more appropriate evasive maneuver. -

Caspar's experience with the church shifts in this book. He

still has his issues with the "powers that be," but he's also struggling with the general "culture" of his congregation, one that isn't particularly empathetic to others' struggles or accepting of people who look different than they do. Even well-intentioned people, with their hearts in the right place, sometimes put their faith in the wrong things. Doctrine, traditions, the way "we've always done it," and the like—and in the process, fail to see how their actions exclude others. Now, with an empathetic bishop, he has a chance to at least attempt to make a difference.

And then there's all the new magic. The trickster fairy, Ensley, does very little that wasn't experienced (either by me, or others) when I was living in college dormitories in the late 1990/early 2000s. Ketchup on my buns... happened more than once. Hopefully, this book will also inspire some light-hearted shenanigans. Because we could all use more practical joking in our lives. So long as we're the ones perpetrating them.

And of course, there's Agnus. Enough said.

I hope you enjoyed reading this as much as I got a kick out of writing it. It was a bit of a hoot to write.

-Theo

AUTHOR NOTES - MICHAEL ANDERLE
MAY 7, 2021

Thank you for reading through this story and the back as well!

I'd like to comment that I did NOT know that the deprecations were directly tied to Theophilus' wife's efforts with little affirmations taped to the walls all over the house. Had I known this little tidbit of wisdom, well, I would have started looking for another collaborator sooner. I fear if his duck and cover skills are not up to snuff, he might not be long for this world.

We shall see.

As you can tell, Theophilus and I share a rebellious streak when it comes to many of the issues with organized religion. While the positive parts are supported, there are many issues that need to be addressed, and we poke a little at those issues. I'm not for throwing it all out just because of the problems, but I support these issues be raised in a story such as this one.

IT'S ALIENS!

I'd like to point out to Marc Stiegler (fellow author and friend) that we have accomplished putting aliens into our Urban Fantasy. Marc and I have a friendly (but passionate) disagreement about the potential existence of alien life.

I can't remember if Marc is strictly a "no aliens have visited Earth" or a "no aliens exist" individual. I'm going to assume the former but reserve the right to correct myself when I ask him in the near future.

(*Editor's note: Since he's my husband and I'm on your side, I'll answer. It's the latter, more shame to him!*)

Anyway, I'm merely putting this stake in the ground that those elves who have traveled from their world to this one are now considered aliens.

Elves are aliens. We might not have been the first, but we are probably the first set of collaborators this *year* to do it.

Maybe.

Orcs are elves

Ok, we have a slight chance that we are the first who are claiming that orcs are a type of elf. Once again, aliens. I might use it as a defense.

(*Editor's note: Have you READ Lord of the Rings? Or seen the movies? Do you remember how orcs were created? Pshaw, I say!*)

Prosecution: "Mr. Anderle, what is your defense when charged with placing two different groups of people in a book and calling them both elves?"

Mr. Anderle: "I claim the 'They are ALIENS!' defense."

Prosecution: "Seriously?" Turns head to the judge. "He can do that?"

Judge: "He can."

Prosecution: "Awww, shit." Throws down paperwork in disgust. "No more questions." Closes briefcase and leaves the courtroom. Door bangs behind him when he leaves.

Mr. Anderle: (Looking at judge). "We done, then?"

Judge: "Yes. Smart move. Nothing gets past the 'ALIENS!' defense."

I hope you have a fantastic week or weekend. See you next book!

Regards,

Michael Anderle

Also by Theophilus Monroe

The Druid Legacy

Druid's Dance

Bard's Tale

Ovate's Call

Rise of the Morrigan

The Voodoo Legacy

Voodoo Academy

Grim Tidings

Death Rites

Watery Graves

Voodoo Queen

The Legacy of a Vampire Witch

Bloody Hell

Bloody Mad

Bloody Wicked

Bloody Devils

Bloody Gods

The Legend of Nyx

Scared Shiftless

Bat Shift Crazy

No Shift Sherlock

Shift For Brains

Shift Happens

CONNECT WITH THE AUTHORS

Connect with Theophilus Monroe

Website: www.theophilusmonroe.com

Social Media
https://www.facebook.com/pages/category/Author/
Theophilus-Monroe-Urban-Fantasy-Author-101469961530864/

Connect with Michael Anderle

Website: http://lmbpn.com

Email List: http://lmbpn.com/email/

Social Media:

https://www.facebook.com/LMBPNPublishing

https://twitter.com/MichaelAnderle

https://www.instagram.com/lmbpn_publishing/

https://www.bookbub.com/authors/michael-anderle